"Marvelous…rapid pace, wonderful prose, and deeply emotional scenes."

—*RT Book Reviews,* 4.5 Stars, Top Pick

"As usual for Ms. Wine, historical facts are masterfully woven into her story, giving it authenticity seldom found in historical romances…a must-read."

—*Night Owl Reviews,* Top Pick

"An absolute delight! You will forever be astounded as well as gratified by reading Mary Wine's Highlander series. Scottish Medieval fans are sure to be in awe."

—*My Book Addiction and More*

"Entertaining and engrossing…Mary Wine weaves a tapestry of a tale with adrenaline-pumping action, sweet and spicy love scenes, a touch of humor, and a twist and turn here and there."

—*Long and Short Reviews*

"Wine's rip-roaring ambushes and beddings make for a wild ride through fifteenth-century Scottish eroticism."

—*Publishers Weekly*

"Wine's crisp writing, intricate plot, and deep insights into clan politics make for a fun and satisfying read."

—*Booklist*

HIGHLAND
SPITFIRE

MARY WINE

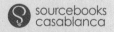

sourcebooks
casablanca

Published by Sourcebooks Casablanca, an imprint of Sourcebooks, Inc.
P.O. Box 4410, Naperville, Illinois 60567-4410
(630) 961-3900
Fax: (630) 961-2168
www.sourcebooks.com

Printed and bound in Canada.
MBP 10 9 8 7 6 5 4 3 2 1

One

"YE'RE AS HEADSTRONG AS YER MOTHER WAS."

Ailis stretched up to kiss her father on the cheek before flashing his captain a smile of victory. Her father rolled his eyes then offered her a hand to help her up onto the back of her mare. The horse tossed its mane as Ailis took the reins in a steady grip.

Laird Liam Robertson's beard was gray and thin, but he still held himself proudly as two hundred of his men assembled to ride out with him. Behind them, Robertson Castle basked in the golden light of morning. The hills were green, and the sound of rushing water filled the air—the rivers were full with melting snow. It was too soon for heather or flowers, but Ailis could smell the changing season in the air. She lifted her face and let the sun warm her nose for the first time in weeks. She was tired of having to huddle close to the hearth to chase the cold from her flesh or pull her wrap up to avoid the frigid wind.

"I was invited," Ailis reminded her father.

"So ye were, but I do no' like the man—even if he is the king's regent—telling me how to direct me own daughter. His business should be with me. No' a woman."

Her father puffed out his chest in a display of authority, but she could see the acquiescence in his eyes. He may not have agreed with the new regent, but he did like to grant her requests when there was no solid reason to deny her.

It made it so easy to love him. She smiled, and he groaned, his Highlander pride requiring some form of bluster to make sure everyone knew he'd at least argued against complying completely with the summons.

"Maybe the man will take the tale of how fetching ye are back to court. It's time ye wed," the laird continued.

"Of course it is, Father," Ailis agreed demurely.

Her father pointed at the twinkle in her eyes. "Just like yer mother," he accused, then climbed onto the back of his horse. "I had to court her for two seasons before she agreed to me suit." He held up two time-weathered fingers. "Two! As if I had naught better to do with me time."

The Robertson retainers making ready to ride laughed with their laird.

The men were looking forward to the journey. They wanted to stretch their legs too. Highlanders might enjoy telling stories by the fireside, but their true love was creating those tales. They jested with one another as their kilts swayed with their motions. The horses shook their heads, adjusting to their bridles and stamping impatiently on the cobblestones in the inner yard. Ailis's mother had insisted on the cobblestones, to keep the mud out of the castle. Ailis had heard the Grants were going to lay stone during the summer because it worked so well.

She lifted her chin and inhaled the scent of new greenery. The last thing she had on her mind was a husband. Ailis was almost sure her father agreed with her, but as a daughter of the laird, it was her duty to think of alliances. So her sire would make the expected comments from time to time. The truth was he didn't want her to go anywhere, and the stack of offers sitting in his study remained untouched. No regent needed to carry tales about her back to court. Offers had been arriving since she'd turned fifteen. But in the last two years, her father hadn't opened a single one, only asked her if he should.

That was a blessing—one many girls didn't enjoy. She looked at the men making ready to ride out with her father, searching among their hard bodies for anything that might stir a longing inside her for marriage.

All she felt was a sense of approval for their forms.

Ailis smiled.

Well, at least she was not repulsed by men. She just wasn't overly interested in them. So marriage could wait another season.

But going out for a springtime ride to meet the Earl of Morton at the abbey sounded fine. She adored her childhood home, but the winter had been long, and she wanted to walk and feel the sun on her skin.

She would be very happy to return when their meeting was concluded.

৵৹

Laird Shamus MacPherson wasn't one to admit that his hair was thinning. But he had taken to wearing a thick wool bonnet, even when sitting at his desk in his study while a fire crackled behind him in the hearth. Bhaic MacPherson watched his father read the message in front of him and growl at it.

"I'll go see the new regent meself," Shamus decided.

Bhaic didn't interrupt. Shamus MacPherson was busy poking the Earl of Morton's summons where it lay on the table. "Bloody waste of time. How like a lowlander regent to think everyone has time to squander on foolish ceremonies, such as riding down from the Highlands to reaffirm the peace. As if I do nae know who me king is!"

"I'll be riding with ye, Father," Bhaic told his sire and laird.

Shamus looked at him and frowned. "I refuse to let that man waste yer time as well. It will fall on yer shoulders soon enough, this duty to ignore what truly needs doing in favor of riding off to meet with whatever man has managed to bribe enough fellow councillors to gain the position of regent. It is nae as if we've had a king that lasted any too long."

"At least we have a king, and no' his mother."

"Bhaic MacPherson—"

Bhaic answered his father in a firm tone. "Do nae scold me for saying what everyone is thinking. I'm a Highlander, nae some lowland Scot more concerned with appearances than maintaining his honor."

His father nodded, pride lighting his eyes. "Ye are right there, me lad. Right as rain in the summer." Shamus stood up, tugging his doublet down. "Mary

Stuart may have been a queen of Scotland, but it's a king we really need. So we will have to put up with regents until young James is old enough to manage. I'll do me duty and ride out to meet his regent, and judge his mood. Maybe this one will last until the boy is grown."

"I would nae count too much upon that," Bhaic warned his father. "The earl is the fourth regent, and the king is only seven years old." He stood and shook out his shoulders. "So I'll be going along to meet this regent. I want a look at him meself."

"Very well, no doubt that's wise," his father said as he came around the table and walked toward the doors that opened into the great hall. Two MacPherson retainers stood guard, reaching up to pull on their bonnets when their laird appeared. Shamus started down the aisle toward the doors with a determined pace, the maids they passed all lowering themselves before returning to the duty of clearing away the remains of the morning meal. The great hall was still full of long tables and benches that welcomed all the inhabitants of the castle at mealtimes.

"Yes, it's wise of ye to ride along with me to meet this regent," Shamus continued for the benefit of those listening. "Ye are making sure ye are seen, so there will be no question who will become the next laird of the MacPhersons."

"There never was a question of that, Father, and it is nae why I am riding out with ye," Bhaic stated. "It's because ye are me laird, no' just me sire."

His father turned and winked. "But, me boy, I fully enjoyed begetting ye!"

There were a few muffled chuckles from the

retainers close enough to hear. Shamus's eyes twinkled with merriment as he finished making his way to the huge double doors of the outer wall.

The yard beyond the open doors of the keep was full of horses already. MacPherson retainers were busy making ready to ride out with their laird. Many of the lowland Scots had taken to wearing britches instead of kilts, but the MacPherson men wore their colors proudly.

Bhaic grinned. The lowland Scots called him a savage, but he enjoyed knowing they feared him. His colors were a constant reminder that he was part of something more than just his own family. No man wore the colors of the MacPherson without earning the right by conducting himself with honor. There was no greater shame to a Highlander than being stripped of his kilt.

The lowland Scots were welcome to their britches. Let their regent see the MacPhersons in their kilts.

He was a MacPherson and a Highlander. Let them worry about his mood.

❧

The Earl of Morton was a rough man.

He'd seen his share of the harder side of life. That fact accounted for the task he was embarking on today. He'd dressed for the occasion, wearing a thick leather over-doublet to protect against smaller blades.

He lifted one gauntlet-clad hand and pointed at the forest surrounding the abbey. "Make sure our men are posted along that line of trees. I want musket and pike there—these Highlanders must know they are surrounded, or we'll have a bloodbath."

"Might have that anyway," his captain remarked. "They *are* Highlanders. Not likely to bend."

"Today, they are going to put being Scotsmen above their clan loyalties."

The captain didn't correct his noble lord, but he surely didn't agree with the man. Highlanders were different. Only a man living inside a palace would be so naive about that.

❧

Ailis leaned low over the neck of her mare when the abbey came into view. The older portion, which had been built a century before, was crumbling. She tucked in her heels and let the horse have its freedom. The animal raced down the hill, across the meadow, and through the remaining arches of the old medieval church.

"Ailis!" her father scolded, still up on the hillside where the forest thinned.

She lifted her arm and waved to him, then slid from the saddle with a happy smile on her lips.

"Ailis!"

The tone of her father's voice had changed. It sent a chill down her spine, and she turned to look back. His retainers were surging down the hillside, their teeth bared and their kilts flapping with the motion of their horses. They were riding hard, but there was no way to reach her before the men waiting behind her made their move.

She jumped back, making a grab for her horse, but one of them had already taken the animal's reins, which left her facing six men. She pulled a small dagger from where she'd tucked it in the top of her sleeve.

They converged on her. She got off only one jab before she was trapped. She struggled against the hold on her arms, straining to break free, but she knew it was hopeless. She'd ridden straight into a trap—and her kin were honor bound to try and rescue her.

Ye are such a fool!

Berating herself didn't change the fact that there were hard fingers digging into her flesh. Or that she could smell the scent of horses and gunpowder on her captors. The sun shone cheerfully, and the grass was growing, but she felt the cold kiss of steel against her throat.

It seemed surreal, like a dream spun in her ear by a fae while she napped on the grass in the afternoon of a long summer day.

But the men holding her were real. Their breeches frightened her the most because it meant they were not Highlanders. She strained against their hold, snarling as she tried to break free.

"Stay back if you do not want her blood spilled!" the one holding her said.

Her heart was pounding, and sweat trickled down the side of her face from her struggle, but the blade against her throat was too terrifying to fight against. She could feel how sharp it was, feel it already slicing into the surface of her tender skin.

"Hold!" her father yelled. The first of his retainers had made it to the arches. They jumped from their saddles and had their swords drawn before her father's voice halted their impulse to rescue her. They froze, pure, raw fury in their eyes.

Guilt fell on her like a stone. It was crushing, burning its way through her as she witnessed the distress she'd caused by being impulsive. There would be blood spilled, and it was her fault for leaving her escort behind.

She'd known the cost of such recklessness since she was eight years old and had made the mistake of wandering during a spring festival. The memory normally chilled her blood; today, it was already near freezing.

"The earl is waiting for you, Laird Robertson," her captor said.

"I will nae be meeting with a man who sends his men to put a blade to me daughter's throat!" her father declared.

"Your daughter is in no danger."

Ailis shifted her gaze to find the newcomer. He stood over to one side, flanked by a dozen men with black-powder guns all aimed at her father and kin.

"I do nae agree with ye, boy," her father retorted. "Tell yer men to get their hands off me child. I thought it was only the bloody MacPhersons we had to worry about."

"How very interesting to hear you say that name." The man gestured to the men holding her, and they marched her toward him. "I am the Earl of Morton, Regent for James VI of Scotland." He studied her for a long moment before looking past her to her father. "Let us go inside to discuss this."

Ailis didn't have any choice. She was muscled through the garden that fed the inhabitants of the abbey and into the kitchens.

The bruising grips on her arms didn't bother her half as much as the knowledge that her kin were being drawn after her. Better her throat had been slit in the garden.

For now, she was the bait.

"Do nae—" She turned her head and screamed, but the man holding her clamped his hand over her mouth, smothering her warning.

Aye, she'd rather be dead than watch her father's men coming after her.

She deserved death for being so foolish.

But she very much feared that she was going to be forced to live through the consequences of her actions.

❧

"Bloody Robertsons," a MacPherson retainer snarled.

"At least we do nae hide behind skirts," a Robertson growled back.

Ailis looked over to see the other side of the church filled with the tartan of her father's enemy, the MacPherson. More men stood guard over them with long muskets. The MacPhersons looked as furious as her kin did. But they were outnumbered by the earl's men, who surrounded the entire abbey, more of them posted in the alcoves above to ensure they had a clear shot at their prisoners.

"Regent or nae, ye're a bloody coward." Her father's voice bounced around the inside the abbey. It was built of dark stone, making it seem like a cave. The stained glass windows served only to darken the sanctuary even further. The earl's men removed the blade from her throat and marched her up the aisle to the front pew.

"What I am is a man set on a course of action," the earl said as he stood at the front of the church. There wasn't a hint of remorse in his expression. Two priests stood at the altar, their fingers moving on the prayer beads hanging from their belts.

"Only a coward uses a man's daughter," her father protested.

"Or a man who is ready to crawl out of the barbaric traditions you Highlanders cling to," the earl answered. "I needed your attention, and now I have it."

"I'll nae leave behind me honor in favor of a man who hides behind a woman," one of the MacPhersons argued. He stood up, boldly offering his chest to the gunners.

"Instead, you would all continue to fight over something that happened more than three generations ago?" the earl asked.

Ailis found herself biting her lower lip. It was the truth, and she was slightly shamed when she was forced to hear it spoken aloud. Three generations was a long time—there was no denying it.

"It's none of yer concern," the MacPherson insisted. He was a large man, with midnight-black hair. Unlike a number of his clansmen, his face was scraped clean. Attached to the side of his bonnet were three feathers, two of them pointing straight up. It was Laird Shamus MacPherson's son, Bhaic, which accounted for his boldness. He would be the next Laird MacPherson. The feathers confirmed that he was the clan Tanis. It was more than blood that put him in line for the lairdship; the rest of the clan's leaders had voted him into the position.

"Join Mistress Ailis in the front pew," the earl ordered.

Bhaic smiled, showing off even white teeth, and crossed his arms over his chest. He had his shirtsleeves pulled up, granting her a view of his muscular arms. A touch of heat stroked her cheeks, and she looked back at the earl.

"Shoot me where I stand," Bhaic taunted. "If ye've got the balls to."

"Mind yer mouth, MacPherson, me daughter is present."

Bhaic shrugged. "I am nae the fool who brought a woman along."

"The Regent is the one who insisted me daughter come along!" her father protested. "For a man who thinks we Highlanders are stuck in the Middle Ages, Lord Morton, ye are the one acting like a savage. I never thought to question the terms of yer message as if ye were some sort of English scum."

"I find myself agreeing with Laird Robertson." Bhaic sat back down in defiance of the earl's demand. "So now that I am completely disgusted, what do ye want, Regent?"

"An end to this feud," the earl informed them.

A ripple went through the sanctuary, the scuffing of boot heels against the stone floor as the men shifted, the reality of their long feud shaming more of them than would be willing to admit it was so.

The earl didn't miss it either.

"The crown and the king will no longer tolerate unrest in the Highlands," Morton informed them.

"What are ye planning to do?" her father demanded. "Kill us all?" He chuckled ominously. "Ye'll nae be the first nobleman who fails at that task."

The abbey was full of laughter, the sound bouncing between the dark stone walls.

"Come here, mistress," the earl demanded.

Ailis wanted to refuse, but that felt cowardly. Bhaic was standing up to the man, so she would as well.

"Stay where ye are, Daughter," her father ordered.

She stood, earning another round of laughter from the MacPhersons.

"Seems ye are as good at teaching yer children respect as ye are at fighting, Robertson!"

Ailis turned around, her skirts flying up to reveal her ankles. She glared at Bhaic MacPherson.

"I am no more afraid of this lowlander than ye are," she said in a tone that would have pleased even her stern tutor. Her chin was steady and her voice even without a hint of sharpness, just clear determination.

The grin on his face faded, and for just a moment, his expression became one of approval. But she turned and walked toward the earl. She had to fend off the impulse to perform a reverence, because it was such an ingrained courtesy. But he would not receive such politeness from her—even if he was a nobleman. There were plenty who would warn her against such prideful ways, but she had been raised in the Highlands. Respect was earned. And the earl had abandoned polite behavior, so she would as well.

She spoke evenly once more. "I'll not be lowering meself before a man who ordered a blade put to me throat."

His lips twitched in response. For a moment, he studied her, running his gaze up and down her length. When his gaze met with hers again, there was a pleased look flickering in them. He was different than the other noblemen she'd met. There was a rough edge to him that struck a warning bell inside her. He was ruthless and unashamed of it. This man had not been raised with servants trailing his heels. He'd dirtied his hands more than once. She was certain of it.

That made him very dangerous.

"Look through those windows, mistress, and tell me what you see."

A knot was tightening in her belly, pulling tighter as she turned and looked where he pointed. Beyond the sides of the abbey, there were more of the earl's men, set apart by their britches. They held a line of horses steady beneath thick tree branches; more men stood ready with nooses above the animals.

She felt as though her throat was closing shut.

"Have you lost your courage, Lady?" the earl inquired.

"I have nae," she countered, but her voice cracked, betraying her horror.

"Enough. Let the lass be." Bhaic stood back up. "If ye want a fight, man, I'll be happy to give it to ye, since ye've gone to so much trouble to get us all here."

"Like hell!" her father shouted. "She's me daughter, and I'll be the one doing the fighting, since me sons are nae here."

Ailis gulped down a breath and fought to find her strength before her father lunged across the pews at Bhaic—and unleashed a bloodbath.

"There is a row of horses with nooses dangling above the empty saddles," Ailis forced out. "Every detail set for an execution."

The abbey went silent as her words reached every last man. All hints of teasing dissipated, and more than one man looked at the gunners and began to judge his chances. Better to die trying to live than wait for someone to slap the flank of a horse while you felt the bite of the noose around your neck.

"This feud ends here," the earl informed them. "None of ye recall the reason it began."

"I do," her father insisted. "It was a MacPherson who murdered me grandfather."

"Only after he tried to steal the bride of me own grandfather!" Shamus MacPherson argued, pointing at Liam Robertson. "But it was the money he was trying to steal the most."

"Me kin are nae thieves!" her father roared. "She found yer grandfather's bed cold, and that's a fact!"

Suddenly the men in the pews didn't care about the guns trained on them. They were ready to tear one another limb from limb. Over three hundred Highlanders began to surge to their feet, but a blast from one of the muskets sobered them. The scent of the black powder was thick, mixing with the beeswax lingering from the morning mass.

"You will end this feud," the earl demanded. "Scotland needs unity. England's virgin queen is earning the wrath of most of the continent with her Protestant ways. If we do not want to find ourselves invaded, we will present a united front to the rest of the world. There will be peace between the MacPhersons and the Robertsons so we might all be Scots."

"I suppose if ye hang us all, there might be." It was Bhaic who spoke up, his voice strong and steady.

"I find meself agreeing with a MacPherson," her father groused. "May me father forgive me and no' rise from his grave to torment me."

The earl was looking at Ailis. She felt the weight of his gaze, the knot in her belly becoming unbearable.

"Your father's fate is in your hands, mistress. I leave the choice to you, since they are still intent on fighting, even with the odds clearly against them."

"I am one person," she answered slowly, a tingle touching her nape. "What is it ye suggest I do?"

The earl offered her a direct look. One that left no doubt in her mind as to how deadly serious he was. If she failed, he'd hang her kin as she watched. She swallowed the lump lodged in her throat.

"Ye are the laird's daughter. Alliances are made through highborn daughters," the earl informed her. He pointed at the altar. "Kneel and take vows of marriage with Bhaic MacPherson, or watch your father and his captains hang. Either way, you shall kneel in prayer."

She gagged. Her jaw fell open, and she couldn't seem to close it. So she clasped a hand over her mouth, trying not to retch.

"She will nae do it," her father snarled.

"Me son will have no part of any wedding with a Robertson!" Shamus MacPherson declared from the pews.

The earl gripped her arm and sent her stumbling toward the priests.

The earl spoke directly to Bhaic. "Then your son will live with the knowledge that he sentenced you and your captains to their deaths. My marksmen have been told whom to spare. If you choose death, your son will live with the knowledge that he stood by and allowed it to happen."

The gunners were looking down the length of their

muskets, the smoldering rope they used to touch off the powder in their weapons held securely in their fingers. They had the ends of those deadly guns cradled in iron holders to help bear the weight and make sure their aim was true. She could see the men in the pews, all trying to calculate their odds of escaping. The first one to move would die; the only chance to flee would be during the melee.

It was a sickening thought, but one she couldn't dismiss. Highlanders had died in groups before, and at the hands of their fellow Scots too. She looked out the windows at the horses, the nooses nauseating her again.

She looked back over her shoulder at Bhaic.

He was everything she detested. Hardened. Huge. Devil-dark hair and ice-cold blue eyes. Her father's sworn enemy, and his father hated her. He was glaring at her, hatred tightening his features. She fought to keep her own revulsion from showing.

She had to. The earl would keep his word. She had no doubt on that matter. None at all.

"It is a simple enough choice, madam. Prayers for the living or for the dead. Make your choice," the earl instructed her.

What a poor marriage it would be. Bhaic hated her: not her nature, but her blood.

But she couldn't be so selfish.

Better to be hated than live with bloodstained hands.

She climbed to the altar and forced herself to kneel. It felt as though her knees broke beneath the effort. Staying there took every last bit of self-control she had.

"A most sensible choice," the earl muttered.

"Me son will nae be wedding that Robertson," Shamus MacPherson insisted.

"That's on account of the fact that MacPhersons are too bloody selfish to think of anything but their own gain," Ailis's father announced. "Me daughter is near gagging, but she will nae put herself above me life. Curse and rot ye, Morton, for using a lass so."

"Me son is naught to gag over!" Shamus growled. "I've got plenty of offers."

"And the only one that matters is mine," the earl interrupted. "I offer to end this feud through a marriage, or wipe out the lot of you who continue to persist in fighting over something your grandparents did. Captain, make ready to fire."

"Ye'll have yer way, Lord Morton."

Ailis flinched, the timbre of Bhaic's tone cutting through her resolve. Panic was trying to take hold of her, the urge to bolt almost overwhelming. She gripped handfuls of her skirt, squeezing until her fingers ached.

"At least today ye will," Bhaic stated, "because ye are right about one thing: I will nae stand here and watch me clansmen die while I do nae face the same danger. But I say ye are a coward to fight yer battles through the use of a woman and a musket leveled at me father."

"Alliances have been made through marriage since the dawn of time. Even in the Highlands," the earl said. "Ye'll wed that girl and end this feud because your children will share blood."

Children…

Oh, hellfire. They would have to beget those babes together.

She couldn't lay with Bhaic MacPherson!

Ailis started to stand, losing the battle to kneel so submissively. She could feel Bhaic closing the distance. Her heart was pounding, feeling as if it might burst.

But a hard hand caught her wrist before she made it very far off the hassock. Bhaic cursed low and long in Gaelic, earning a scathing look from the priest.

"Keep yer hands off me," she hissed and jerked her hands in front of her.

He cut her a mocking look as the priest began the opening prayer. "That will make for an agreeable marriage as far as I am concerned," he replied.

She felt the color drain from her face. Ailis looked toward the priest, but seeing him perform the motions of the sacrament of marriage gave her no relief at all. She glanced back toward Bhaic, and saw once again the horses waiting beneath the row of nooses.

Trapped.

She was caught, just like a rabbit.

It was a horrible feeling, made even worse by the sight of Bhaic MacPherson kneeling next to her. His tartan was something she'd been raised to hate and fear. She'd seen many a widow weeping because his clan had fought with hers. The great hall of Robertson Castle rang with curses against them so often, the priest on Robertson land no longer gave out penance for them.

And she was wedding the worst one of all. The laird's son, the next leader of raids against her own kin. At least he didn't want to touch her. But he reached down and squeezed her hand. She jumped and made eye contact. His eyes were a startling blue. Not the color of the summer sky, but a vibrant blue that struck her as more intense.

"The priest is waiting," he growled, startling her back into the moment.

She looked at the priest and nodded, because she couldn't recall what he'd asked her. The older man frowned but smoothed out his expression quickly.

"Ye must answer with yer voice," he admonished softly. "Do ye swear to be an obedient wife?"

She bit her lip, rebellion flashing through her. But it was followed quickly by the memory of the horses and the waiting nooses. "Aye." She had to force the word past her lips. It practically stung. For the first time in her life, she doubted she was going to be able to keep her promise.

She was lying in the house of God.

Breaking a commandment.

And all because of the MacPhersons.

"Aye." Bhaic's voice broke through her mental turmoil, the harsh note in his voice grating on her pride.

Why should he be so furious? The answer was simple: she was as hated on his land as he was on hers. The idea punctured her anger and left her feelings unguarded.

As much as she'd not been in a hurry to wed, kneeling beside a groom that detested her had never worried her. Her father had always placed her tender feelings above cold-blooded business transactions that might be sealed with a wedding.

The Earl of Morton was not adverse to such things, apparently.

The priest elevated the golden chalice and brought it toward them. Her throat felt swollen tight, but the burn of the wine made its way down to her stomach anyway. The last of the Latin prayers echoed through the stone abbey as the priest made the sign of the cross in front of them.

"Go in peace."

Ailis was certain she had never heard three more impossible words in her life. Bhaic jumped up as though the kneeling bench was studded with spikes. His kilt swayed back, giving her a glimpse of his hard thighs before it settled into place.

Why are ye looking at the man's thighs?

She had no idea and chided herself for mentally lingering on something she saw often enough.

"I will be providing the wedding banquet," Morton informed them.

More of the earl's armed men surrounded Bhaic and took him off through the side of the abbey. They gestured her after him.

She went, but she refused to think of the man as her husband.

He was nothing of the sort.

He was a MacPherson.

⤝⤞

The Earl of Morton knew how to celebrate.

The banquet was lavish. A short ride from the abbey took them to a tower belonging to the earl. His staff offered platters of new spring fruit, brought from the shipyards servicing lands far away, where spring came earlier than it did in the Highlands. A full boar had been roasted until it was golden brown, the scent teasing her nose, but Ailis refused to eat any of it.

She was not celebrating.

Bhaic seemed in agreement with her, leaving his plate untouched as the staff continued to carry in platters meant to tempt.

Below them, at the long tables that filled the hall, both of their kin brooded. The only relief from their scowls came when one of them gave in and tasted some of the rich fare offered, grinning as they tasted the fine food. Musicians played merry tunes in alcoves surrounding the hall. The tempo would have normally tempted Ailis to tap her foot, but she felt as stiff as a tree.

There was a pretty tablecloth beneath her plate and beeswax candles burning. Someone had made her a wreath of heather and greens for her hair, but she'd tossed it in front of her plate, and it sat there looking sad. Maybe she shouldn't be so surly. The Head of House cast her a reprimanding look from where she was overseeing the banquet. It wasn't hard to tell what the older woman was thinking. She was judging Ailis a brat. A girl in a woman's body, still throwing tantrums because everything was not as she wished.

Life was often unkind. A wise person learned to take joy when they could find it.

The staff had no doubt been working for days to prepare the decorative foods being presented. Every dish set before her and Bhaic gleamed from recent polishing. Yet no one gave the staff any word of gratitude. All her kin wanted was to fight with the MacPhersons.

The MacPhersons had exactly the same thing on

their minds. Scathing glances flew between tables as muffled curses mixed with the music. Ailis looked up at the musicians in the alcoves. Music was a rare treat. Most of the time, the days were too full of chores for anyone to have the inclination to play an instrument during supper, and here her kin were, wasting the moment. Ignoring the pleasures while they plotted more bloodletting.

Perhaps the earl had a point.

She felt guilty for even thinking it, but she could see the logic in ending the feud that had gone on for so many years.

Ailis sighed. She reached for the wreath and put it on.

"Pleased with yer circumstances after all?" Bhaic asked, cutting her a hard look. "Was this all a plot yer father hatched to further steal from the MacPhersons?"

Her eyes grew round as her temper boiled. He was a huge man, intimidating. He was scowling at her, but that didn't change the fact that they were both being rude to the staff.

And she was done with it. She focused on that thought because ill manners were more than MacPherson or Robertson, more than even a Highlander opposed to a lowland Scot. Manners were civilized and the mark of a good upbringing, as well as the mark of an unspoiled child.

"I'm thinking I'm past the age of sulking." She reached for her goblet and took a swallow, forcing a serene look upon her face.

Fury flickered in his eyes, and he leaned closer. "Is that why yer father had to resort to plotting with the earl to get ye a husband? Because no one in their right mind would want to steal away a Robertson harpy who is long in the tooth?"

The tiny bit of contentment she'd managed to cultivate shriveled and died. But instead of allowing her temper to rise, what she felt was a twinge of hurt that he might judge her so harshly.

His voice grew louder, causing the men below them to look up at the high table. Some of her father's men growled, and there was a clear answer from the MacPherson.

Bhaic stiffened and looked at their audience.

The goblet shook in her hand as she faced the very real circumstances of their union. Morton's words rose from her memory.

Prayers for the living or for the dead…

"I've made my choice, so make yers…" Ailis whispered. "All they wait upon is a small quarrel between us to begin the fighting. I confess I would rather no' give it to them. Being agreeable is no' too much for me to accomplish, no matter what insults ye care to bait me with."

He tilted his head toward her so their eyes met. Something in his eyes sent a ripple of awareness through her. Her heart accelerated as she realized there was no hope of success unless he joined her.

"Ye are more woman than lass." There was a touch of something that might have been admiration in his tone, if she were given to entertaining the idea that he could feel anything but hate toward her.

"I'd rather no' see blood spilt either," he said slowly as he made an effort to soften his expression. She could see the resistance glittering in his eyes and knew he saw the same in hers. Yet she maintained her soft smile, and he forced his lips into an easy line.

A Robertson and MacPherson, united in a common goal. Inconceivable, yet it sat on both of their shoulders in that moment. A moment of unity she'd never imagined, but discovered herself proud of. Yet it was a shared achievement.

She had no idea what to think of that fact.

He muttered something profane under his breath and reached for his goblet. He raised it high. "To me bride." The MacPherson and Robertson reached for their goblets out of habit, many of them looking surprised when it sank in that they had just toasted to the union.

With each other.

"It seems we have both been assigned roles to play that we do nae favor, Ailis." His lips had quirked into what might actually be considered a grin. If only a minor one. "Ye do so with grace, madam."

For a fleeting moment, she felt the most unexpected thing: a sense of commonality between herself and a MacPherson. It was shocking, numbing her wits enough to keep her staring at Bhaic. The lapse allowed her to notice how fair he was. His cheekbones were high, his jaw strong. She liked the way he kept his chin scraped clean of whiskers. Somehow, the lack of beard made his lips look sensual. A flutter went through her belly, and she looked away, the unexpected response making her uncertain. There was the unmistakable touch of heat in her cheeks.

Her gaze landed on the Earl of Morton. He

bestowed a small, pleased look on her, then stood up and signaled to the men standing guard behind the high table. "I bid you good night."

The musicians had been replaced by gunmen. They pointed their black-powder muskets down at the men sitting at the tables. Her father wasn't intimidated, instead climbing to his feet, his face red with rage.

"Bloody bastard," Liam Robertson raged. "Me daughter is nae going above stairs with a MacPherson!"

"She is going above stairs to consummate her marriage," the earl informed them.

"Me son will have naught to do with any Robertson wench, even if she strips down and spreads herself out for him!" Shamus MacPherson hollered to the delight of his men. They cheered and pounded the tabletop.

"Then I will shoot the lot of you right here. I offered you a choice. Make no mistake, I will have peace between you. If this is not a valid marriage, I will wipe out the generation that cannot see the wisdom in building a future free of feuding."

The earl's tone was harsh. Seeing the muzzles aimed at her kin, Ailis pushed her chair back and stood. The Head of House rushed in front of the guards and took her by the hand, pulling her across the raised platform the high table stood on. Ailis didn't look back, but she felt Bhaic's gaze burning into her.

The lump was back in her throat. No matter how many times she swallowed, it remained. The Head of House was patting the back of her hand, advising her to "bear up." Wasn't that the plight of women and wives? To shoulder what must be endured in a world run by men? The Head of House sent her approving looks, as did the maids that followed. None of them wanted the chore of mopping up blood from the floor or to lay their heads down in a keep haunted by the ghosts of those gunned down inside its walls.

But the thing that horrified Ailis most was the certain knowledge that the worst was yet to come.

෴

The earl's tower boasted a fine new slipper tub.

Sitting near the hearth at the back of the kitchen, it was made of copper and had a high back. The Head of House had set her maids to making sure it was full of water. The moment the woman pulled her into the kitchen, the maids working at the long tables pointed the boys toward the doors.

With only women left, the maids began to untie the laces holding Ailis's dress closed. She tried to shy away, but they surrounded her, one working on the lace that closed her bodice in the back and two more loosening the cuffs of her sleeves.

"We are only women here," the Head of House insisted firmly before pulling the wreath off Ailis's head. "No need for modesty. And all the better for ye if there are witnesses aplenty to swear ye are nae misshapen."

Ailis froze, stunned by the Head of House's words. The woman nodded with approval as the maids lifted off Ailis's bodice and began to open her stays.

There had been no midwife to inspect her.

Without such an inspection, Bhaic MacPherson might send her back to her father, claiming she was misshapen.

No doubt the earl thought himself so high in authority that such a detail would not matter. The man was certainly a lowlander, for no Highlander would have made such an error. Ailis enjoyed the thought, for at last, she was able to see the earl's failings instead of the very tight trap he'd managed to set.

Of course…

She suddenly smiled, the lump in her throat dissolving. Bhaic wanted no more of their marriage than she. Of course he would send her back to her father. The earl and his guards would be long gone, and her father would not trust any further meetings with the regent.

The marriage would be annulled.

Relief flowed through her.

"There now…" the Head of House said in response to the smile that lifted Ailis's face. "Ye're a levelheaded one and no mistake. Seeing the blessing ye have in being wed to the son and no' the father."

Her smile faltered. Ailis looked at the woman as some of the maids made low sounds in their throats.

It would seem matters could be worse after all.

Her stays were opened, and the maids took the garment away. Her skirts followed quickly.

"Likely the earl worried Laird MacPherson might be too old to consummate his vows," the Head of House continued.

"Likely," Ailis agreed. It was another reason for her to be hopeful. An old man might just keep her, but Bhaic was young and wouldn't care to have her shackled to him.

No, of course not. She'd seen the resentment in his eyes.

So, there was naught to worry about.

Even being stripped of her remaining garments

didn't bother her—she was still basking in the certainty that Bhaic MacPherson would happily send her back to her father as soon as the earl was gone.

The Head of House produced a comb and brushed out Ailis's long hair. The blond strands were wavy from the tight braid she'd worn all day, but straightened as soon as Ailis climbed into the tub and submerged her head.

The soap they handed her was made with rosemary. Ailis happily rubbed it along her arms and legs while the maids tried to hurry her.

She resisted their prodding, lingering in her bath and rinsing her hair twice before standing up. With her stress dissipating, she grew tired. There was no resistance in her as the Head of House guided her up the steps to the second floor.

But the knot in her belly returned when she realized some of the earl's guards had fallen in step behind them. She'd not escape completely from this marriage. There would always be whispers clinging to her skirts.

The sun was setting, the last crimson rays making the windows glow. The woman kept going, pulling Ailis up another flight of narrow stone steps. At least the earl's men kept back enough to keep from getting a clear look at how thin her chemise was.

They reached a door and the Head of House stopped. "It's a fine chamber the earl had prepared for ye." She pulled the ring of keys hanging from her waist and fitted one into a lock on the door. It made a grinding sound when she turned it.

Ailis looked down at the two guards waiting behind

her. They wore breastplate armor and helmets, and each one had a sword and a smaller black-powder gun. They inclined their heads before looking away because she wasn't dressed. The Head of House had brushed out her hair and put the wreath back on her head before deeming her ready to meet her groom.

He wasn't that.

Bhaic MacPherson wasn't going to be her husband. Yet it appeared that they would have to share a chamber for the night. Try as she might, Ailis couldn't stop her heart from racing at the thought.

But the Head of House took her into the chamber, and Ailis froze when she saw the earl sitting in a chair next to the bed.

"The bride, at last." He motioned to the Head of House. "Remove that chemise. I will bear witness to her health myself."

∽

Ailis felt as if her lungs had frozen. She needed to draw breath but couldn't. She was locked in the horror of the moment, unable to look away from the hard conviction in the earl's eyes. Unable to recall how certain she'd been that everything would be righted by the next day.

The reason was simple. She had to deal with the present first, and the Earl of Morton was a harsh reality indeed.

"Ye'll do no such thing," a male voice said.

Her deliverance had come at the hands of Bhaic MacPherson. She was hugging herself, intent on keeping the chemise on as the Head of House tried to comply with her master's order. But she was also trying not to stare at Bhaic MacPherson.

He was stripped to his shirt and boots, the edge of the shirt falling to just above his knees. She stared at his groin, unable to help herself, but the dark room didn't allow her to see anything.

Bhaic stepped in front of the woman and pointed her toward the doorway they'd entered the chamber through.

"Did ye bathe me bride?" he asked.

The Head of House lowered herself. "Aye, Laird."

"In naught but her skin?" he pressed while Ailis felt her cheeks burn.

"Indeed."

He grasped Ailis by the upper arm and sent her toward the large bed.

"With other experienced women in attendance?" Bhaic continued.

"That has naught to do with my request," the earl interrupted. "I'll see the wench for myself, so there will be no cry from your father that the girl is unfit for marriage."

Bhaic pointed the Head of House toward the doorway again, and she took the opportunity to hurry out of the chamber.

"Ye've had yer way enough today, Lord Morton." Bhaic faced off with the man. "Ye will nae be looking on me wife."

"This marriage will stand, or I will return with enough soldiers to destroy your clan."

"I've heard enough threats out of ye too," Bhaic informed the earl. "Ye have no guards here."

The earl stood and grinned unpleasantly. "Thinking of trying me, Highlander? You might find it harder than you think to choke the life out of me."

Bhaic smiled menacingly. "The only thing I'm worried about is that I might enjoy it and have to account for it to St. Peter someday."

The two men began to circle each other. Bhaic moved toward her and slapped her bottom. "Get up on the bed, lass, so ye're out of the way."

Her cheeks were on fire now, an instant reaction to the idea of climbing into the large bed at Bhaic's command.

He'd be a demanding one in bed, for certain.

The thought was misplaced. It was also exciting, if she was willing to admit it. Which she wasn't. But she climbed onto the bed. The mattress was filled with goose down and the sheets scented with expensive ambergris, but she was focused on the two men glaring at each other.

"My guards are below"—the earl spoke softly, ominously—"with their muskets aimed at your father's heart. If I don't return, they have orders to fire."

Bhaic only grinned in the face of the earl's threat.

"Ye will nae be the first man to discover his authority fading with his death," Bhaic responded. "Once ye're dead, they will look for the next leader who is still among the living. That's the way with ye men who worship position and power."

"And ye'll go back to fighting over something yer grandfather did." The earl straightened, abandoning his fighting pose. "Tell me something, Highlander, is it better to fight for yourself or for a man who is long dead? You will be Laird of the MacPherson soon. Are you going to happily condemn hundreds of your own kin to death because you want to continue a feud that is three generations old? And one that started with a jilted groom and a fat dowry? Where's the honor in sending your clansmen to their deaths over something so very done with?"

There was a long silence in the chamber.

"I'll be remembering who I am," Bhaic answered, but his forehead furrowed, and he straightened up.

"Thinking about it, aren't you?" the earl questioned smoothly. "Do that, son of the MacPhersons. Think long and hard about the fact that right now, you can choose a brighter future for your clan. You claim to put them above all else. Consider doing it instead of just talking about it."

"I married the Robertson wench to protect them, did I nae?"

The earl nodded. "Words mean little without action. Unconsummated, your vows mean nothing. I am not a fool. I will know if you send her back to her father. I also know it will not be an easy union. Your clan will accept her as their mistress only if you make it clear she is your choice." He turned to look at Ailis. "You wanted peace enough to wed, but it will take far more than words spoken in front of a priest."

The earl walked to the door and pounded on it. His guards pulled the small view hatch open and looked at him before opening the door.

"I may not be a Highlander, but I assure you, I am devoted to Scotland as deeply as you are. I'll see this country united, even if I have to snuff out the life of those who cannot move into the future. Marriage or destruction. Make your choice, future Laird and Lady of the MacPhersons."

The earl left the room, and his men closed the door. The sound echoed inside the chamber like a gunshot. Ailis tightened her hands around the foot post of the bed, holding her breath as she waited to see what Bhaic would do.

Well, what are ye planning to do, Ailis?

She really had no idea. Matters had seemed so clear while she bathed. Now, the earl's words were echoing inside her head. It was as if her mind was unable to focus on anything else.

"I suppose the man has a valid point," Bhaic said, his tone clearly displeased but nonetheless accepting. "A very good one."

Two

AILIS JUMPED OFF THE BED.

The stone floor was cold beneath her bare feet, but she preferred to shiver rather than wait in the bed.

"He's spouting nonsense." She moved away from the bed, looking for wood to start a fire, but there was none.

Bhaic chuckled, sitting down in the chair the earl had been in. He ran his hand through his hair before stretching out his legs.

"He may be, but the man is no fool." Bhaic leaned down and started loosening the ties on his boots. "This chamber has been prepared very carefully to ensure that the only comfortable place to spend the night is in that bed."

"Together?" Her voice cracked again. She hugged herself and backed up, but a gust of wind blew in the window, chilling her to the bone. She stared at the openings in the stone, completely perplexed by the inability to cover them.

"The shutters are missing," he confirmed from behind her.

Ailis was looking through an iron screen that would

have been used to darken the chamber for a lying-in or while someone was ill. On the other side, there was no glass and no shutters to seal out the night.

"No wood either," she remarked after staring at the fireplace for a full minute because she just didn't want to face their circumstances.

She turned and locked gazes with him. She was beginning to shiver, and it was the chill of the night, not her company, causing it.

There were windows all around the chamber. The night wind blew in, stirring her hair as she looked back at the bed.

"No bed curtains," Bhaic added.

There were still rails where the fabric would have hung. Bhaic stood and grasped one.

"The canopy is gone as well." He released the rail with a disgusted grunt. "The bastard planned this well. His bully boys took me kilt while his staff had ye delivered in that transparent chemise."

Her cheeks warmed. "It is nae transparent."

He glanced toward her, his lips curving. "It is when ye walk near that candle."

She gasped and crawled right over the bed to the opposite side of the room, leaving the single candle behind.

"Ye can stop playing the innocent," he said in a tone that sounded as though it was edged with disgust.

She discovered herself stammering and fought to make her tone even. "I am nae playing at anything."

He reached for the bedding, flipping it back to reveal only the single comforter and sheet. "Ye're the one who decided this was a good idea."

Her temper rose, burning away her shyness. "Compared to watching me kin killed, it was."

He caught her in a hard look, but at least there was a flicker of agreement in his blue eyes. "It seems we are both victims of our fathers' stubborn natures."

"Aye," she answered.

He very slowly slid his gaze down her body, truly looking at her like a woman instead of a Robertson. It stole her breath, sending a bolt of heat through her that she'd never experienced before.

"So why are ye blushing now, Ailis Robertson?" he asked mockingly. "Did ye nae think on just what marriage involves?"

She looked away, unable to hold his unsettling stare. Her emotions felt as if they might spill over all the boundaries she had always lived by. There was something about him that made her nervous. And to be sure, she was uncertain how to have a civil conversation with a MacPherson. Yet being rude seemed wrong. So she floundered as she tried to answer him.

"I was a bit more focused on the musket aimed at me father's heart," she said in a rush.

His eyes narrowed. "Ye're forgetting I knelt beside ye for the same reason, lass."

There was a tone in his voice that shamed her. She drew in a deep breath and let it out. "Why are ye tormenting me with accusations about not thinking on what marriage involves?" She ended up looking at the bed again, a sense of defeat pressing against her heart. "I certainly had no thought I'd be wed today."

"We have that in common." Their gazes met once more in a moment of unexpected agreement. He made a low sound of frustration, but his features lost their stern edge. For a moment he contemplated her, look-ing as uncertain as she felt. "How old are ye, Ailis?"

She wasn't sure she liked hearing her name on his lips. It was oddly intimate. Yet they stood facing each other in their underclothes, so fitting as well.

"Twenty-two," she answered.

"Old enough to be thinking of marriage," he said.

"But with ye?" she asked before realizing she was insulting him. It really wasn't wise, since the man was locked inside the chamber with her. It was just second nature; he was a MacPherson.

"Me own delight is near impossible to contain."

His tone left no doubt that he was displeased with her. She lifted her chin, but it was only a show of bravado. She felt the distinct sting of her feelings being injured.

He was just a MacPherson. But it still hurt to realize she was hated for nothing more than the fact that she was a Robertson.

He muttered something low and moved around the bed, closing the distance between them. Her belly twisted in alarm. She scrambled over the bed again before even thinking about why he alarmed her so much. But the candle flame illuminated her the moment she stood up, so she backed away from it. That left her facing him without the bed between them.

"I will nae rape ye."

There was something new in his tone, something that calmed her. It was disgust, but not the sort he'd aimed at her before. This was injured pride. Even if he was a MacPherson, he still had a Highlander's honor.

But that admission left her nothing but gratitude. And duty. Men were not the only ones who had to shoulder their share of life's burdens. She looked back at the bed, her mouth once again dry. "Ye...ye... do nae have...to." She forced the words through her resisting lips. "I keep me promises."

"As do I," he confirmed in an unrelenting tone.

The urge to cry filled her. She shook it off and ordered herself to go toward the bed. At least it was dark and he wouldn't see the tears shimmering in her eyes. Small comfort, but better than none.

She sat on the edge of the bed, finding it impossible to lift her feet.

He moved closer, sending her heart racing. She was so keenly aware of him. Her skin felt alive and eager for contact with his. Beneath the smooth fabric of her chemise, her nipples slowly drew into hard points.

Ailis raised her chin, needing to understand why he affected her so intensely. She found him watching her, his blue eyes full of something she could not understand, but it sent a bolt of heat through her. He was only a pace from her, and studied her for a long moment before he reached out and stroked her cheek.

The contact was shocking. She jumped, scooting back to the center of the bed.

He chuckled. "Noble sacrifices are nae to me taste either, Ailis."

He placed one knee on the bed, looking as if he was testing her nerve.

"I do nae know what to do." And she didn't care to admit it to him either. "It is nae a shame that I am

nervous. Ye are the first man I have been alone with…
in a bedchamber."

"Aye, ye're skittish." His expression softened for a
moment; warmth that looked like compassion flickered in his eyes. But a gust of wind blew in and flattened his shirt against his lower body. For a moment,
the fabric molded over his member. She stared at it
and felt her cheeks burn.

"Yet still bold." He laughed, throwing his head
back and shaking with amusement.

It grated on her nerves, wounding her pride and
pushing her into action. She grabbed one of the pillows
and rose on her knees to swing it at his head. It made a
soft "woof," turning his head and silencing him.

"Stop mocking me, ye brute."

He retaliated with a lightning-quick motion of his
arm, sending the pillow flying across the chamber.
She gasped, but he was already reaching for her and
had her hauled up against his body before she finished
drawing in her breath.

He clamped her against him, his embrace as strong
as steel.

"Perhaps I am enjoying ye, Ailis." He ran one of
his hands down her back and cupped one side of her
bottom, pulling her against his lower body. His cock
pressed into her soft belly, sending a twisting sensation
through her insides that left her breathless.

"Even if ye are a Robertson, I'd be a fool if I did
nae admire the fact that ye are innocent. Nae every lass
has the restraint to keep herself pure."

"Nae every man either," she accused as she pressed
against his chest. All she accomplished was a new

understanding of how his chest felt. There were ridges of muscle beneath the fabric of the shirt, and she enjoyed the feel of them.

"Certainly nae ye," she continued, lashing out. She knew it but couldn't seem to temper her anger. It was flaring up inside her, overriding everything else. She suddenly realized that she wasn't angry. She was frightened. Of herself. She liked his embrace, his scent, and the way he touched her.

Sweet Christ. How could I?

"A man weds later than a woman." He threaded his fingers through her hair to cup her nape. "His nature still demands the comfort only a woman's body can provide."

The flicker of heat in his eyes fascinated her. Along with a knowing glint that suggested he knew exactly what she was thinking. The hard outline of his cock was turning her insides to molten liquid. She felt empty, her hips twitching toward his out of pure instinct.

"It seems ye are quick enough at learning the art of seduction," he said, his hand smoothing down her back to cup her bottom for a long moment. She felt suspended in that moment, so aware of him she ached.

Bhaic suddenly released her as though he was fighting against opening his arms.

Ailis fell back, tumbling into the center of the bed in a jumble of limbs. She rolled over and felt the brush of the night air on her thighs. With a kick, she turned over again and pushed her chemise down to cover her legs.

"I do nae care how sweet ye smell. If I bed ye, I must keep ye," he said through his teeth, looking every bit as ferocious as she'd been raised to believe he was.

"Brute," she accused softly. "Ye should keep yer hands from me, since ye do nae care for me as yer wife."

He shrugged but reached down to pull something out of his boot. "Perhaps I am, but ye will nae snare me into consummating this marriage. The earl may claim he'll return, but I doubt he'll march an army into the Highlands when he hears we've annulled our union. We need only wait a season."

The candlelight flickered off a thin blade. He lifted his leg and placed his foot in the center of the bed. A quick motion of his hand, and bright red blood dropped onto the creamy surface of the sheet. The fabric soaked it up, making each drop wider as the fibers absorbed the fluid. When there was a good-sized splotch, he pulled his leg back and replaced the dagger.

The scent of fresh blood mixed with the beeswax of the candle. The wind blew in, but she didn't shiver with cold. Instead, she shook with relief. It swept through her, leaving her nothing but a quivering mass. She sat down, unable to hold herself up any longer.

"Thank ye." The words left her mouth before she realized she was going to speak. It was another one of those uncontrolled responses he seemed to be able to solicit from her. It was frustrating, but she was too relieved to worry about the means of her deliverance.

Only that she had been rescued. He was a most unexpected champion, but welcome nonetheless.

She looked up and found him watching her, curiosity and a question in his eyes. So she looked away and slid her feet beneath the comforter. The goose down was wonderfully heavy and warm. She shivered and reached for the edge of it to pull it up.

He made a small sound under his breath that drew her attention. He was frustrated, his face set into hard lines as he contemplated her. Understanding hit her.

"We're both relieved to know each of us craves an annulment, and yet shamed by the fact that we continue our fathers' discontentment," she offered softly, unable to think of a remedy for the situation. She certainly wasn't going to suggest consummating their union.

"Aye, *shamed* is the proper word," Bhaic agreed, "for the earl is correct. Marriages have been the traditional method of ending such feuds. I should be more open to the idea."

He stared at her for another long moment, clearly trying to decide if he should change his mind. Ailis found herself holding her breath as he pondered her.

He sent the comforter up and over her. The edge of the bed sagged as he sat down and finished unlacing his boots. She heard him set them aside before he picked up the candle and set it near the door, leaving the bed in semidarkness. The bed ropes groaned as he lay back and settled himself beneath the comforter.

"Me brother..." she said, "is no' an unreasonable man."

There was a grunt from Bhaic.

"Ye both can choose what future there might be," she continued.

The bed moved. Bhaic had rolled onto his side and propped his head into his hand as he watched her. "As I noticed before, ye are more woman than lass, Ailis.

For all that I should praise ye for it, it would be best if I did nae take notice of it." He settled back down beside her. "At least no' while ye are wearing so little, and I have the church's blessing to enjoy it."

A bubble of amusement escaped from her. She just couldn't help it.

"And now ye're pleased with the fact that ye tax me," he groused.

"I admit I'd never have thought such a thing before this moment," she answered. "Ye are Bhaic MacPherson, after all."

"And ye, Ailis Robertson are in bed…with me," he said good-naturedly. "A brow-raising situation if ever there was one. Any man that might have suggested such a possibility would have earned himself the title of liar from me."

"Aye." He was warming the sheets up nicely. "Perhaps that is what to take away from this event. A willingness to welcome change."

"Aye," he agreed.

They didn't touch, but their body heat mingled. The scent of his skin teased her senses, in spite of the wind blowing through the chamber.

She'd never expected a man to smell enticing.

Yet she could not deny it or ignore it. She was still awake when the moon climbed high enough for her to see it through the window. Her body was still pulsing with strange yearnings that excited her more than she cared to notice. Yet she'd be lying if she didn't admit she had a new knowledge of her own nature. One she liked. One that gave her hope for her future, as well as a solid confidence in what had just that morning been her worst enemy. All in all, the earl had managed to begin bringing about the change he wanted.

Even if their marriage was going to be annulled.

There was still hope for a bright future.

⤜✦⤛

"Sweet."

Ailis shifted, enjoying the soft word spoken so close to her ear. She wiggled closer, drawn by the warmth. The darkest part of the night brought howling winds that chilled her nose.

So she had buried it against a warm body.

A little sigh of contentment left her lips, and she heard an answering grunt before she was pulled closer.

Still locked in sleep, she didn't bother to consider what she was doing. There was only impulse and reaction. She was being drawn toward that warmth. Seeking it out to satisfy some yearning inside her. It felt bone deep.

"So sweet…"

This time, the words brushed her neck, followed by warm lips pressed against the sensitive skin. She twisted, her body alive with pleasure. She reached for him, sliding her hands along his chest and delighting at the feeling of his crisp hair between her fingers.

He shifted, pressing her onto her back. She rolled easily, happy to take his weight. It felt so good, so very right as he pressed a kiss against her lips. His mouth was softer than expected, his lips smooth and silken.

He tasted good.

The knowledge burst inside her head, bringing her closer to consciousness.

Men didn't taste good. But Bhaic did.

Bhaic MacPherson.

She pulled away from the kiss, but he cupped her face and pressed his mouth over hers again. This time his kiss was demanding and harder. She struggled to recall why she had to resist. It wasn't because it was distasteful. Pleasure was flowing down her body from the sweet contact. She wanted to kiss him back and lost the battle to think at all for several long moments. Beautiful moments of their lips slipping across each other's, sparking a hundred different sensations that both shocked and surprised her.

But it was Bhaic MacPherson.

Her husband.

It was the word "husband" that broke the last of sleep's hold over her. She tried to back away from him, her knee connecting with his member.

He snarled, bolting up as he woke completely.

"Ye…must…not." She meant to sound stern but managed only a soft plea. Her tone was breathless.

He recoiled, taking the comforter with him. It was pitch-black in the room, the moon on its way to the horizon. She strained to see him, but in the darkness, the only hint of his presence came from the sound of his breathing.

The wind howled, and she shivered, her teeth chattering. It was the slap she needed to return to reality.

"Ye're a dangerous creature, Ailis."

The bed ropes creaked as he sent the comforter back over them both.

"Ye kissed me," she retorted as she dug her fingers into the bedding to hold it against herself.

"Because ye pressed up against me. I warned ye. I am a man who enjoys the comfort of a woman's body."

"Even when it is a Robertson? I heard ye enjoy Grants." It was her wounded pride talking. There was no other possible reason for her to crave his response to such a question.

"So that's the game, is it?"

He rolled onto his side and propped his head with his hand. She could feel him watching her. She should have kept her mouth shut.

He suddenly chuckled. "Brenda Grant was me mistress, and she enjoyed the position well. Her husband was a selfish bastard, and once she was widowed, she was woman enough to want to know if there was pleasure in bed sport. I assure ye, I did nae disappoint her."

His tone was wicked but at the same time enticing. The darkness only added to the temptation brewing inside her to needle him until he lost control again. Perhaps she'd not be disappointed either.

The desire shocked her. She shouldn't want anything at all from him.

"Is that why the earl thought I'd fall for this plan?" he asked softly. "Did the man think all he had to do was get ye into me bed and I'd lose all control?"

She scooted away from him, shivering as she touched the icy-cold sheets. "I did nae know of the earl's plans. I'd be a poor daughter if I let my sire be hanged when there was something I might do to prevent it."

"Unless yer father was never in any danger."

His tone was thick with accusation. She sat up. "I would nae have wed ye for any other reason."

Her tone was equally as distrusting. The peace she'd fallen asleep dreaming of was nothing but a forgotten fantasy.

"The Robertsons do nae have the strength to defeat us," he growled. "It's only our mercy that keeps yer land from being overrun and burned. Little wonder ye joined with Morton to lock me into this marriage."

"I did nae." She lost control, reaching out to slap him. "Brute."

The sound popped loudly, bouncing between the walls of the chamber.

"Harpy," he snarled, capturing her wrist and pinning it to the surface of the bed.

He was strong, holding her wrist down easily. In the dark, he seemed even larger than he had during the day.

"I do nae lie." Her voice cracked, tears easing from the corners of her eyes. She knew she had no right to expect mercy from him. By divine law, her body was his. Submission and obedience her duty.

He snorted before releasing her wrist. The bed ropes groaned as he landed on his back. "Maybe, maybe no'."

The icy night air was a balm for her overheated skin, carrying away the heat of his body. She rolled over, scrambling to escape. The chill made her suck in her breath, but she wasn't staying in the bed with him.

"Come back here… 'Tis too cold, lass."

He caught a handful of her chemise and pulled her back. The fabric ripped, her body weight too much for the thin cotton.

"We shall have to suffer each other for a few more

hours, Ailis." He dropped her in the center of the bed and tossed the comforter over her. He locked an arm around her waist and settled against her back. She tried to wiggle away, and he snorted next to her ear.

"Be still, woman. Yer flesh entices me, so stop struggling, and we might yet make it to see the sun rise without being stuck with each other."

As far as compliments went, she had never heard a worse one.

Yet she had never enjoyed one more. For without a doubt, he was sincere.

It completed her humiliation. Tears escaped her eyes.

Bhaic shifted, his touch becoming something very unexpected.

Tender.

Comforting.

But she knew it could so easily change. Despair clawed at her, making her breath catch on a silent sob. Helplessness was a cruel beast that threatened to crush her as the wind howled through the open windows, making her cringe with the cold.

"I owe ye an apology, lass." He smoothed his hand along her cheek, capturing her tears. "Ye called me brute justly."

"I did."

His chest rumbled with a soft chuckle. "Agreement between us. What would our fathers say?"

She choked on a laugh. "Naught civil, I imagine."

She heard a chuckle behind her. For one insane moment, they laughed together.

He rubbed her arms, and she relaxed. She didn't plan to; his touch just seemed so enticing.

"I hope yer father might think kindly upon the fact that I have nae enjoyed the treat Morton tried to make of ye."

Her insides felt as though they were tightening again.

"Yer father as well," she countered, trying to sound as unconcerned.

He grunted. "Aye." She was trying to edge away from him again. He released her, and she made it a few inches before the cold became unbearable. She ended up on her back, so very aware of him. It was pure insanity. Her very skin seemed more sensitive than it had been when she awoke that morning.

He chuckled softly. The sound drew her attention.

"I have never been in bed with a virgin."

She lost her resolve to ignore him. "I should think there are worse fates."

He laughed softly.

He reached out and picked up a lock of her hair resting near his elbow. "I'll say this for Morton, he baits his traps well, for ye are a bonny thing."

His words shouldn't have pleased her.

Yet they did.

He raised the lock of hair to his face, inhaling the scent of it. Something shifted inside her. A jolt firing off some place deep inside. She looked away from him, uncertain to say the least.

A moment later, he'd captured her hand and lifted it into the air between them, their fingers mingling intimately. Her breath lodged in her throat. His touch was intense, igniting a storm of sensation that flowed through her more freely than French wine.

He was a MacPherson.

He raised her hand to his lips and pressed a kiss against it. "Aye, ye're likely right."

"I did nae say anything."

He released her hand when she withdrew it, but her skin continued to tingle where he'd kissed it.

"Yer wide eyes say plenty, Ailis. Intimate conversation is something ye have no practice with."

"Certainly no'," she muttered, feeling her cheeks heat. "No unmarried girl is."

He shrugged. "Do nae be so naive, lass. There are plenty of daughters in the Highlands who have nae kept their innocence for their wedding night. Ye are no meek maid, so it stands to reason that ye might have followed yer passions."

She shifted, shaking her head before she thought better of letting him know so personal a detail about her.

His grin faded, his expression becoming pensive. "Ye deserve respect for holding on to yer virtue. It means ye have integrity and deep respect for yer father's name."

He lay down on his back. For a moment, she couldn't quite believe he was truly going to leave her in peace.

Respect from a MacPherson. Truly, it had been a day full of surprises.

She was certain she couldn't take another one.

❧

Ailis woke to the sound of the door being unlocked. She blinked, still groggy from too little sleep and too many thoughts churning inside her head.

"At last," Bhaic growled next to her. "Damned night lasted a month."

"It did," she agreed and then regretted her words when she witnessed the hard glint that appeared in his eyes. Clearly she wasn't ready for marriage, for men needed meek words when they woke. Bhaic's pride was wounded, and no mistake.

She had rolled onto her belly sometime during the night and had to push herself up. The door opened, and the Earl of Morton appeared in the doorway. He was wearing a fur-lined half coat and a thick, felted wool hat. She glared at the warm clothing.

"Chilly night," he remarked as he strode boldly into the room.

"It was warm enough," Bhaic remarked before standing up.

Two other men entered the room, and she realized one was her father. His lips were white from being pressed together so tightly. The other man was Shamus MacPherson, and he went toward his son with his kilt.

Her father held out a dressing robe for her. Ailis sat up and eagerly left the bed behind. But her father froze, his gaze on her. She looked down to see her chemise gaping open where the sleeve had been torn. One cuff was secured around her wrist, while the edges of the sleeve fluttered loose.

"Ye bloody bastard," her father accused.

Ailis reached for the dressing robe and wrapped it around herself.

"There is nae a mark on the lass," Bhaic responded. He was pleating his kilt on the edge of the bed, folding it with a practiced hand before slipping a belt beneath it and buckling it around his lean waist.

"I am fine, Father."

"And wed," the earl announced.

With both of them out of the bed, the earl had pulled down the comforter to expose the sheet. The blood had dried, turning a dark brown that stood out plainly.

"You are free to return to your land, Laird Robertson," Morton informed him before he looked at Bhaic. "You'll be expected to take your new bride home."

Bhaic brushed past the earl and captured Ailis's upper arm. He swept her from the chamber without a word. She squelched the impulse to protest.

What was she going to do? Stay in the chamber? Admit she was a maiden still?

No. Every fiber of her being rebelled against that idea. The morning sun was bright, and she itched to get into it. Escape filled her thoughts as she spied the Head of House.

"I'm off to find me dress," Ailis said.

Bhaic made no protest. She felt an odd little twinge of regret, but it wasn't enough to stop her from following the servant to a chamber where her dress was hung up neatly. There were times she didn't care for the long stays in fashion, but today, she enjoyed feeling the laces closing the stiff undergarment tightly against her body.

She felt buffered against the harsher facts of reality.

But when she emerged, the Head of House led her to the high table once more. This time her father sat there, and so did Shamus MacPherson. The two spaces between the lairds were for her and Bhaic. There was something symbolic about the scene at the high table, and she would be lying if she said she didn't think it was attractive.

Never once in her life would she have even jested about seeing her father and his enemy sitting down at the same table.

That was a sad thing to admit, a lack on her part not to see the merit of peace.

She should have thought about it, should have longed for it. The feud claimed lives every year, staining the fresh season of spring with death. Thinking of a way to end the feud should have crossed her mind and stayed as something she could not dismiss.

Perhaps she should have continued kissing Bhaic last night.

It was a strange, alien idea, but not without its merits. The earl was right about alliances ending feuds.

The regret was hard to ignore, leaving guilt to chew on her as she entered the hall and felt everyone watching her. She lifted her chin and forced her lips into a sweet curve. At least she might make sure there would be no reason for Bhaic to accuse her of blackening his name by appearing abused.

It was a beginning. A step away from the hatred she'd always accepted as the only way to think about MacPhersons.

The Earl of Morton watched them throughout the meal, his keen stare soaking up details. Ailis took the broken bread from Bhaic's hands, once he'd blessed the meal and passed it to his father and then her own. The men watching stroked their beards and grinned. She witnessed the mood in the hall lightening, astonished by how much her actions influenced her father's men.

"Well done, Ailis," Bhaic whispered beside her. "Ye have shamed me with yer show of unity, and I thank ye for showing me the error of me ways."

There was a note of appreciation in his tone that warmed her on a deep level, but she shied away from acknowledging it completely.

He wasn't her husband, not truly.

And she was pleased. Yes. Very pleased.

Unless she thought upon the matter too long.

⁓

The Earl of Morton watched them all mount. Ailis felt a lump form in her throat again when the MacPherson retainers surrounded her. But she kept her expression serene and her thoughts on riding out of the yard.

One step at a time.

She wouldn't think about dealing with Bhaic tonight. No. She'd focus on escaping the earl first. Bhaic was no more interested in being her husband than she was in becoming his true wife. There was no other reason for him to have left her a virgin.

She held that thought tightly, using it to fend off the panic trying to claim her.

They rode off toward MacPherson land. Her father followed them for a time before heading inland. She fought not to look after him longingly.

"I think I might accuse ye of being a skilled actress, Ailis." Bhaic had come up beside her, looking power-ful on his stallion. He didn't linger inside the ranks of his father's men but rode along the sides, keeping his eyes on the horizon for trouble.

"Is that because ye wish to find a new insult?" she questioned.

His eyes narrowed. "I have the right to be suspicious of ye."

"As do I, of ye," she countered, feeling bone tired of their clashes. "Yet that leaves us trading barbs."

She expected him to take insult, but he surprised her by reaching down and catching her mare's bridle. He had her reins in his grasp before she realized what he was doing. He dug his heels into his stallion's sides and led her mare away from the MacPherson retainers. The road was surrounded by thick forest, the trees hiding them within moments of their exit from the road.

"What are ye doing?" Ailis asked.

She ordered herself to remain calm, but the idea that he might murder her still rose up to horrify her.

He turned and faced her. Ailis tried to gather her courage as she waited for him to answer her. The afternoon sunlight shone off the pommel of his sword where it rose above his left shoulder. She couldn't help but stare at it. The earl's men had worn swords on their hips, but Bhaic clung to the Highland ways.

"Do nae insult me by thinking I've brought ye out here to kill ye, Ailis."

She jerked her gaze away from the sword to find him glaring at her.

"I am a Highlander. I do nae fight me wars through women." There was truth edging his words.

"Then what are ye about?" she asked.

He closed his mouth and contemplated her. She

could see him considering something, the look in his eyes serious.

"I witnessed something this morning I never thought to in me lifetime," Bhaic began.

She nodded, still unsure as to how to accept the idea of seeing MacPherson and Robertson retainers breaking bread together. Truly, it might have been easier to grasp seeing a true fairy.

"I should have thought of it, and that is my shame," Bhaic said gravely. "As the next laird, I should have considered leading me clan away from constant bloodshed. Morton spoke a solid truth: 'twas three generations ago and certainly no' the first time a bride was stolen away in the Highlands."

"True, as much as I detest his methods," she admitted. "We'll all be better for having been made to see it."

"Aye," Bhaic agreed.

"But I did nae plot to help him," she added quickly. "I knew naught of his schemes."

Bhaic wasn't sure he believed her. She saw him considering her with doubt in his eyes. Such amazing blue eyes. They seemed full of life in a way she'd never noticed a man's eyes might be.

"What I'm thinking about most is the fact that I saw me clansmen breaking bread with Robertsons. Something ye did much to encourage by smiling sweetly and sitting by me side with grace."

Now he was complimenting her again, and she warmed beneath his praise.

"It was the right thing to do," she whispered. "Since ye…treated me gently."

He drew in a stiff breath. "It disturbs me to see

ye grateful for such a thing. I am nae a monster. I do nae rape."

"Ye're a MacPherson." The words were out of her mouth before she thought on them. His face darkened. "Sorry. It's just… I do nae know any other way to think of ye. Is nae that why ye called me a liar? Because I am a Robertson?"

He nodded, conceding the point. "That brings me back to the shame of nae thinking about ending this feud. Ye did nae expect me to behave honorably."

"Ye did." A surprise, but a pleasant one. A dear one. Truly. She offered him a smile of gratitude.

He leaned forward. "I want ye to come home with me, Ailis."

She recoiled, pulling on the reins out of reflex. Her mare stepped back in response. Bhaic eased his stallion forward.

"Ye did nae have to bring me out here to tell me yer will." Disappointment edged her words and twisted cruelly through her.

He spoke slowly. "I'm asking ye."

She eyed him suspiciously. "That did nae sound like a question."

He shrugged, unrepentant. "I did nae have to bring ye out here and give ye a choice. So do nae quibble over the wording. I'm as shocked as ye are that I'm saying the words. Yet I would prove meself the brute ye've labeled me if I gave ye no choice."

Shock held her silent for a long moment. By rights, she belonged to him. His retainers would make sure she arrived on MacPherson land even if she went bound and gagged.

But the memory of the past night rose up to torment her with how volatile their reaction to each other was. It was like some sort of combustion; when together, they lost their wits and all sense of control.

She shook her head. "We are nae good together."

"Perhaps it was a mistake to leave ye a maiden, lass." He eased his stallion up beside her, setting off a ripple of awareness that traveled down her body. "There is passion between us, and ye are too innocent to realize it is no' a common thing. Ye kissed me sweetly, lass."

"'Twas lust."

He reached out and cupped her chin, his eyes bright with hunger. It made her breathless, when she knew it was wrong.

"Aye, but there is something more." He leaned closer, until his breath teased the surface of her lips. "There is something deeper."

She shivered, turning her head to avoid his lips. "Something wicked."

He chuckled, the sound low and menacing. A warning bell went off inside her mind, but it was too late. He'd leaned over and scooped her off her mare before she could react.

She gasped and grabbed for the only solid thing she could reach. Which was Bhaic. It was instinct, the need to feel something solid instead of being suspended in midair.

When she landed in his lap, his stallion sidestepped nervously.

"Nae wicked if we're wed, lass."

"Well... I suppose..."

He captured her head and tilted his to the side so

he might fit their lips together. This time, there was no hold from slumber to interfere in the intensity of the kiss.

His kiss.

It was shattering. The connection so hot, she felt her insides melting once again. Her heart began to pound, but she didn't care. She wanted to kiss him back and mimicked the motions of his lips as she learned the art. He growled softly through the kiss, startling her with the ferocity of his response.

She pushed against him, ducking beneath his arm and sliding down the side of his stallion.

"Sweet Christ, Ailis!"

The horse danced away, screaming with displeasure. She ran after her mare and used a rock to mount.

"That was a bloody insane risk to take!" Bhaic scolded her.

He was right. Her father would have thrashed her for being so careless near a stallion. One kick could have split her skull.

But a lifetime of sense had abandoned her the moment he kissed her. It was overwhelming and suffocating. She gathered up the reins and pointed her mare in the direction of Robertson land. She leaned low over the horse's neck as it took off. Once they cleared the forest, Ailis gave the mare free rein.

In spite of the pounding of her mount's hooves, she heard Bhaic giving chase. She refused to look over her shoulder, forcing herself to believe she could outrun him.

He truly was the monster she'd been raised to fear.

If she stayed near him, he'd devour even her soul.

The head of his father's retainers drew up beside Bhaic. Ronald watched Ailis as she rode across the borderland between Bhaic's father's and hers.

"Are we pleased about the little lass's escape or no'?"

Bhaic resisted the urge to smash Ronald in the jaw. The impulse soured his mood even further.

No woman had ever affected him so violently. And he'd never been unhappy to see a Robertson fleeing from him.

It was a sensation he wasn't sure he was comfortable with. Women were enjoyable but never too distracting. He had matters to see to, important ones that didn't allow for any sort of obsession.

So it was better that Ailis Robertson was on her way.

"I'll have the marriage annulled next year," Bhaic told his captain. "That should give the councilors surrounding the king enough time to become disenchanted with the Earl of Morton and his ideas on ruling the country."

Ronald cocked his head to one side. "That will be difficult, what with the stained sheet."

"It was nae the lass's blood. She'll agree. As ye can see, she has no taste for this union."

Surprise widened Ronald's eyes before he grinned. "In that case, ripping her chemise was a fine bit of trickery."

"Aye," Bhaic answered even as the memory surfaced to needle him.

Convincing a female to share his bed was a favorite challenge, and he'd enjoyed having Ailis in his bed. The moments of the night replayed across his mind,

tempting him to set his heels into the sides of his stallion and run her down. Ronald was watching him,
picking up the indecision on his face. Bhaic cursed.
The lass would have a right to call him a brute if he
chased her down with half his men along.

The Earl of Morton was right about one thing
though: it was a changing world. Ships were sailing
farther, discovering new lands, and Rome was losing
its grip on the world. Still, he wasn't willing to resort
to forcing a woman into his bed. He knew she'd
enjoyed his kiss, and the thought made him chuckle.

She was a virgin all right.

And one who had been sheltered when it came to
the coarser nature of men. Her father truly was to be
commended for making sure his men kept their dallying from her eyes. No' just any laird could manage
such a feat. Castles were large, and Highlanders were
lusty by nature. Sundown offered dark passageways for
liaisons. Even the laird's daughter was bound to see
the blunt realities of life if someone wasn't minding
her chastity.

He grunted, his respect for his father's enemy growing again.

Ailis had cleared the ridge and disappeared down
the other side of it.

She had the right idea. It had been insanity to ask her
to stay. She would have distracted him. What he needed
was a wife who would bear his children and welcome
him into a warm bed when he had time for her.

Nothing else.

But it was still the first time he'd been displeased to
see a Robertson fleeing his father's land.

"Only a MacPherson would fail to see what a gem me daughter is."

Ailis sent her father a stern look, but he ignored her.

"Mind ye, I was dead set against the marriage, but me daughter is a true Robertson. She puts her clansmen above herself," Liam Robertson continued. His captains hung on his words, and the servants nodded as they performed their duties. Young lookouts fidgeted behind the captains, their eyes glowing with hatred for the MacPherson.

It sickened her, and unleashed a wave of guilt powerful enough to drown her.

Perhaps she should have taken Bhaic's offer. A shiver worked its way across her skin. A month later, she shouldn't have been so sensitive to the memory.

But she was.

It played and replayed in her dreams. She woke swearing she smelled Bhaic in her bed, detected his warmth between the sheets. Felt his kiss lingering on her lips.

It was the cruelest sort of torment, which bred a growing longing inside her. It made no sense, unless Bhaic had been correct about her being old enough for marriage.

Was it so simple?

She hoped so.

Fleeing from him wasn't sitting well with her. It was cowardly, and there was no way to soften it. She'd run from him. Fled from the intensity, from the overwhelming sensation his touch unleashed.

Maybe she was ready for marriage.

"Father, I am looking forward to May Day."

Her father paused, looking at her as he tried to drop the subject of how terrible the MacPhersons were. A renewed sense of guilt assaulted her when she witnessed how much effort it took. It was sad indeed to see that they didn't know how to talk about anything except the feud. She felt a hint of responsibility for keeping the fighting going, because they never stopped fanning the flames. Well, it was time.

"Aye, it will be a fine market fair."

He returned to talking to his captains, but Ailis felt a bit of relief.

May Day was the perfect time to begin looking for a husband.

Three

MAY DAY WAS ONE OF THOSE FEW DAYS WHEN CLAN rivalry was abandoned. At the crossroads of the MacPherson, Robertson, Grant, and Gordon lands, merchants arrived to set up their stalls. There were metalworkers, cloth sellers, and leather craftsmen. The time when a castle produced everything for itself was passing into the pages of history. Now, there were merchants who made their living by bringing exotic fruits inland from the ports. Even so early in spring, there were oranges and pomegranates brought by ship from Spain. There were spices brought in from faraway lands.

The merchants were joined by jugglers and musicians. The air was festive, and the four clans mixed freely, their animosity displayed only in games of strength. Instead of wielding swords against one another, they tossed cabers—long poles as big as trees—and tried to get them to flip end over end.

Ailis brushed out her hair and put on a wreath of spring greens to celebrate the new season. Many girls had risen at dawn to wash their faces in the morning dew to ensure their youthful beauty. More than one young maiden had celebrated spring with more than dew.

She hadn't, because she was a laird's daughter and expected to remain a virgin until she wed, so she wasn't allowed to join the other girls in the predawn hours. At least she was able to go to the fair every year. The rest of the castle inhabitants had to take turns, because it would never do for the castle to be left empty.

But for some girls, taking a lover on May Day was a way to decide upon a husband. Ailis envied them the opportunity to make sure they would have no unpleasant surprises on their wedding nights.

She'd certainly had a shock on hers.

Ailis shook her head. She would not think of Bhaic MacPherson or her wedding night. She was not married. But only because she hadn't been bedded.

She shivered, but she honestly wasn't sure if it was caused by revulsion or excitement.

Yes, ye do know.

Heat teased her cheeks as she admitted it was excitement. She had enjoyed his kiss. It would be a lie not to admit that she had also wondered what else she might enjoy.

Which was why she wandered out into the fair, smiling at the men who passed. It was time to apply her attention to getting some offers she was actually interested in receiving.

❧

"Ye're a beast of a man, Bhaic MacPherson," Symon Grant shouted across the green where they had been tossing cabers. Bhaic smirked and bent his arms at the elbows to show off his muscles. His chest was bare, sweat trickling down his abdomen.

Symon closed the distance and offered him a slap on the back. "Damned lucky too. I thought I had ye on that last toss."

"Almost," Bhaic admitted.

"Which is nae enough, so ye can buy me some ale."

Bhaic chuckled and bowed. The winner bought the ale. He scooped up his shirt, but didn't put it on as they walked toward the food merchants. There were Robertson retainers sitting nearby, but they only cut him and his men stiff glances.

Bhaic gestured his captain forward. The merchant's eyes lit up as Bhaic counted out the silver. The man snapped his fingers at the serving wenches, and they began to bring out frothy-topped wooden mugs.

Bhaic drew off a long swallow and grinned. The men surrounding him raised their tankards high, toasting him before they tasted the brew.

But he lost focus, his gaze settling on the cloud of blond hair floating around the shoulders of Ailis Robertson. There was a happy smile on her lips as she spun around and around in a dance. She laughed when she reached the end of the row and picked up her skirts to run back to the beginning of the set.

"Now there is something interesting," Symon remarked as he stood beside Bhaic. "Is nae that yer wife?"

"Maybe."

Symon cut him a somber look. "Marriage is nae one of those things ye say *maybe* about."

"In this case, it's true."

Symon drew off another sip of ale. "I suppose that accounts for why Lye Rob Gordon is dancing with her so openly, and her with her hair down. So a wedding but no' a bedding? Was that the way of it? And ye're happy to have it known by one and all?"

Bhaic felt his body stiffen. There was more than one man looking at him. The news of his wedding had traveled fast. People gathering around the dancers, pointing at Ailis and her unbound hair.

A tradition that only applied to maidens.

It was a public declaration of the truth of their union. Lye Rob Grant was making a bold statement by dancing with her for all to see. Ailis had on a different dress today, one that left no doubt she was a woman. It had a square neckline, and her plump breasts were clearly on display. Lye Rob looked at them often, reaching out to cup her slim waist every time the steps of the dance allowed him. Bhaic felt his nostrils flare, a surge of possessiveness filling him.

She belonged to him.

It wasn't about facts or words spoken in a holy place. It was a feeling rooted deep inside him, that place where he still recalled what she smelled and tasted like. A recognition that had taken root in the darkest hours of the night, when she had shattered his control like he was an untried lad.

Lye Rob pulled her close and tried to kiss her.

Bhaic abandoned his ale and went after what he truly craved.

❦

Ailis laughed and shook her head.

"Do nae leave me now, lass!" Lye Rob pleaded.

She shook her head again, her heart racing too fast for her to draw enough breath to answer him. She backed away from the couples dancing, lifting her chin so the breeze might cool her neck. She did not want his kiss.

It was disappointing, because she wanted to find a man who stirred her the way Bhaic had. But it was clear it wasn't Lye Rob. He was fun to dance with, and his brown eyes were warm, but they did not excite her.

Not like Bhaic.

She turned around, and her skirts spun up. Cool air teased her ankles and calves before the fabric settled.

"Are ye enjoying putting the horns of a cuckold on me head?"

She stared at Bhaic in stunned silence, wondering if she'd conjured him with her daydreaming. But the men at his back confirmed that she was not locked in another memory of their wedding night. "I'm nae doing anything of the sort."

He snorted and reached out to finger her hair. She jumped, the single touch setting off a reaction that rippled throughout her entire body.

"Unbound hair is the right of a maiden."

The truth of his words rolled through her, stunning her at just how foolishly she'd betrayed the facts of her unconsummated vows.

"It's so nice of ye to make sure everyone knows." He jerked his head to get her to look beyond him. People were standing three and four deep, many of them whispering as they looked at her.

"She was dancing with me," Lye Rob interrupted.

Bhaic turned on him with a soft growl. "Unless ye're a fool, ye know she's wed to me."

Her temper flared up, the public declaration feeling like a collar going around her neck. Perhaps she hadn't made as clean an escape as she'd thought.

"Enough bickering," she admonished. "'Tis May Day. Everyone is dancing."

Bhaic was crowding Lye Rob, towering over the other man by at least a foot. Somehow, she'd missed the fact that Bhaic was bare chested.

That was a sin, to be sure.

One ye enjoy...

The man was sculpted to perfection. She'd felt the ridges of muscles on her wedding night, but seeing them let loose a whole different surge of excitement. This time, her nipples puckered behind her stays, longing for the chance to be pressed against his bare skin.

It was a red-hot craving, one that felt worse than any hunger she'd ever endured.

"There is little point in bickering," she said.

He turned to face her. "Aye, enough is right, Ailis."

He captured her hips and pulled her forward. She ran into his chest, raising her hands out of instinct to break her collision with him. He leaned down and pressed his mouth against hers, running one hand up her back to capture her head and hold her still.

The kiss was ravishing. It bore little resemblance to the tender ones he'd given her before. This time he demanded, and her will crumbled beneath the hard motions of his mouth. This was the kiss she'd truly wanted.

The crowd watching them cheered, the men roaring with approval.

Bhaic lifted his head, and she glimpsed his pleased expression right before he tossed her up and over his shoulder.

She squealed, her skirts flying as she kicked, but the crowd applauded and cheered him on.

"Put me down!"

He smacked her bottom instead.

A bolt of hot need pierced her in response. Her cheeks flamed, making her grateful no one could see her face. The sounds of the music diminished into the distance as he climbed into the forest that surrounded the crossroads.

He tossed her down the moment they were hidden from the fair.

She'd forgotten how mesmerizing he was. She wished she might forget again. But he was huge, and for some reason, she found his dark hair extremely appealing. He was a beast.

He was also virile…

"Perhaps it was a mistake to leave ye a virgin."

Her temper sizzled, and she propped her hands on her hips. "What happened to yer notion that I was in agreement with the earl's plot? I would think ye would be pleased to see me making it plain that I have no claim on ye. Do ye no' feel liberated?"

Her argument hit a soft spot. He paused, his eyes narrowing.

"It does nae please me to see ye dancing with Lye Rob Gordon."

"Since ye made it plain ye want naught to do with me, I'll dance with whoever I please," she informed him.

Her heart was beating fast, and he looked down at her breasts as they heaved. "Lye Rob wanted something to do with ye alright, and it had a great deal to do with the tempting display ye've made of yer breasts."

His possessiveness irritated her. She felt as though he was trying to put a bridle on her, and she was not going to submit. "Ye are the one who noticed I was old enough for marriage. Ye should begin the annulment, nae spend yer time harassing me. Since ye do nae want to be me husband, ye have no right to dictate how I behave."

He locked gazes with her. "And what do ye think the good earl will think of me annulling our union this soon, my sweet Ailis?"

"I am nae yer sweet."

But she hadn't really thought about what would happen when the earl found out she was back beneath her father's roof.

"I asked ye to stay." His tone had deepened, hinting at his true feelings.

She lowered her arms, no longer feeling the need to face off with him. "Ye did, but ye spent far more time accusing me of plotting to chain ye to me."

His lips curled up, flashing his white teeth. "So, ye are here to prove ye can get a man on yer own?"

She didn't care for how right he was. "Ye do nae need to know me private feelings, Bhaic MacPherson. Men are no' the only ones with pride. I would like to think I could do better than having a man forced to wed me."

He chuckled, surprising her as his eyes danced with merriment.

"We're more alike than I would have thought." There was something flickering in his eyes, which looked a lot like understanding. "Me pride was stinging the night of our wedding, no mistake. I said a few things I should nae have."

A sharp giggle interrupted them, coming through the trees. A moment later, a girl appeared. She was looking back over her shoulder, her eyes sparkling with mischief and her bodice loose, allowing her breasts to fall and bounce with her motions. A man chased after her, drawing up when he saw Bhaic. He let out a whistle, and the girl turned to see them in front of her. She flashed them a saucy smile before diving off into the forest with her companion on her heels.

Ailis's cheeks flamed. "Sweet Christ, everyone is going to think ye carried me off to…to…"

"To ravish ye?" he supplied with a mocking grin.

She propped her hands on her hips again. "Ye have no right! I am nae your wife."

The words were spoken before she realized she was challenging him. She witnessed it flash through his blue eyes before his lips thinned.

"Do nae let yer pride become involved again."

He shook his head. "Ye are something worth being proud of, Ailis." His gaze lowered to her cleavage. "A woman of character." His lips suddenly curved into a rakish grin. "Ye're a fine-looking woman too."

"And a Robertson."

His eyes narrowed. "Aye. Ye're that. Yet, as ye brought to my attention, yer blood has advantages."

There was a promise in his tone now, one that made her shiver. The urge to flee filled her again, but her pride rebelled. She didn't want him to label her a coward.

If she ran, there would be no doubt she was scared of him.

She had to admit to being curious as to what might happen if she stayed.

But that left her facing him, watching him move closer, each step increasing the intensity of the moment. All of her senses felt keener, sharper. Time itself felt frozen, the seconds feeling like hours in which she was able to notice all the tiny details she might have normally missed.

He reached out and stroked her cheek. It was such a simple touch, but her senses were so heightened, she wasn't sure she could have endured anything else. The moment his skin connected with hers, sensation exploded inside her. She jumped, unable to contain it all.

"As I said, Ailis, there is passion between us." He wasn't mocking her any longer. His tone was deep and almost compassionate. It sounded as if he were just as bewildered as she.

He reached back and slid his hand along the side of her jaw. Her breath caught as delight spread across her skin. She was mesmerized, intoxicated by him. He didn't stop until he'd threaded his fingers into her hair. The gentleness of the touch transformed into a firm hold that kept her steady as he took the last step between them.

"Ye smell sweet." He didn't kiss her, but leaned down and inhaled her scent. "Touch me, Ailis. I see the desire in yer eyes."

He'd stopped with just inches between them. Her breath was rapid, drawing in the scent of his skin as she felt his body heat teasing the bare skin of her chest. Temptation was drawing her in.

She was reaching for him before she could think about it. His words rang in her ears, combining with the need churning inside her. His skin was smooth, beckoning her.

He drew in a sharp breath when she touched him. The response stunned her but quickly transformed into confidence.

She wielded the same power over him.

It was a prideful thought, but one that filled her with boldness. She flattened her hands against his chest, unleashing a surge of excitement inside herself.

It was astonishing and exhilarating.

"Look at me." His tone was harder, more demanding.

She lifted her chin, locking gazes with him, and felt as though he could see right into her soul.

"Now kiss me."

"Me?" Her tone was so breathless, she wasn't sure he heard her.

But he did, his eyes narrowing slightly. "Aye." He massaged her head, sending little ripples of delight across her scalp. "Kiss me. Reach for what ye crave, Ailis."

She hesitated, not sure if she wanted to crave him. It was a demanding word, but it suited the feelings swirling inside her too well. She slid her hands up his chest, savoring the feel of his skin beneath her palms and fingertips. Kissing him was harder than she'd thought it might be. She'd kissed him back, but now, she had to stretch up, and even on her toes she wasn't tall enough. So she slid her hands along the strong column of his neck and gently pulled him toward her.

He bent down, allowing her to press her lips against his. She trembled, the sensations overwhelming. She felt as if she were spinning around, but didn't really care if she dropped to the ground in a dead faint.

All that mattered was kissing him.

She craved the taste of his mouth and moved her lips against his. Her grip wasn't firm enough, so she reached up to lock her fingers behind his neck, trying to secure him, control him.

He groaned, using his hands to tilt her head so their lips met together more completely. He was losing patience, his mouth beginning to move against hers. But *she* wanted to kiss *him*. The urge pounded through her, overriding everything else.

She tried to remember how he'd kissed her, moving her lips in what she thought was the right way. She increased the pressure and opened her mouth.

He growled and took command. There was no missing the moment when he stopped allowing her free rein. The kiss he pressed on her wiped all thoughts aside as delight took over. It didn't matter how they kissed, only that they did. She felt as though she might perish if she didn't get a deeper taste of him.

He teased her lips, tasting them before sweeping across her lower lip with the tip of his tongue. She shivered again, the touch more intimate than anything she'd ever experienced. It set off a throbbing between the folds of her sex.

She pulled back, startled by the hunger gnawing at

her insides. She understood with shocking clarity that she wanted him deep inside her. So carnal. So blunt.

"Do nae be alarmed, I'll nae ravish ye, Ailis."

"Maybe that's what I want." She snapped her mouth shut when she realized she'd spoken aloud. "I did nae mean that!"

He cupped her chin and made her look into his eyes. They were ablaze with hunger, mirroring the yearning burning inside her.

"Ye did," he assured her. "Ye simply do nae know how to enjoy it yet."

He scooped her up, stunning her with his strength. He controlled it so well, it was simple to forget how strong he was.

That knowledge made her tremble. He lowered her to the forest floor, the scent of grass rising up, wrapping her in the moment of new growth.

"It is going to be me pleasure to teach ye, Ailis."

"But…the annulment…"

He settled beside her and bent one of his knees so he might place it over her thigh. She thrust her hands out to keep him back, but once again, the feeling of his firm chest distracted her from everything else.

It simply felt so right. The sensation was intoxicating.

"Are ye enjoying me touch?"

He leaned down and kissed her throat, the soft pressing of his lips taking her further into bliss. Her eyelids fluttered shut as she stretched her chin up to expose more of her neck.

"Honestly, lass, ye do nae want me to stop any more than I want to." His words were a whisper against her ear.

It was so tempting to just let him do as he pleased. It felt so good.

Nothing had ever felt so intense before.

The knot of her bodice loosened. She opened her eyes, but he'd pulled the lace through the first few eyelets before she turned to look at his face.

His expression sent a shudder through her.

"Ye are more than comely, lass."

She blushed.

His lips curved into a possessive grin. It was presumptuous, but it also made her feel attractive in a way she never had before.

He pulled the lace through a few more eyelets, until he could open her bodice. She was in her simplest dress, one that didn't have a set of long stays behind the bodice. The only thing shielding her breasts was the thin linen of her chemise. Excitement twisted through her. She felt pinned to the spot, caught in the moment as she waited to see what he'd do next.

What was the next step? She wanted to know.

Now.

"Ye have no doubt haunted the dreams of more than one man." He cupped one breast through her chemise, sending a bolt of excitement into her core.

She twisted, the sensation too great. "No…no one thinks about…me…parts."

She was trying to think, because it gave her stability. Bhaic brushed his thumb across her nipple and shattered every last bit of conscious thought she had.

"I do," he whispered next to her ear. "I think about ye more than I like. I have never been jealous of a man like I was just now of Lye Rob."

He lifted his head and let her see his eyes. They were full of possessiveness.

"I was just dancing."

Bhaic slid his hand beneath her chemise, his fingertips teasing the skin between her breasts and setting off an ache to be touched in both mounds.

"Nae, lass, he was getting close to ye because he wanted to do exactly what I am doing now." He cupped her breast, closing his fingers around one tender mound as victory shown in his expression.

"I would nae have let him...touch me."

He massaged the globe of her breast, setting off a renewed throbbing at the top of her sex. It was harder now, more insistent. Keeping her thighs together felt awkward and uncomfortable, so she let herself relax.

"But ye'll welcome me."

"I—"

He didn't wait for her to finish. Bhaic leaned down and licked her nipple. It had already puckered but drew tighter as she arched up to offer it to him. A soft moan escaped her lips, the sound renewing the blush stinging her cheeks.

"It gets better, lass."

He cupped her breast, holding the soft mound still before closing his lips around the puckered tip.

She cried out this time, the heat from his mouth flowing down to the apex of her thighs. Something was throbbing incessantly, making her lift her hips in a quest.

He sucked harder on the point and slid his other hand across her belly. Her passage gave a desperate twist as she reached for him and held him to her breast. She wasn't close enough. Wasn't pressed against him tightly enough.

Her damned dress was too heavy against her legs.

"So sweet…" He kissed his way to her other breast and teased her with soft licks along its side before he claimed the nipple. She arched and lifted her hips. He slid his hand lower across her belly, grabbing a handful of her skirts and jerking it up.

She sighed as cool air reached her legs. It was invigorating, and she reached for him, no longer content to just be touched. She wanted to stroke him too.

Ailis flattened a foot on the ground and used her leg to push her body up. She rolled into him, pushing him back as she sought out one of his flat nipples. She licked it, purring as she tasted a faint salty tang left behind from his sweat.

He rolled back, letting her have her way, and it filled her with confidence.

"That's it, lass, ravish me in return."

"I will."

She wasn't sure why she sounded so bold. She kissed one of the ridges on his chest and then another. He gathered up her hair when it settled around them and pulled it out of her way. Teasing motions were no longer enough.

He slid his hand along her thigh, lifting her skirts higher. She was too hot, but the contact between their flesh felt perfect.

She reached for his neck, purring as she detected the steady throb of his pulse beneath the soft skin. He was strength incarnate, yet smooth and soft too.

It felt as though she was made to fit against him. She wanted to melt until she fused with him completely.

Her skirt went flying above her waist. One powerful motion of his wrist had sent it up to bare her lower body.

She gasped, startled by the sense of vulnerability sweeping through her. It conflicted with the sweet intoxication holding her hostage.

Bhaic didn't let her senses recover. He cupped the side of her face and leaned over her, the heat from his body pushing aside her modesty. He kissed her, restoring her to the perfection of the moment. She pushed her hands through his hair, delighting in the feeling of the threads sliding between her fingers. There were so many tiny details she had never thought might be so enjoyable. Little things she did every day, but when Bhaic did them, sensation surged through her. She was sinking deeper and eager to experience more.

Bhaic didn't disappoint her. He settled his hand on her thigh again, his grip possessive but filling her with a sense of satisfaction.

It also unleashed a sense of anticipation that left her breathless.

Remaining still was impossible. She reached for him, boldly seeking out what she craved. His thighs were just as hard as his chest, the muscles clearly defined and covered in more smooth, hot skin.

"I swear I've never enjoyed a woman's hands on me like I do yers."

The admission was torn from him in a harsh tone. She detected the protest from his pride and found companionship in it.

At least she was not alone in the madness.

She slid her hand higher, seeking what she'd only had a teasing glimpse of on their wedding night. She was frustrated by that fact, irritated that she didn't yet understand completely what it was she craved.

She was empty and wanted to know what he had to fill her.

Someone cleared their throat.

Someone male.

Bhaic growled but gathered up her chemise and covered her breasts while shielding her with his body.

"Go to hell, Symon."

The tone of his voice cut through the intoxication dimming her wits. It was like waking up from a dream, and her body protested the return to reality. She wasn't ready to come back yet.

"I figured ye might say something like that."

Ailis looked past Bhaic to see a huge man wearing the Grant colors in his kilt. He was looking away from them, but her cheeks burned with shame all the same. She scrambled to push her skirts down and sit up.

"Someone better be dying," Bhaic warned as he pushed to his feet with remarkable ease. He reached down to hook her upper arm and lift her.

The man's strength was amazing.

"So who's dying?" Bhaic demanded, his frustration plain.

"Yer father and hers," Symon responded as he turned to face them. "It seems they are trying to kill each other over the pair of ye disappearing into the woods for a tryst."

"We were nae—" She stopped when Symon's

gaze lowered to her open bodice. Bhaic reached out and cupped her shoulder to turn her away from his friend's view.

"Cover yerself, Ailis, and do nae deny what is plain."

She grasped the ends of the tie that had closed her bodice and shot Bhaic a hard look.

But what she saw stopped her. His blue eyes were lit with a hunger that fascinated her almost as much as it frightened her.

She turned around before he read the fear on her face. He was so confident, so full of determination, she didn't want him to witness her reaction.

She could not give him that power over her.

But her hands shook as she tried to thread the lace through the eyelets to close her bodice. The fact that both men were waiting while she adjusted her breasts sent her temper sizzling.

Her breasts were no man's concern.

But ye enjoyed what Bhaic did with them, sure enough.

She yanked on the lace and tied a firm knot. It took another few moments for her to adjust herself before she was fit to turn around.

Symon's topaz eyes were brimming with amusement when she met them.

Bhaic slapped him on the shoulder. "Now what was the urgent need that sent ye after us?"

"Well now, there are urgent needs and urgent needs, it would seem."

Bhaic growled, earning a smirk from Symon. But the man pointed at the fair they'd left behind. "Yer father claims she enticed ye into the woods—"

"I did nae—" Ailis said.

Bhaic reached out and curled a hand around her face to cover her mouth. In one swift motion she was trapped against his side, his fingers smothering her retort.

Symon nearly choked on his laughter. Ailis lifted her foot and kicked him in the shin.

He yelped and jumped back, out of her range.

"Feisty," Symon observed before shrugging. "And her father is demanding satisfaction for the slight of labeling his daughter a harlot. The pair of goats are fixing to ruin May Day with a melee."

Ailis bent her knees and twisted free of Bhaic's hold. "They loathe each other. We have to stop them."

She grabbed the front of her skirts and began running.

"Ailis!"

She froze, Bhaic's tone ringing with authority. It sent a shiver down her back—she understood now just what gave him the fierce reputation she'd heard about near the hearth during the winter months.

"Ye'll stay away from the fighting." He was shrugging into his doublet.

He passed by her, moving with purpose toward the edge of the forest. The longer length of his kilt in the back swayed with his motions as Symon joined him, forming a wall she was stuck behind. Their longer strides made her run to keep up.

But the quiet beyond the forest made her double her efforts.

The musicians had stopped playing, some of the merchants quickly pulled their wares off the counters of their booths. Women were herding the children away from the massing members of her clan and the MacPhersons.

The Grants and Gordons were doing their best to keep the two separated, but the expressions of her clansmen warned her that their tempers were short.

And not likely to last much longer.

Her father pointed his finger at Laird MacPherson. "Me daughter is pure! Ye'll be taking back that insult, or I'll beat it out of ye!"

Shamus MacPherson tossed his head back and laughed, the men behind him following their laird's example. "Everyone saw yer daughter dancing with Lye Rob, making sure he got a good look at her ankles! Ye can nae expect me son to ignore a free tumble!"

"Ailis Robertson is me wife!"

Both lairds turned to see who was shouting. Shamus MacPherson's face darkened when he found himself facing his son.

"And it's May Day, the time for dancing on the green," Bhaic said.

Liam Robertson wasn't going to be satisfied with such an explanation. He tried to push past the Gordon retainer holding him back from Shamus MacPherson. The man let him through but closed the gap quickly to keep the Robertson captains from following their laird.

"I never agreed to this marriage!" He stormed up to Shamus and poked him in the chest. "Me daughter is too good for the likes of a MacPherson! I won't have it!"

"But me son has already had her, and did nae see fit to keep her!" Shamus shouted. "I'll nae stand for her weaving her spell over him because she can do no better!"

"Ye bastard!"

"Enough!" Bhaic shouldered his way between the lairds, Symon joining him. "The lass is nae part of this feud, Father."

He tempered his tone, but his father still took offense. "She's a Robertson!"

"I know it well, but there is a measure of wisdom in the Earl of Morton's idea to end this fighting."

Neither laird was willing to soften their stance, but the men behind them found it to his liking. Expressions lightened, and dirks were replaced in the tops of boots with looks of relief.

Her father glared at Bhaic. "Ye sent me girl back to me. The union is dissolved by yer actions. Ailis? We are heading home!"

It felt as if someone had stuck a dirk through her.

It shouldn't have. Robertson Castle was her home, and she adored it, but Bhaic's silence stung her pride and something deeper. Something she never would have considered ever feeling for a MacPherson.

But she refused to show it. If Bhaic was going to watch her leave, she would not grant him any last looks over her shoulder.

She reached down and grabbed her dress so she wouldn't step on it. Bhaic grasped a handful of the back of her skirt and pulled her to a stop.

"I was giving her time to adjust to our union," Bhaic said. "The earl sprang it upon us so suddenly, I thought to spare ye and her a harsh parting."

Liam shook with rage. "Is that so?"

Bhaic nodded curtly a single time.

Her father raised his finger into the air. "Then why did yer father call me daughter a harlot? Why does yer own sire know naught of yer plan to claim yer bride?" he shouted. "Because a MacPherson does nae know how to speak the truth! They are born with lies on their lips!"

"Father!" Ailis ducked around Bhaic and pushed her father away from Shamus MacPherson. "Yer words are too harsh."

Her sire looked at her as if she'd gone insane.

"Too harsh?" Liam demanded. "They are… MacPhersons!"

She was suddenly bearing the weight of all her clansmen. There were more than two hundred burly Highlanders leaning in to hear for themselves what she would say. The women farther up the hill edged closer and cupped their hands behind their ears. Whatever she said, it would be branded upon her forehead for the rest of her life. If blood flowed in response, it would stain her hands for certain.

She swallowed and lifted her chin.

"No child is born hating." Brows lowered among her kin, their lips pressing into hard lines. "I detest the way the earl made his point, but he was right about one thing, we've all learned to hate one another over something that was done generations ago." She lowered her voice. "Maybe it's time to look to what sort of future we can build if we are nae consumed with the past."

"How dare ye say such a thing!"

The two lairds had spoken simultaneously, and were now stunned into silence. They stared at each other, sticking out their chests, but neither could take back what he'd spoken. Her father started to stroke his beard, until he realized Shamus MacPherson was doing the same.

Neither was happy about having anything in common with the other, but they could not deny it.

"How nice to know ye both agree." Symon Grant raised his voice so it might be heard by all those straining to hear. "I'll admit that's a surprise, but one I'm happy to witness."

"Mind yer tone, Grant," Shamus snarled. "Ye are too newly weaned from yer mother's breast to be thinking ye can use that sort of voice with me."

Symon reached up and tugged on the corner of his bonnet. Shamus grumbled, but turned and began conversing with his captains.

The tension dissipated, the men watching them relaxing.

Everyone except for her.

Her father's captain had a hand on Liam's shoulder and was talking quietly in his ear. Her father's lips were pressed into a hard line, but she could see him beginning to relent.

That made her throat go dry.

It made sense, and would benefit all of the men and women watching, but it would mean she had to be Bhaic MacPherson's wife.

She couldn't do it.

The thought chilled her, sending her back, away from the men deciding her future. It was for all the right reasons, yet it horrified her.

Do nae be so selfish!

She had to maintain control, but it felt as though the tighter she closed her resolve around her emotions, the more cracks they found to escape through. The very fabric of her life was shredding, leaving her exposed and unprotected against the unknown.

Shamus MacPherson suddenly lifted his hand, and every man wearing his colors went silent. Her father looked at him, and the Robertsons followed their laird's lead.

"I was…overly harsh…in me comments about yer daughter's dancing."

Shamus looked as if the words had taken every bit of strength he could muster. He drew in a huge breath when he was done, and wiped his forehead on his sleeve.

Ailis felt her jaw drop. She was frozen in silence as her father stiffened, looking as though he was holding his breath. His face turned red before he gasped and replied, "Yer clansmen are nae born with lies on their lips."

The captain behind Shamus patted his laird on the shoulder, increasing his strength until there was a soft "thud" every time his hand landed on the older man's back.

"I'm getting to it," Shamus snapped and sent his captain a hard look before picking up his feet and stomping toward Liam with his hand extended.

Her father made him wait. His own captains were leaning into him, pressing him forward. Liam Robertson held out until he stumbled forward beneath their weight. He ended up facing Shamus and clasped his wrist.

The men watching let out a cheer. It was deafening, and echoed by the women looking on from afar. There was suddenly music, pipers sounding as the fair resumed with a fervor. The merchants applauded as her father roared, "I need me a drink, lads! And something to wash it down with!"

Ailis was sure she needed one more than anyone else.

&

"I never thought to see the day," Bhaic remarked.

Symon Grant was standing next to him as the Robertsons and MacPhersons celebrated in joyful excess. Full hogsheads of ale were opened and drained. Men lined up to have their mugs filled and then returned for another measure. As the ale flowed, the men began to swing the women up and around. They practiced the art of hefting, by throwing the women from man to man along a long line. The women squealed, and their eyes sparkled with merriment.

"Neither did I," Symon responded. "But ye were jealous of the little lass dancing with Lye Rob and no mistake, me friend. I saw it with me own eyes."

Bhaic sent a punch into Symon's shoulder. "I was nae speaking of that."

"Still trying to deny it?"

"Ye're making too much of it," Bhaic informed him.

"Now that's a shame," Symon responded, a smirk on his lips.

Bhaic shot him a hard look. "No, it is nae."

Symon's smirk widened into a smile, tempting Bhaic to punch him again.

"It's a shame, because it looks as though ye will be taking yer wife home, and it might be best if the two of ye liked each other. But"—he glanced around—"it looks as if young Ailis has escaped ye, so it's likely a fine thing that ye were nae jealous. Otherwise, ye might take her absence as a personal rejection."

Bhaic stiffened. He scanned the women, searching for Ailis.

Damn her.

All the good she'd done would be reduced to rubble if she didn't appear at his side when his father's men mounted up to ride home.

The little fool.

He refused to allow her to destroy what had been built. The bridge between their fathers was fragile, but with time, it would strengthen.

So his wife would just have to become accustomed to his company.

৵

She just needed a moment.

Ailis moved back into the forest, seeking shelter.

It wasn't something she had decided to do; it was some instinct that flickered to life as she watched the celebration grow louder and louder.

Nothing came from nothing. Her father had raised her to know there was a price for everything. Her throat felt as if it was swelling shut—she was the price being paid for peace. Not that it should surprise her. She would be joining a long line of brides sent to their clans' enemies to stop bloodshed. It was a noble cause, one she agreed with. But that didn't stop her from feeling like a prize mare.

Ye'll feel more like one when Bhaic gets the time to mount ye.

The worst part of that was the knowledge that she was just as interested as he was.

Oh, for Christ's sake! Get a grip on yerself! What are ye? A lass of sixteen?

That thought sobered her. She was twenty-three and obviously ready to become a woman.

She drew in a deep breath and straightened her back. She was going back. Aye, back to keep the bargain she'd struck.

"Ye do nae have to go with him."

For a moment, she thought she imagined the words. But she turned her head and caught Lye Rob coming through the forest.

"I was planning to try me hand at courting ye, but it seems I am going to have to move forward to asking ye to wed me, Ailis Robertson."

"I am already wed." The words felt clumsy, but she held her chin steady.

Lye Rob shrugged, his lips set into a pleasant grin. "Me father has no liking for the MacPhersons. He's made it plain he would favor a match with ye. Do nae be so naive as to think this bit of peace will be lasting. The Robertsons and MacPhersons have been enemies for too long. Once the ale has been slept off, they will be fighting again. If ye wed me, the Robertsons and Gordons will have the numbers to match the MacPhersons."

It was a horrifying thought, packed with enough truth to nauseate her. Her choices were clear, and she had to make the right one. "I am going with me husband."

His expression remained cajoling, but something flickered in his eyes that chilled her. It was cold and hard and very calculating. There was a crunch behind him, and she noticed his retainers moving closer. She took a step back, and Lye Rob's grin faded into a hard line.

"Come with me, and I swear ye shall have time to consider me offer." He offered her his hand. "If ye go with Bhaic MacPherson, ye'll be in his bed tonight."

"Ye've got a clever way of twisting words, Lye Rob Gordon."

Bhaic's voice was menacing and coming from right behind her. Ailis jumped, but he'd already reached for her, and she ran into his hand. Pain went through her shoulder, stopping her retort.

"Ye say time to consider," Bhaic said, "but what ye truly mean is ye will give her until ye reach yer father's holding."

Lye Rob shrugged. "I did nae lie."

Bhaic gripped her shoulder and pulled her behind him. She stumbled. Lye Rob was focused on Bhaic, his men guarding his back.

"Mind ye," Lye Rob said, "I'm glad to see ye. Wedding a widow is simpler than proving her marriage to ye is unconsummated." He pulled a dirk from the top of his boot. "It will save me the trouble of making sure someone sees me fucking her."

Her eyes rounded with horror. "Ye toad!"

The calculating glow in his eyes burned brightly. He tossed the knife from hand to hand as he closed the distance between himself and Bhaic.

"Get to yer father's side, Ailis," Bhaic said.

"But—"

"Now," he ordered sternly.

He was a man accustomed to being obeyed. She

backed up, but stopped when she realized they were surrounded by Gordon retainers. More had closed in behind them while Lye Rob distracted them. She bent down and picked up a branch—a thick, heavy one—and gripped it as if it were a club.

Lye Rob laughed, looking past Bhaic at her. "Do ye think ye can hurt me?"

Ailis didn't get the chance to reply. Bhaic took advantage of Lye Rob's inattention and charged. Bhaic had his arms open wide and got them around Lye Rob's chest. He surged up, lifting the other man off his feet, and twisted around to drop him on the ground.

Lye Rob snarled, but Bhaic had his arms locked around his throat. His arms bulged as a muscle on the side of his jaw twitched. Lye Rob thrashed, desperately trying to gain enough leverage to upset Bhaic.

The Gordon retainer near them lifted his arm to join the fight. Ailis never really decided what she was going to do, but she leaped forward, the branch lifted over her head. She brought it down on the retainer's raised arm. The shock shook her bones and made her elbows ache, but she carried through with the blow.

The retainer yelled, his scream startling several birds above them.

"Not man enough to take me on yer own, Lye Rob?" Bhaic swung him away but pulled the knife from his hand. "Ye're a coward, and yer men lack honor."

Ailis moved in a circle, two burly retainers stalking her. They had their arms stretched out wide, their stances low. She had to keep shifting her gaze from one to the other to keep the branch aimed at them.

"Kill Bhaic MacPherson, and the prize is ours, lads!" Lye Rob yelled as he lunged toward Bhaic.

The retainers made a grab for her, but she swung the branch in a wide arc and hit one of them on the side of the face. He twisted around and landed on the forest floor in an unconscious heap.

Lye Rob let out a hoarse cry, and she turned to see him cradling his arm. His wrist was bent at an odd angle, clearly broken.

"Now this is an interesting scene." Symon Grant appeared beside her. He lifted one foot and kicked the retainer still threatening her in the groin. "I almost do nae have the heart to interrupt. It seems fitting to have Gordon cowards brought low by a woman."

The woods were suddenly full of men. Symon's retainers and Bhaic's came through the forest, their expressions deadly.

Lye Rob turned and ran, his kilt bouncing until he was hidden from sight by the trees. His men followed, and Bhaic grabbed the branch Ailis was still holding in front of her. He tossed it aside and pulled her against his body.

"Ye could have screamed, lass, but I admit, I think I enjoyed yer response more." He pressed a hard kiss against her mouth to the delight of his men.

"Come, me lads, it's time to head for home. I have a bride to settle."

He clasped her wrist and pulled her along behind him. Her feet felt clumsy, but the weight of his men's stares were on her. Lye Rob was right about the peace being a fragile one. She forced a smile onto her lips and picked up her feet so Bhaic wasn't dragging her.

It was obviously the last May Day where she'd be wearing her hair down. Her gaze settled on the wide expanse of Bhaic's shoulders and then down to where his fingers closed all the way around her wrist.

God help her.

❧

"Me boy, ye need to stop going off as ye please," Shamus MacPherson admonished his son. "Ye're me son, and as sure as the Blessed Mother was pure, there are men who would like to send ye home to me dead."

"No doubt that's why ye gave him a captain," Symon supplied with a wink.

Bhaic's eyes narrowed, and he tugged Ailis closer. "There are times a little privacy is in order."

Ailis watched Shamus MacPherson look at her. Really look at her. His face was wrinkled from the harsh climate of the Highlands. His beard had gone completely white, but his eyes were still the same brilliant shade of ocean blue. Just like his son's.

"Aye, I suppose I can understand that." He was the last man she'd ever expected a compliment from. Yet it was there, in the twinkle in his eyes. He lifted a hand and waved her off. "Go on and bid farewell to yer father."

She lowered herself, placing one foot behind her and bending the knee to give him deference.

She heard his captains making soft sounds of approval. Some of them were stroking their beards in contemplation as she rose. Gaining respect from them would not be simple.

Bhaic stepped into her path.

"Ye'll be watched this time, Ailis."

His tone was low enough to stay between them, but there was no mistaking the rage. If she did miss it, all she had to do was look into his eyes to see the anger glittering there.

The man was furious with her.

And she was going home with him.

May Day was the worst day ever to look for a husband.

❧

"Ye scared her away," Symon observed. "Nae exactly a good way to preserve the peace."

"She was off in the woods with Lye Rob."

Symon crossed his arms over his chest. "Ye know, it's a fine good thing ye are nae jealous of the lass."

Bhaic growled and shoved his friend, but Symon only rocked back on his heels, regaining his balance with a smirk. "Ye're so busy being mad at the facts that have landed her in yer hand, ye have forgotten to look at what a pretty little treat she is."

"Shut yer mouth, Symon."

Symon raised one finger instead. "On second thought…"

"The devil take ye," Bhaic said. "I've got a fine memory. Mark me words, yer day is coming, me friend. The day when a lass twists yer insides with naught more than a look."

His friend sobered. "It's that intense?"

The disbelief in his friend's tone was only a fraction of what Bhaic felt. He looked at Ailis, his gaze running along the length of blond hair cascading down her back. She had a pert nose and twin dimples in her cheeks. But it was her curves that made him ache the worst. His cock began to stiffen again, hardening enough to press against the heavy wool of his kilt. The damned thing had risen too quickly and too often at the sight of Ailis.

Of course, she was his wife.

That fact made his lust far less unseemly, at least in theory.

But the application was going to be tricky.

His lips twitched.

He tried to fend off his amusement. There really were too many complications waiting for them if they tried to make a go of their marriage.

But all he wanted to do was grin at the jest fate was dealing him. All of his adult life, he'd been told chasing skirts was a sin. Now he had a wife, one the church would agree was his for the taking, but she was the only woman in the Highlands he had no business craving.

His enemy's daughter.

The ghosts of his grandfather and great-grandfather were no doubt planning a nighttime appearance to let him know what they thought about him bringing a Robertson bride home.

Even the thought of the specters wasn't enough to cool his passion.

But all the passion in the Highlands didn't make for a good marriage.

❧

"I'm drunk," Liam Robertson declared.

Ailis studied her father for a moment. "No, ye are

nae," she corrected him gently. "Ye never drink so much that yer wits desert ye."

Her father sniffed, a guilty flush darkening his complexion. "Well now, Daughter, ye do know me well. The times have been few, and only yer brothers were present."

"How would ye know?" Ailis questioned. "If yer wits were dulled, how would ye recall the number of times?"

Her father puffed up. "Because of Highlander honor!"

"Aye, honor." The word left a sour taste in her mouth. She would be upholding the family honor in a far different way.

Her father sighed. "Are ye sure ye want to do this, lass? It's true I planned to decide the matter of yer future soon, but I would nae see ye frightened of yer groom."

"I am nae frightened of Bhaic."

At least not completely scared of the man.

That would have to do.

Her father raised one of his gray brows. "Bhaic, is it?" He frowned. "I'm nae so sure I like the way that name crosses yer lips so easily."

She felt her own face darkening, and lifted a shoulder in a shrug. "We are wed."

"No, ye aren't," her father stated firmly. "Words uttered by a servant of God do nae make ye wed. Nae in the Highland tradition. Ye be married, I agree with that, but to be wed, the union must be consummated."

There was a question in her father's tone, which the answer to might set her free, but it would also start the fighting again.

"Ye would have chosen a groom for me based on alliances."

"Aye," her father agreed.

Ailis looked past her father at the men who were still enjoying the newly forged peace. "MacPherson and Robertson retainers at ease in one another's company, it's a fine alliance."

But it also reminded her of just how little she factored into the arrangement. Bhaic didn't value her, only what she brought to his clan.

As if that's anything new when it comes to marriages…

It wasn't, and she needed to stop thinking like a child. A laird's daughter kept her mind on what she might do for her clan.

Ailis nodded.

"Ye look as though ye are trying to convince yerself, Daughter."

She resisted the urge to shrug and stood steady. "It is the first time I've had to face such an arrangement, and it is a bit…sudden. I will do just fine."

It was also intense, the way Bhaic affected her.

"Aye, it is sudden," her father agreed and hugged her tight.

His embrace was a familiar one, and it almost broke her control. But she managed a smile when he released her and turned around to face her future.

The sight of two MacPherson retainers behind her made her pause.

"You'll be watched…"

Of course she would be. The peace was too new, too fragile to chance her being scooped up by a rival clan.

Highlanders.

She was one of them, proud of who she was, but for the moment, she was sick unto death of their feuding ways.

But her feelings were irrelevant. She was the vessel used to secure peace.

So she would have to play her part.

She was a Robertson, and she was no coward.

❧

MacPherson Castle.

Ailis stared at the dark stone structure, absorbing the reality of seeing something no one else in her clan ever had. It had towers that rose four stories, and at least four of them, from what she could see. It was perched on the edge of a peninsula that jutted out into a huge loch. The dark water surrounded the structure on three sides, making it rather ominous.

They rode through the village in front of the entrance to the castle. People came out of their homes to see the laird returning, but they glared. The dress she'd been so excited to wear to the festival this morning felt revealing, her unbound hair some sort of sin.

A few of the clansmen leaned over and spit when she passed, the scowls on their faces making their position clear.

She bit her lower lip and forced her chin level.

Her mare felt her discontentment, pulling on her reins and trying to refuse to follow the line of MacPherson retainers. Ailis reached down and patted her neck gently, wishing it would be so easy for someone to reassure her.

The memory of Bhaic kissing her neck surfaced.

But that only served to unsettle her more.

By the time they reached the gate, her heart was racing. Her lungs were working hard to keep pace. Her mare carried her beneath the huge gates into a massive keep at the center of the castle. Women were spilling out of its huge double doors, calling out to the returning men. Children clung to their mothers' skirts, older ones coming down some of the steps as Shamus and his captains happily smiled and began to dismount.

The cries suddenly died away. Shamus looked up at the women, trying to deduce what had deflated their joy. He followed their stares to Ailis.

"Aye," he said as he climbed up the steps of the keep. "Me son's wife. Ailis Robertson."

That seemed to be the extent of the welcome he could manage. Her name drew more than one hiss. She slid down from her mare and ended up facing a young lad, maybe ten years old. He was one of a small army of boys who had rushed out to take the horses. He stared, his jaw hanging open and his hands frozen in midair on the way to take the mare's reins.

"Here now." Bhaic suddenly appeared, thumping the boy on the back. "It's a horse, lad. I'm pretty sure horses do nae have clans. Get on with yer duties."

The boy jumped, his cheeks darkening with the reprimand before he grabbed the reins and led the mare away.

It left her facing Bhaic. He'd hooked his hands into his belt and stood contemplating her. Around them, activity stopped, everyone waiting to see what would happen.

Well, at least she was not the only one trying to decide what to make of their union.

He offered her his hand. There was naught to do but take it; still, she felt as if every muscle she had was frozen. The tension around them tightened. She forced herself to move, lifting her hand and placing it into his waiting one.

The connection of their flesh made her shudder.

He turned and led her through the frozen ranks of retainers and up the stairs of the keep. The women parted, but what turned her stomach was the way they pulled their children behind them.

"This is Duana, me father's Head of House. She'll see to ye."

Duana wasn't pleased with her assignment. The older woman was plump, and surely her features could be called kindly. At least when she wasn't scowling.

Bhaic gave her only a short nod before moving away down one of the passageways with the rest of his father's captains.

Which left her facing Duana.

The woman's lips were pressed into a hard line. She had dark eyes, and dark hair peeked out from beneath the linen cap she wore. Her apron had several spots on it, and the scent of fresh bread clung to her skirts, but that was the extent of welcome coming from her.

"God save me," Duana uttered, but the heavens were silent, leaving her staring at Ailis. "Come along," Duana said with a jerk of her head. She didn't wait for a reply but turned and started down a passageway. The sun was sinking, making the passageways dark. No one had lit the lanterns hanging every so often from large iron hooks.

Ailis shivered.

It was a silly, childish response. Robertson Castle looked very much the same at twilight. Yet tonight, it felt as though the darkness was creeping up the walls from the shadows to engulf her.

"This will do ye well enough."

Duana fit a key from the large ring that hung from her belt into a door and turned it. Ailis tried to control the urge to gag.

The door had a lock on the outside of the room?

Her mind was racing, jumping to conclusions that were horrifying. The Head of House grunted when the lock opened. "Go on with ye. I've supper to see to getting served."

Duana was gone with a grumble.

At least she wasn't going to be locked into the room. *Stop being childish.*

The door had stopped half-open. She pushed it open and saw nothing but darkness. There wasn't a window in the room at all. The air was musty from the door being closed. Moving inside, Ailis used the little light left in the passageway to investigate her surroundings.

It was a modest room, to say the least. The reason for the lock became clear as she looked at one side of the room and saw a long worktable there. On it were stored several boxes and lengths of fabric. She moved over to it, smiling when she spotted a small pewter plate with a pile of dry thatch on it. Lying on the edge of the plate was a flint and a length of iron. A half-burned candle was there as well.

Ailis picked up the flint and struck it. Sparks flew, dropping down into the tinder. She blew softly on it until a taper of smoke rose and at last a flame. She held the candle to it, smiling when it lit.

"That's better."

Her voice echoed around the room, if she could really even call it a room.

Well, do nae call it a cell...

No, that would only clear the way for her resolve to crumble. And honestly, that was all she had. So holding tight was essential.

On the other side of the room...

She smiled and walked across the bare stones that covered the floor to where a bed frame sat. Rope was threaded through it to support a pallet.

Better than a hard cot...

Better?

She snorted. There was nothing better about the entire *room*.

And she wasn't going to stomach it.

But when she turned, her hair fluttered like a wave. That stopped her. If she wanted to be taken seriously, she'd need to look the part. At the moment, she looked like a half-grown child. Certainly not the new mistress. Little wonder the Head of House thought it a simple matter to humble her in such a way.

Well, Ailis would just have to set her mind to showing Duana that she was woman enough to take her place.

She went back to the table and opened the boxes. One held an assortment of sewing tools. Tiny silver needles that she couldn't help but admire. There was also a fine pair of cutting shears that had been recently sharpened. More than five dozen pins and an entire box of fancy silk threads for embroidery.

Little wonder the room was locked.

The fabric was all linens. Lightweight, thicker ones, but all of it intended for shirts and chemises. There was a box that had all the scraps folded neatly inside, to be made up into caps or used for patching.

She opened another box and smiled when she spied a comb and small mirror. There were hairpins too, and several cosmetics. Ailis ended up unrolling the pallet and sitting down on it, because the only other item in the room was a stool she perched the mirror on. Her hair was tangled from being down all day. It took some time to work the comb through it and braid it.

By the time she'd finished, her temper had cooled. She replaced the items and sat down on the bed to think. It was all well and good to march into the kitchens and demand her place. Bhaic could hardly blame her.

Or would he?

Honestly, she knew very little about him. What did he want from their marriage?

Peace?

Aye. That was their common ground, yet it was a very undefined thing. Clearly Duana didn't think very highly of her presence. No, she would have to think hard and long about how she was going to approach winning the respect of the MacPhersons. Demanding her place was her right, but such would be expected.

Far better to earn her place. It would take time and resolve.

She giggled, rolling back onto the pallet as she dissolved into a fit of laughter. Never, ever had she thought she'd be contemplating how to impress MacPhersons!

God had a very funny sense of humor, it seemed.

❦

"I've been lied to."

Bhaic turned his head as his half brother sat down next to him. Marcus was older than him by six seasons and the product of a handfast that hadn't made it to marriage. His bonnet had one black feather raised on it, proclaiming his status as War Chief.

Marcus flattened his hand on the table. "I was told there was a Robertson in this castle. A pockmarked hag, with blackened teeth and breath that could make a demon faint—"

"Ailis is nae—"

"I am no' finished, little brother," Marcus interrupted. "She has hair as course as straw and the shriveled mounds of a grandmother. So"—he pounded the tabletop—"where is this creature you've been saddled with? Ye know I enjoy watching ye suffer."

Shamus looked down the table. "Aye…where is the lass? Did ye leave her passed out in yer bed already? She'll have to be building up some strength if she's going to be yer wife." His father chuckled. "Just like me, he is! A beast with the lassies."

The captains at the table roared. Bhaic didn't join them. Marcus was the only one to notice, his brother's face sobering.

"Mistress Duana," Bhaic said.

The Head of House looked up from where she was directing two serving girls behind his father.

"Where is me wife?"

Duana's expression tightened. "I did nae know she needed shepherding. Forgive me. Me attention was taken up by prayers for me murdered husband."

There were grumbles in the hall from those listening in. The name Robertson was spat out.

"My marriage is about making sure there is nae any more blood spilled." Bhaic stood up, his body tight with fury. "Now, what manner of welcome did ye give to me bride?"

Duana lost a little of her confidence, but only so far as to look somewhat less than annoyed. It was a far cry from being ashamed of her lack of attention. "I took her on down to one of the sewing cells. Making yer shirts is a fine place for a Robertson to begin life here. She has much to atone for."

There were chuckles in response. Bhaic sent a hard look toward some of his father's captains. They didn't suffer his reprisal gracefully. One of them, known as Angus, spit on the floor in open protest.

"There will be no more of that." Shamus spoke solemnly. His father glared at his captains. "She's a lass. One doing her duty. So she'll be given the respect such deserves."

"If she has no' the courage to face this hall, I say send her home before she whelps weakling babes," Angus said.

"I apologize for being late."

The hall went quiet. Bhaic froze as Ailis made her

way down the center aisle. His father's retainers glared at her.

Damned if she didn't ignore them all.

Bhaic found himself watching her with pride. She made her way forward at a steady pace, stopping only when she made it to the base of the stairs that led up to the laird's table. Her expression hardened just a tiny amount before she lowered herself.

His father grunted. "See now? There's the lass."

"A truly hideous hag…" Marcus muttered under his breath. "I'll weep for yer fate."

Ailis had put her hair up. Somehow, she looked more mature, more confident. When she made it to his side, Bhaic realized she'd used a light coating of cosmetics too. Gone was the allure of innocence that seemed to define her, and in its place was a promise of something very enticing.

The scent of a woman.

"Weep for yer own fate, Marcus," Bhaic said softly, "for she belongs to me."

"And they call me bastard."

⁓

War Chief.

Ailis knew the MacPhersons had one, and the man sitting next to Bhaic had two feathers raised on the side of his bonnet, only one was black and the other white. Bhaic had two white feathers facing up on his.

The man was slightly older than Bhaic. He made way for her and the two boys bringing another chair to the long table. She sat down, feeling as if every motion she made was too clumsy or loud. Everyone was watching her, judging her.

Well, let them. She was no coward.

But getting food down her throat was going to prove rather challenging. A smattering of conversation started up, but everyone was clearly trying to hear what she said.

She looked over the hall and cringed. There had to be over three hundred retainers alone. The massive keep made sense now—it was the only place they could all break bread together. The MacPhersons were more powerful than her father ever suspected. They sat at long tables on benches, as a continuous stream of women brought food in from two passageways.

"I'll have words with Duana about showing you to a cell." Bhaic spoke softly, but the moment he opened his lips, the conversation died. Proving she was correct to think everyone was listening to them.

Well, she'd begin as she intended to continue.

No hint of weakness.

She replaced the goblet she'd been drinking from and offered him a smile. "Duana was very kind."

"Kind?" Bhaic questioned. "By showing ye to a cell?"

"Aye." Ailis shot Angus a soft smile. "She neglected to lock me in when she departed. Kind of her, as there wasn't even a mouse in there to catch for supper."

Bhaic stared at her for a long moment before his lips twitched. His father's captains choked on their amusement, even as they tried to cover up their lapse with coughs. He stabbed a piece of meat on his plate with a small eating knife but paused with it in the air. "Yer sense of humor is going to serve ye well."

Exactly what she was afraid of.

Ailis covered her moment of fear by looking over what had landed on her plate. She should have been hungry. Ravenous actually, since she'd taken to dancing on the green instead of feasting. The food looked well enough, but her appetite was missing, likely due to the lump lodged in her throat. It was growing too. But everyone was watching her, waiting for her to make some error that they might cry insult over. She reached for the bread and chewed on it. Forcing it down her throat.

Duana would not be claiming she'd insulted her fare.

Too soon, she realized she'd drained her cup. With an empty stomach, the wine was speeding its way through her body. Bhaic reached for a pitcher to refill her goblet.

"I think I've had enough. Thank you."

"The lassie wants to be taken off to bed," Angus said with just a little too much mirth. There was a gleeful note of enjoyment in his tone. He eyed her from where he sat closer to Shamus and smacked his lips. "Since ye're no' eating and no' drinking...ye must be ready for yer duties."

Her cheeks heated, but so did her temper. Angus snickered at her discomfort, while a good number of his clansmen joined in. She pushed her chair back, the feet skidding loudly.

"There is naught here that distresses me," she said.

It was a straight-out lie.

Bhaic's very presence distressed her.

She offered them the briefest courtesy before shooting the Head of House a hard look. "If you would be so kind as to show me the way above stairs?"

Duana nodded and dropped her what might have

been a courtesy, but the Head of House's eyes widened as she was bending her knee, and she shot straight back up, blinking for a moment in astonishment. Clearly it was a habit, but one Duana wasn't happy to discover herself performing for a Robertson. She covered it by snapping her fingers at several of the serving women.

Ailis followed her down the steps and through a passageway opening.

"Isn't it just like a Robertson to be taking me away from the high table during supper service?" Duana complained loudly.

One of the maids stifled a snort badly.

"If ye had shown me to me proper place to begin with, I would nae have bothered ye."

Duana stopped and turned on her. "Do nae ye have any manners at all?"

"More than ye." Ailis stepped right up. "For if me brother brought home a bride, I'd no' show her to a cell."

"Ye're a Robertson." Duana's tone made her disdain clear.

"Yes, I am." Ailis kept her tone even, because she wasn't going to give the woman the fight she craved, only a look at just how well Ailis could stand firmly in her place.

Duana jammed her fists onto her ample hips. "Me husband died at the hands of a Robertson."

Ailis stared at the anger flickering in the Head of House's eyes. "A feud I am here to end."

Duana snorted at her, sweeping her from head to toe and clearly finding her lacking.

"Did yer husband court ye?" Ailis asked.

The question caught Duana off guard. She titled her

head to one side as she considered it. "Well…aye, he did." Her lips curled into a saucy grin. "No one knows how to tickle a lass's fancy like a MacPherson."

"I wouldn't know," Ailis said softly. "I was wed at gunpoint, to a man who would rather have been hanged, but took me in favor of seeing his father fitted with a noose. It tickled something inside me for certain, but it was no' me fancy."

The Head of House lost her poise, appearing uncertain for a long moment as the maids around them looked away to avoid making eye contact with Ailis.

"Aye," Duana muttered, attempting to recover. "I suppose…suppose…this way."

Ailis followed the woman up three flights of stairs. There were another two stories above that, but Duana stopped and slid a key into a door. The grating sound of the lock opening echoed down the stone stairway. She pushed the door in and revealed a sizable receiving chamber. The maids went around lighting candles and hastily pulling covers off the furniture. Two of them disappeared through an arched opening, and a moment later, the warm glow of candlelight illuminated a bedchamber.

The maids worked to dress the bed, while two more maids arrived with pitchers of water and a stack of fresh linen cloths. There was a crackle from the hearth as wood caught.

"Well now, off with that dress," Duana said firmly. "Ye'll need to be ready to greet yer husband if he decides to share yer bed tonight. There's a dressing robe in the wardrobe if he sends one of his lads down for ye."

One of the maids opened a double-door wardrobe

and pulled out a thick robe. She laid it over the arm of a wooden chair.

"Thank you. I can see to myself." She was suddenly weary. All she wanted to do was hide.

Just until she wasn't so tired.

"Oh? And why would that be?" Duana was in the mood to stand her ground again. The three maids all looked toward her. "Have something to hide, do ye?"

All four of them lifted their chins in defiance. She might have dressed them down for it. Truly thought about it. Lord knew her temper would have enjoyed returning spite for spite.

And where would that take them all?

Ailis reached up and tugged on the tie that kept her partlet closed at her neck. It slid open easily. She unfastened her cuffs next, and then popped the knot at the front of her dress. The maids started to shift uncertainly, looking between the Head of House and Ailis as more of her clothing began to gather on the floor. She kept at it until every last bit of her skin was on display.

"Leave when ye've seen enough to satisfy ye." Her tone reflected how much determination she had.

Two of the maids started to pick up the pieces of her dress in response. "I said leave. I'll see to myself before putting a single one of ye to the trouble of suffering me."

Eyes widened with shock; cheeks turned red. The Head of House let out a huff. "Well, see now what comes of the kindness I attempt to show ye."

"May someone be as kind to yer daughter," Ailis

said as she gathered up her clothing to shield herself. "When circumstances turn challenging."

Duana's expression changed. It became grudging. "Ye're no weakling."

She shuffled out of the chamber a moment later. Her maids followed, closing the door behind them.

It was a sweet sound.

Ailis closed her eyes and let the soft click wash through her. The fire crackled behind her, but there wasn't a single other sound.

Thank Christ.

She just needed a moment.

Well, perhaps more than one moment. But she'd be fine.

Ye are such a liar…

❧

"I was wed at gunpoint, to a man who would rather have been hanged, but took me in favor of seeing his father fitted with a noose."

Harsh words.

True words.

Bhaic hung back in the hallway, keeping to the shadows as Ailis faced off with his father's Head of House. Duana was a buxom woman who had several inches on Ailis, but his bride wasn't intimidated.

And cut him to the bone with her words.

They chafed because he'd always enjoyed seducing his bed partners. Any man might corner a lass, but it took cunning to draw one into the shadows for a bit of sport.

"Perhaps she's no' as much yers as ye think,

Brother." Marcus was hovering a few feet
behind him.

Bhaic shot him a withering look. "Do nae ye have
something better to do?"

His half brother smirked and shook his head.

"The devil take ye."

Marcus chuckled, low and ominously. "I was born
in sin, Brother, so I've never been very far from
Lucifer's reach. But"—he sobered, looking at the
darkened passageway the women had gone down—
"tonight I'm thankful. I'd no' care to hear how
much strife was between me and the one woman the
church blessed me to have in me bed."

"Aye." Bhaic turned and headed back toward
the hall.

"No' going up?"

Bhaic shook his head. "The lass is correct. I've no'
courted her."

Marcus reached out and caught his shoulder. "But
the union is consummated?"

Bhaic looked both ways before shaking his head.

"That complicates matters." His brother's tone had
gone hard. Marcus would always put the clan first.
"Unconsummated means we're open to reprisals."

Bhaic shrugged. "I was nae going to prove meself
the monster she's been raised to think me, by jumping on her and demanding me rights. Besides, to be
truthful, I was hoping to be free of the union. Lye
Rob Gordon has complicated matters."

"Oh…well now…" Marcus started. "She looks to
be such a terrible fate."

"Ye would no' have cared for being forced to yer

knees either, Brother. Ye've got yer mother's stubborn pride."

"Aye," Marcus conceded. "Which is why ye're the Tanis. The art of mediation is no' one I'm very accomplished at. That's a skill a laird must be willing to cultivate."

"Aye." Bhaic turned to go back toward the hall. Marcus stood firmly in his path.

"A Tanis must also see to securing alliances," his brother stated firmly. "So turn around and get to it."

"The lass and I have had enough of being told what to do," Bhaic stated firmly. "There's time enough for us to get to the particulars of our arrangement. I prefer me women feisty, no' worn down by a day that has been too long."

"Lye Rob will take advantage of that mercy, make no mistake," Marcus warned. "Yer kindness will become a horror the lass will have to suffer if he gets his hands on her."

"As War Chief, that is yer concern," Bhaic shot back. "Keep the bloody Gordons off our land. So I can focus on making sure me marriage does nae form another chain in the feud, because me wife learns to hate me and all me kin."

He only passed through the hall, going to the other set of stairs and climbing up to the fourth floor. His chamber was warm and welcoming. A fire going in the hearth and his bedding turned down, with a hint of rosemary coming from the sheets.

He ground his teeth, frustrated by the lack of welcome Ailis had received. It was his responsibility to see to her. She was his.

Well, no' completely so.

His gaze returned to the bed.

What a welcoming sight it would be to have Ailis in it, her golden hair spread out over the creamy linen sheeting.

His cock twitched, thickening as he indulged the moment of fantasy.

There was a scratching on the door.

"Aye?"

The door was pushed in slowly, and a maid peeked in. She smiled as she noted he was halfway out of his clothing. Her gaze roamed boldly over his bare chest as her teeth appeared in her bottom lip.

"Would ye care for…anything, my laird?"

Bhaic paused with his hands on his belt. To his shame, he couldn't recall if he'd had her.

And it was a shame when Ailis came to him a maiden. Feisty and passionate but still pure for the sake of honor.

The girl was licking her lower lip. She was halfway across the floor before he could stop her.

"Take a message to me bride," he said.

The girl froze, disappointment twisting her features.

"Tell her I wish her a pleasant night's rest."

The girl smiled brightly and lowered herself. "It will only take a little bit of time, and I will return."

"Nae."

Her expression darkened.

"And make sure ye speak to her with the respect me wife should have."

The girl turned around, but not before Bhaic saw her eyes widen. He cursed when the door shut.

He was being forced to see the Earl of Morton as a man with vision and insight. How could his own people be spiteful to one wee Robertson lass who was all but imprisoned inside the MacPherson castle?

There was the savage side of a Highlander's nature that one could be proud of, and then there was the behavior of his own kin. Meanness, for the sake of being unkind. It shamed him.

Yet Ailis had faced them all down. Damned if he hadn't been proud of her. She might have complained; instead she stood up for herself. Willing to earn her place.

Mercy? Nae. She deserved courting. No' the cold reality of being claimed.

He unbuckled his belt and gathered up his plaid before it fell to the floor. He took the time to lay it on a table, folding it into pleats and threading one belt beneath it before he turned to take his ease. If there was trouble during the night, he'd need his kilt ready.

He lay back in his bed, his cock stiff and unsatisfied.

But he was pleased.

Aye. He was.

For tomorrow, he'd set about chasing down his bride.

❧

Someone knocked on the door.

Ailis sat up, crumpling the sheet. Her heart jumped into a rhythm that she was sure would make it burst. Her attention flew to where the dressing robe was still lying over the arm of the chair.

Was the day not yet finished?

A girl came into view, looking around the outer receiving room.

"I am here."

The maid turned to look at her and moved to where the two rooms joined under a double-wide opening. There were thick velvet curtains that might be drawn, but Ailis had left them pushed back to have the light from the fire. The darkness had felt too lonely, the glowing red embers offering small comfort, but comfort nonetheless.

"Yer husband did send me to ye."

Her heart was definitely going to burst.

"He bids ye a restful night."

The girl offered her a shrug and started to leave, but then turned back and lowered herself, looking as though she was as uncertain of the gesture as Ailis was in receiving it. She scurried out the door the moment she was finished.

A restful night?

Dare she embrace relief or dread the fact that everyone would soon know Bhaic hadn't wanted her?

She groaned and lay back down. How was it possible to be granted what she craved but then be dissatisfied?

Ye're fickle...

Maybe. Honestly, she was too tired to ponder anything. The bedding was thick and warm, luring her away into the embrace of slumber.

She'd puzzle it all out tomorrow.

Four

FIRST LIGHT SHOWED HER MORE EVIDENCE OF THE MacPherson's superiority.

From the windows in her room, Ailis could see the outer buildings that supported the castle. The kitchens were huge. She counted at least seven chimneys, all of them in use. There was a well-worn road that led up to those kitchens. Even so early in the morning, there were wagons arriving. Beside the kitchen were hen-houses and a byre with cows. Young boys were moving around, sitting down on short stools to milk those cows.

Her belly rumbled, low and long.

Farther down the road were more buildings, likely belonging to the butcher. In the distance, she could see the stables. It was a misty morning, and chilly. Ailis pulled up her arisaid to fend off the chill, since she didn't have a wrap to fill in the neckline of her dress.

More than one person turned to stare at the Robertson colors when she passed by the passageways. She hurried by, not giving them time to start an argument with her. This early, the hall was still full of retainers sleeping on its floor. The men were rolled in their plaids, slumbering side by side, the tables and benches pushed to one end.

Being in the employ of the laird was a good life for many. The keep kept the snow out better than a rough hut, and men who served as retainers might enjoy three meals a day. They would all be fiercely loyal to Shamus and Bhaic. She stepped lightly as she went through the passageway toward the kitchens.

The hearths were fired up, the ovens hot as more than two dozen women worked lumps of bread dough on long tables. Flour floated in the air, tickling her nose. Ailis let her arisaid down, grateful to be able to blend in.

She stopped and selected a small round of bread resting on a cooling rack. After her meager supper, it smelled delightful. Her belly rumbled, and she walked through to a storage room where she selected a small chunk of cheese. The storeroom smelled delicious and slightly of wax, but inviting. There were pottery bowls with wide leather caps that held softer cheeses and perhaps fruit preserves from the last spring. Maybe honey too.

Had she really been gone from Robertson land for only one day?

Was it only yesterday that she'd been greeted as a member of the household?

"Here now, can ye nae wait for the laird to bless the bread?"

Ailis turned to find a woman standing in the doorway to the storeroom. She had her sleeves pushed all the way up her arms and a huge apron that was covered in flour. Her hair was tied up behind a length of fabric, with just a few wisps having worked their way free.

"Oh…well now, ye are nae who I expected to see in the storeroom, mistress."

Ailis was holding the bread and cheese to her body. The woman pulled off a length of toweling hanging from her belt and gave it a snap. Flour flew off it.

"Here, tie it up in this." She handed over the toweling and disappeared into the main kitchens. But she returned, offering a small knife and pottery jug. "I suppose I can nae blame ye for wanting a bit of peace while ye eat. I do nae know how ye managed to swallow anything last eve. The last time I felt that much tension in the hall was during the monthly court."

"Helen? What's keeping ye?"

Helen smiled before she turned and went back to the kitchen. There was good-natured conversation at the worktable. Someone broke out in song, and others joined in. It was tempting to stay, but when she appeared in the door frame, half the women snapped their mouths closed.

Ailis turned and walked through the back doorway. She pulled her arisaid up again, grateful for the length of Robertson wool that she'd worn tucked into her belt to show her clan affiliation. It was a good length, wide enough for her to wrap around her shoulders without pulling it from her belt. If it rained, she might make a hood of it to shelter under.

Today, it granted her privacy from the MacPhersons peering at her as she passed. She climbed up to the stables before sitting on a stump. The sun was in sight now, stretching out its golden rays. The mist was rolling in wisps, retreating to the valleys where the streams ran full of melting spring snow.

The length of toweling proved useful, covering her dress as she pulled the bread apart. Since she didn't have anything else to wear, keeping the front of it from stains would be best. She pulled the cork from the pottery jug and sniffed at the contents. It was water.

She could hear the horses as they woke and greeted the day. Wagons were making their way along the road, and in the distance, she could hear the church bell calling everyone to worship.

She muttered a quick prayer, asking for forgiveness, because going anywhere near stone walls chafed at the moment. Her breakfast finished, she shook out the toweling and tucked the knife into her belt before walking into the stables.

Her mare was at the end of one long row of stalls. She tossed her head when Ailis greeted her.

Tugging her skirt up, Ailis climbed up onto the crossbeams of the stall and sat on the top rail. Her mare was chewing her breakfast but nuzzled against her, looking for affection.

Ailis gave it freely, needing someone, or something, to help drive the loneliness from her heart.

"See? I told ye!"

Ailis jumped in surprise and slipped off the rail. Four burly retainers were coming down the row of stalls, their strides long and purposeful. They had doublets on with their kilts, and sword belts. Each man kept a sure hand on the hilt of his weapon as they moved to control the swing of the weapon behind him.

"No Robertson lass is going to be too hard to find."

"What are ye doing?" Ailis demanded. The retainer who appeared to be in command inclined his head toward her, but reached out and clamped his hand around her upper arm.

"Taking ye back to the castle."

She pulled against his hold, but only succeeded in wrenching her shoulder. "Do ye suppose ye might just ask me to accompany ye?" The urge to panic was hard to resist, but she fought to maintain control over her emotions.

His companions lost their scowls for a moment, one of them fingering his beard. "Would ye, then? Just come along quiet like?"

"Ye'll no' know unless ye try," she snapped, jerking on her arm again.

The leader released her and fixed her with a skeptical glare. "I am Lyel. Would ye be so kind as to return to the castle with me and the lads?"

Her arm smarted. She resisted the urge to rub it and let him see that he'd pained her. "May I ask why?"

One of the others spoke up. "That's what ye get for asking. Now she's going to pester ye to death with questions."

"Shut yer jaw, Finley," Lyel said. "Well, mistress? Are ye coming, or are we hauling ye between us?"

"Hauling?" She stepped back, and they all followed her. "Why ever would ye haul me?"

Was she a prisoner then?

"Marcus set us to looking after ye." Lyel indicated his comrades. "Finley there, Skene, and Kam. Since ye were no' at table to break yer fast, there was a bit of a concern for where ye might have slipped off to.

A Robertson unaccounted for, well now, there's the reason for concern."

"I was just here…seeing me mare."

Lyel's lips curved in a smug grin. "Aye. I thought to myself, where would she go but up to where she might get herself a horse, to be quicker away to her father's lands?"

"That is an unfounded charge."

"It is." Bhaic suddenly appeared. The four retainers all reached up and tugged on the corners of their bonnets. "The lady would be long away if that were her intention. According to the kitchens, she was gone just after first light. Helen will nae give her food again."

She'd just been enjoying a moment of relief when his second comment stole it away. "Good Christ," she swore. "What does it matter?"

Bhaic gave the retainers a gesture. They nodded and headed back down the aisle toward the doors of the stable, but they didn't leave. He'd started to turn back toward her but looked back at the retainers.

"Can I no' be alone with me wife?"

Lyel cleared his throat and looked down.

"Be gone," Bhaic ordered them.

"The thing is"—Lyel cleared his throat again—"we can nae do that."

"And why no'?" Bhaic demanded.

"Well, ye see, Marcus gave very clear instructions."

"Aye, clear they were." Finley came to his comrade's aid. "Ye two need…witnesses." He gestured to himself and his friends.

Bhaic's face darkened with understanding. "Would it suit ye if I just toss her skirts right here?"

Ailis felt as if she'd been punched in the belly as the retainers all started nodding.

"That would do it sure enough."

"Right well."

"Better done quickly, I always say. Settles the lassies down when they're skittish."

"With a fair lass like that? I'd be in favor of tossing her skirts," Kam finished up.

"Ye will no'!" She lifted her foot and kicked Bhaic straight in the backside. He hadn't been watching her, and stumbled when her blow landed. The retainers hooted with amusement.

"Skittish and spirited!"

"Better get a bridle on her!"

Bhaic flipped around. "I did nae mean it like that, Ailis." He'd landed in a fighting crouch but recovered quickly. She'd be wise to recognize just how deadly the man might be, but all she could hear was the choking sounds his father's retainers were making.

"I am no' a strumpet to be spoken of so freely for sport."

He held his hands up. "I know ye are nae. Men talk…more crudely."

She'd made it away from the stall. He started to follow her and she just couldn't control the urge to edge away from him.

He didn't care for the way she was backing away from him. His eyes narrowed, his lips pressing into a hard line. "If I was going to handle ye roughly, I'd have insisted on sharing yer bed last night."

She stopped moving, realizing she was far more trapped by the union she was in with him than anything else. There was nowhere she might go, no place on earth that wouldn't recognize the rights of a husband to his wife.

It left her feeling hopeless. Trapped.

But he had shown her kindness. She tried to hold onto that fact.

"I simply woke early," she said. "I was nae leaving."

"But ye are here…in the stables."

She felt him closing the distance. It was the oddest sensation. A tightening of her insides and a ripple of awareness across her skin.

"Me mare is the only creature I was certain would welcome me."

His lips twitched, curving into a confident grin that sent her blood racing. "Ye may depend on a warm welcome when ye come to me, lass."

"Come to ye?"

He nodded.

Wouldn't that be too bold?

He'd made it close enough to clasp her wrist. She jerked when he closed his fingers around her limb. His expression was harsh.

"I know me strength," he muttered softly. He stood a full head taller than she. He might have tucked her head beneath his chin. "Ye needn't flinch."

"Yer touch is…unsettling."

He lifted her chin with two fingers, making her look into his eyes. She'd been avoiding it. Because she knew she'd get lost again.

She was right. There was something about the way he looked into her eyes that made her feel as though he could see her most intimate thoughts.

"Aye." His tone had deepened, clearly pleased, but in some dark, wicked way. "Since we're wed, it's as it should be, lass. I plan to teach ye how to enjoy it."

She liked the sound of that.

Her mouth went dry, and her lips felt as if they were recalling exactly what it felt like to be kissed.

Oh, it was a terrible, craven thing to like, but she couldn't very well lie to herself.

He was leaning toward her, making ready to kiss her.

"Why…why didn't ye…insist last eve? If ye are so convinced I am no' trustworthy, why leave the matter unsettled?"

He made a soft sound under his breath. "Because I do nae wish to be the brute ye accused me of being."

"I called ye that justly."

"Aye." His tone had become a husky whisper. "So grant me some notice for the fact that I am trying to please ye."

She nodded. But with nothing to quibble over, all she was left with was the knowledge that he was stirring up her senses.

His breath teased the surface of her lips, sending a ripple of awareness over the delicate skin. He eased closer, his scent filling her senses. Her heart accelerated, beating with hard, deep, pounding motions. She wanted his kiss, and he leaned down, his blue eyes focused on her mouth. She started to rise onto her toes, intending to meet him.

Something snapped beneath a boot at the other end of the stable. She stiffened, landing back on her heels with a jolt.

"I told ye to stay still! We're going to be stuck

trailing the pair of them until they get this finished,"
Finley barked. "Don't mind us…"

Bhaic cursed in Gaelic. "I needs speak with me
brother. They will nae leave us in peace, since his
word holds the same weight as mine."

Ailis withdrew, but he pulled her to a stop with the
hold on her wrist. She lifted her arm and started to pull
against his grip. Their gazes locked as she increased her
resistance. He didn't want to let her go. She witnessed
the flash of rejection in his eyes before he relented and
opened his fingers.

"I'll take ye back up to the castle, lass. I do nae
know what women spend their days doing, but I know
it is no less demanding than me own responsibilities."

He offered her his hand.

Time felt as though it froze. He stretched just
another inch closer to her.

"Take me hand, lass. Trust that I only mean to put
it on me arm."

Trust. It was an enormous idea, one that felt as if it
had the ability to crush her.

Yet part of her wanted to touch him again.

Her heart skipped a beat as she laid hers into his grasp.
He settled her hand on his forearm and started off.

Ailis discovered herself lost in the moment. One
she'd daydreamed about, because to stroll so intimately
on the arm of a man was something the maiden
daughter of the laird simply did not do. She'd seen
other girls enjoying such, their cheeks pink and their
eyes glittering with enjoyment.

Did she like it?

For certain, it was far different than she'd expected.

Her breath felt caught and labored. Thinking took massive amounts of concentration, and even then, her thoughts were muddled. Her insides were twisted into a strange concoction of excitement and anticipation. She ended up laughing softly under her breath.

"My escort amuses ye?"

She laughed harder and pulled her hand off his arm as she tried to explain herself. "The situation…being on a man's arm…well, it is nae…exactly what I thought it might be. When I got the chance to experience it meself."

He chuckled and caught her hand and returned it to his arm. "Aye."

They were making it closer to the castle. More people were there. They looked up, pausing as Bhaic brought her past them. She started to pull her hand off his arm, but he covered it with his own, gently rubbing the back of her hand.

"We're in this together, lass."

They were kind words, but not entirely true. She looked at MacPherson Castle, noticing all of the things about it that were unfamiliar.

She knew Robertson Castle like the back of her hand. She was the stranger here, not him.

Ahead of them, Marcus was watching a group of youths practicing with wooden swords.

"Excuse me, lass. I needs have words with me brother, and they will likely be too rough for yer ears."

Bhaic turned to face her, slipping his hand behind her head and cupping it gently. She gasped, but he captured the sound beneath his lips as he pressed a kiss onto her mouth. It wasn't overly hard or deep, but there was a reaction around it.

He pulled away, the look in his eyes sending a shiver down her spine. She had spent more than a few hours thinking on the day when a man would consider her his, but she wasn't prepared for it.

The intensity in his eyes curled her toes.

He turned and started across the yard, giving her too much time to admire what a fine figure he made. His shoulders were broad and packed with thick muscle. No hint of a belly, only a trim waist where his kilt was secured.

"Robertson…"

The slur caught her attention.

No, it wasn't a slur, it was her father's name, and it was time she did something about making sure the MacPhersons stopping using it as such.

She turned toward the kitchens, her escort falling in behind her.

❧

"Brother."

"Do nae brother me, Marcus." Bhaic braced his feet in a wide stance. "Ye know what I'm here about."

Marcus had his arms crossed over his chest. It was his favorite pose for keeping his thoughts to himself and driving Bhaic insane.

"Ye are the Tanis."

"I bloody well know that," Bhaic said.

"Then why is that lass still yer bride and no' yer wife?" Marcus turned to face him. "She's an educated woman, likely reads at least three languages. And she was loose in our halls without a single pair of eyes on her, with the legal right to annul her marriage.

I would have posted someone at her door last night if I'd thought for a moment ye'd be so stupid as to leave her alone. If she makes it back to her father, the information about our defenses she might carry with her would be catastrophic."

Bhaic was fuming, but he couldn't very well accuse his brother of having no grounds for his concerns. "She's the one who saw the wisdom in our union before I did, Marcus. Do nae color the lass so guilty. Notice that she is trying to make this work, and no' many are willing to see it an easy task for her."

His brother only gave him a half grin. "'Tis my place to be suspicious. Yers to make alliances."

"Would ye have me be rough with her?" Bhaic demanded. "She's a delicate lass."

His brother chuckled ominously. "Aye, I've seen her. Her sweet face makes a man forget everything. The perfect makings of a spy."

"You go too far with that word."

Bhaic challenged Marcus's gaze, but his brother didn't retreat.

"I mean it, Marcus, take it back."

His brother considered him for a moment and shook his head.

The youths started to notice, halting their practice. Bhaic didn't back down, and neither did Marcus.

"Alright then…" Bhaic said as he pulled his sword belt off and tossed it to one of the boys behind him.

Marcus's expression lit with savage enjoyment. They both stripped down to their shirts, the youths clearing out of the training yard as Bhaic and Marcus took up positions.

"Ye're going to take that word back," Bhaic promised.

"I would love to see ye try to make me."

A lot of others wanted to see too. They began spilling out of the buildings as he and Marcus circled each other. People started calling out wagers, but all Bhaic saw was the gleam in his brother's eye.

One he was going to smash.

They collided with a crunch, the crowd groaning. Marcus's jaw was as hard as a boulder, but Bhaic smashed his fist into it anyway. His brother didn't give easily but ended up staggering under the force of the second blow Bhaic landed. He came back with a vicious snarl, ramming himself into Bhaic and lifting him off his feet.

They slammed into the ground, raising a cloud of dust. People surged forward, trying to get a good view. Marcus tried to pin him on his back, and Bhaic strained and tossed him over. He flipped and launched himself at Marcus, the pair of them grabbling, rolling, punching, and doing their best to lock an arm around the other's neck to choke him into compliance.

There wasn't going to be any quarter.

❧

"Mistress…come out of the kitchens…*please*."

Ailis looked up to find Finley dancing from one foot to the other like a little boy on Twelfth Night.

"We're missing the fun," he implored her. "And I can nae go without ye."

The head cook made it clear she'd be happy if Ailis went somewhere else.

"It will be over soon," Finley said.

There was something going on in the yard. People were cheering.

"Very well."

At least someone might be pleased with her at last. Finley ran the few steps to the kitchen door and pushed it open for her. The cheering was louder now, along with some sort of snarling and grunting.

She came up into the yard and blinked as she took in the sight.

"Whoo…hoo…ye've got him now!" Finley roared.

As far as she could see, there was no way to know who had whom. Bhaic and his brother were a tangle of limbs and snarls. They'd raised a huge cloud of dust, and both of them had blood brightening their shirts. The crowd roared with approval as they tried to kill each other.

She started forward, but Finley shot his arm out and stopped her. "Stay here now, lassie. That's no place for a wee thing like yerself."

"Ye have to stop them."

Finley looked at her as if she'd lost her mind.

Well, at least they had something in common.

"Here now…What's all this?" Shamus MacPherson suddenly appeared.

The crowd parted for him but groaned with disappointment. The old laird made his way to the edge of the circle surrounding the two fighting men and scowled.

"Get up, ye sons of the devil!" he hollered. He turned to his captains. "Haul those dogs off each other."

Bhaic got in one final blow with his elbow before Angus dragged him off Marcus.

"I said enough," Shamus insisted.

Marcus and Bhaic both abandoned their spite as they faced their father. For all that the bloodlust had cooled in their expressions, there was no hint of remorse for their actions. Their father shook his head.

"I've a mind to send ye both to the monastery for good penance." He shook his head. "But ye're likely both lost causes, since ye're me sons."

Bhaic and Marcus both snickered in response.

"What's eating at the pair of ye?" their father demanded. He turned and looked at the crowd. "And is there nae a single better thing the lot of ye might be doing with the daylight?"

People started scattering. The youths began to train again, the sound of their wooden swords connecting filling the air.

"Now answer me," Shamus insisted.

"He insulted me wife," Bhaic said plainly. "Harshly so."

Marcus wiped blood off his chin with his sleeve. Shamus pegged him with a hard look. "Perhaps I did."

Bhaic curled his fingers into a fist.

"Enough," Shamus said. "Seems we do nae need the Robertsons to overrun us. All it has taken to set us on our ear is one wee lassie."

Everyone suddenly turned to look at her. Shamus followed the direction of the crowd's attention. He pointed at her.

"Go on then, see what manner of nursing yer husband needs," Shamus ordered before looking at Marcus. "And ye sit down and cool yer temper."

Helen was suddenly there, with a bowl and a pitcher of water. She pushed Ailis forward, other women from the kitchen arriving. One set a stool down, but Bhaic looked at it with nothing more than a disinterested glance.

"I do nae need tending."

He was glowering down at Ailis, looking as intimidating as she'd always been told he was. Everyone was watching them, seeing if she'd fold beneath his stern glare.

"The blood wetting yer hair says otherwise. Now sit down before ye and I have to *discuss* the matter," Ailis admonished him.

His eyes lit with enjoyment, a glitter that warned her he was very interested in her attempts to make him bend. She stared straight back at him. He chuckled softly before lowering himself to a stool.

"Far be it for me to argue about ye wanting to put yer hands on me."

Helen grunted and clicked her tongue as she poured the water into the bowl and added a pouch of herbs.

❧

"Ye have an odd way of talking to yer brother."

Bhaic started to get up, but Ailis shoved him back down and used her fingers to push his hair back from the cut on his scalp. "Sweet Christ, this needs stitching."

Marcus snorted at him, making kissing motions with his lips. Bhaic started to send him an obscene gesture but got distracted by Ailis's cleavage. She was so busy looking at his head, she hadn't yet realized his nose was darn near in the valley between her breasts. He slowly grinned and heard his brother snort again.

"Are ye going to tell me yer brothers are so very different?"

She was still looking at the cut on his scalp. He was still enjoying the sight of her plump breasts.

"Well, nae. I suppose ye have a point. Duncan and Bruce are forever at each other's throats over something or another."

She suddenly realized where his attention was. "Bhaic Gordon Matthew MacPherson."

"So ye were paying attention during our wedding," he said smugly.

"It's branded into me memory."

How could it not be? The thought sobered her, dredging up the dread and uncertainty her wedding had been made of. It certainly had not been a happy moment. By the time she cut the thread on the row of stitches, her mood was gloomy indeed.

Bhaic stood, looking as though he'd suffered through the stitching only to please her. He was every inch the warrior she'd been raised to fear. Hardened. Savage.

And ye belong to him…

They were still the center of attention, with a good number of folks still lingering in doorways and in the yard. Bhaic's eyes narrowed as he caught her gaze for a moment. Ailis turned, using the excuse of washing her hands. She felt him watching her.

"I'll see ye at supper, lass."

It was more warning than invitation. She looked up to see him walking away, the longer pleats of his kilt swaying.

How could it still be before noon? She felt as though the day had been so very much longer.

❧

Her reluctant escort clung to her skirt hem.

Their patience wore thin as the day went on. Ailis went through the large kitchens, familiarizing herself with how the storerooms were organized and just how the huge number of MacPherson retainers were kept fed.

Duana wasn't in a much better mood today. The Head of House was stiff, and a little unwilling to meet Ailis's direct gaze. But at least her cutting remarks were missing some of their sharpness.

"Helen there can spend time playing nursemaid," Duana finally said, "since it seems she has a liking for Robertsons."

Helen dropped her superior a courtesy, but there was a disapproving set to her lips. Duana ignored it as she went back to supervising the evening meal.

"I'll be happy to answer yer questions, mistress." Helen raised her voice just a bit on the word "mistress." It sent a ripple through the women working at the long tables and the men set to watching Ailis.

But a young maid suddenly let out a shriek and dropped a large ceramic pitcher. It smashed into the floor with a loud cracking sound. Cider went splashing over the floor as the girl pointed at Ailis. "She's wearing a knife, she is. Going to slit our throats with it, no doubt."

Ailis looked down at her side, having forgotten about the knife Helen had given her that morning.

She turned away from the girl but found Finley in her path with his hand out. "Give me the knife."

"Sweet Mary and Joseph," she exclaimed. "As if every woman here does nae have a blade stuck through her garter."

"Perhaps so, but they are nae Robertsons."

Ailis turned to find Marcus in the doorway, his body blocking out the sun. He surveyed the mess on the floor and grunted before closing the distance between them.

"Let's have it, lass."

He and Bhaic had a lot in common. It was there in the commanding way they spoke. She tugged the knife free and dropped it on the table instead of his hand. His lips twitched in response.

"As for that, it's me brother's dilemma how to deal with yer nature."

She held her chin steady, feeling the weight of everyone watching them. Her pride was chafing.

"Is this to be the way of it, then?" Ailis gestured toward Finley and Lyel.

Marcus folded his arms over his chest and spread his feet, making himself look huge and impossible to move. "Aye. I can nae have ye carrying secrets back to yer father and brothers."

"I am nae going home." Even if it was sounding more and more like a necessity.

Marcus shook his head. "But ye still call it home, now don't ye, lass?"

She tried to bring her tone under control. "Surely ye can nae expect me to call MacPherson Castle home when I have been here but a day."

"I do nae," he answered gravely. "Which is why ye'll be watched."

He started to turn his back on her. "Heaven forbid I should feel welcome, like a bride."

When he looked back at her, his lips were twisted

into what might have been called a grin, but on the War Chief of the MacPherson clan, it looked far more menacing.

"Ye are exactly that, Mistress Robertson. A bride, no' a wife. So long as ye leave the matter open for annulment, I will have ye watched. Ye can nae tell me yer brothers would do any less if it were me sister walking freely through Robertson Castle."

She wanted to hate him.

Wanted to curse him.

But she knew he had a valid point, and no matter now angry or lonely she was, she couldn't form an argument against it.

❧

"I'm taking a bath, so get ye gone."

Finley snorted, but it was Lyel who answered. "We do nae answer to ye."

Behind her there was a splash as the last of several buckets was emptied into the tub she'd had brought up the stairs. Two boys hurried out of the room, crossing themselves out of fear.

Her teeth were ready to break from how hard she was clenching her jaw.

It wasn't so much that she needed a bath. What she was needed was a place to hide from the cutting looks and snide comments. For sure, there would be grumbling over her asking to have the tub filled, but she honestly didn't care anymore. The sun was starting to set, tightening the apprehension that had been brewing in her since Bhaic had issued his command that morning.

"Here now…" Helen appeared at the top of the steps. Her arms were full of toweling and several bundles. "What are ye two doing inside the mistress's chambers with her making ready to bathe? Go on, before I set the priest on ye for trying to spy a glance of another man's wife."

She brushed right past them and jerked her head at them. "I told ye…get. And close that door all the way. I'll tear a strip off yer backs if I hear the hinge creaking."

Finley was bending, moving to the other side of the door. "We'll be right here." He paused with his hand on the door pull. "And I mean, right here." He tapped the floor with his foot.

Helen turned around and sent the door shut with a push from her backside. There was a snort from the other side as it closed.

"They're just trying to put ye in yer place…" Helen muttered. "As if either of those great gobs knows a bit about what yer place is."

"Well, I would nae want to crush them by telling them that."

Helen smiled and offered her a wink. "That's the way to think about it all. Lord knows ye'll go daft if ye try to make sense of it."

"I'm sure I'm nearly ready for Bedlam now," Ailis confessed, feeling as tired as she sounded.

Helen moved over to a long table against one of the walls. She set down her bundles and began opening them. "Aye. I suppose ye are. But it will get easier, when the castle folk get tired of their game. They will."

Helen moved over to the hearth and poked at the fire, making sure the two kettles were being heated.

When she turned around, she caught Ailis staring at her.

"Ye're likely wondering why I'm kind to ye."

Ailis shrugged and sat down on a stool to begin taking off her shoes. "In truth, I'm too much of a coward to ask ye, fearing ye'll realize yer error and turn mean."

Helen's face lit with a smile as laughter spilled out of her. She wasn't that old. Possibly even the same age as Ailis herself. She had hazel eyes with golden highlights and sable-brown hair. She kept it hidden under a kitchen cap, but wisps of it had escaped to frame her face with tiny ringlets.

"I was born a Grant." Helen made her way back to the table and rummaged through the things she'd brought. "Me father had a dispute with some MacPherson retainers. It was sorted out, but they stole me away to make sure me kin would nae retaliate, in the event they were not as satisfied with the settlement as they said they were."

"That's why yer arisaid is no' a plaid."

Helen looked over her shoulder and sent Ailis a satisfied smile. "Indeed. For certain, some will call me stubborn, but I'll be keeping everyone guessing as to me true thoughts."

"Is that why ye called me mistress?"

Helen shook her head and gave her a disbelieving look. "I called ye what ye are."

"Mistress of a castle full of my enemies."

Helen sent her a sidelong look. "Ye look fit to take them on. In truth, I believe I am going to enjoy being near ye. It's been too long since I've had a good bit of amusement."

Ailis burst out laughing.

Helen tossed a small cream-colored item up and down as she came back toward Ailis. "Soap. Duana wanted to tell me I could nae have it for ye, but I made sure to ask for it in front of witnesses. For all her spite, she's not stupid. The young Tanis was fighting for ye today. She'll no' risk having him displeased with her over something like a piece of soap."

"I suddenly see the merit in this union if there are truly people willing to take spite so far as a lump of soap."

"Aye, 'tis a sad state of affairs," Helen agreed.

Ailis dropped her shoes and untied her garters. She pushed her stockings down and stood up. Helen helped her untie and unlace until she was in just her skin. One of the kettles started to sputter, the water inside it boiling and sending just enough of it out of the spout to hit the flames.

Helen went to fetch it. She used her arisaid to protect her hand as she lifted the kettle and brought it over to the tub. The water flowed from the spout in a steaming stream, hissing as it hit the cold water. Helen dunked the empty kettle back into the tub to fill it and set it over the fire. She added the second kettle before using a paddle to stir the water.

"Come now. We'd best get to it, or we'll be late to supper table. Yon retainers will likely use any tardiness as an excuse to break down the door."

"No doubt," Ailis agreed.

Ailis left her hair up, because there wasn't time to wash it. The hot water had taken the chill off the water in the tub, but it was still only tepid. That didn't stop her from enjoying it. The soap had lavender oil in it, and she smiled as she rubbed it along her arms and legs.

A bell started to toll in the distance.

"Out with ye now. That's the cook telling everyone she's beginning to set supper out."

Helen had warmed a length of towel in front of the hearth. She wrapped it around Ailis as she stepped out of the tub.

There was a rap on the door. "Mistress...supper is on the table..."

Helen smothered a giggle. "Men are simple creatures. They want their hungers satisfied. Remember that, and ye'll be just fine."

She wasn't likely to forget it.

"I brought ye a new chemise. I suggest we rinse out yer other one here, for there's no telling if the laundress will take her spite out on it if we give it to her."

"Aye." Ailis lifted her arms, and Helen helped her into her chemise. It fluttered down her body, but the moment she could see again, she gasped.

Bhaic was standing inside the open door.

"Whooo...now that is a fine set of bosoms!" Finley exclaimed.

"I warned ye." Helen grabbed the paddle she'd stirred the bath water with and went tearing after Finley.

Bhaic jumped out of her way as the two retainers stumbled, trying to flee down the stairs.

"I suppose that's one way to deal with them," he said with a chuckle.

Bhaic kicked the door shut and turned back to face her.

"Ye might have knocked." Ailis propped her

hands on her hips. "I realize everyone in this castle seems to think they need to know our personal business, but did ye truly need to let that fat, smelly fart see me bare?"

Bhaic peered at her with an incredulous expression for at least one minute before he started chuckling. "Fat, smelly fart?"

Then he was laughing so hard his eyes squeezed shut.

She groaned and picked up her skirt to shield herself. "Go on with ye. I'll be down as soon as I've dressed. Ye did nae need to fetch me. I am no' spying."

So accustomed to being trusted, she felt keenly the suspicion surrounding her.

He sobered. "I suppose 'tis been a long day for ye."

There was a hint of compassion in his tone. She shied away from it, unwilling to let him see her wounds. She gestured him toward the door with her hand. "I'll be along, and in any event, I'm sure yer brother's men will make sure of it."

"Helen seems to have run them off."

"I'm sure ye'll feel the need to warn her against doing that as well." She hadn't meant to let the words out, but the day had worn down her resolve.

Bhaic slowly grinned. "I'm pretty sure she'd ignore me. Figures ye'd manage to find the only lass in the kitchens with a reason to want to needle me and me brother."

"It's no' as if either of us has many options as far as finding pleasant company." She forced herself to drop her skirt. The man had seen her in a chemise before. "But she's the one being kind to me."

Now he's seen ye without it too…

Well, that was just fine as well. She sat down and pulled her stockings on, tying her garters to keep them secure. She pushed her feet into her ankle boots before tugging the laces tight and standing up.

"I believe I am going to owe her a boon." Ailis secured her hip roll as Bhaic spoke. Next came her skirts. Her fingers were shaking as she reached for them.

Stop being a ninny; ye're dressing, not undressing…

Not that being clothed would keep him from having her if he wanted.

"Because I came to ask ye to run away with me. Having her chase off yer escort is right timely."

She'd lifted her skirt up and had to pull it down before she might look at him. He'd bent down and picked up her overskirt.

"Have a notion to try yer luck at me father's table?" she asked. No matter how nervous she was, she couldn't help but laugh at the idea.

Bhaic grinned. "Nay. I'm no' sure I'm as good at holding me temper as ye are."

She took her overskirt from him and got into it, tying it closed before he handed her the bodice.

"I've no taste for the scrutiny either," he offered as she worked the laces through the eyelets on her bodice.

"So I came up here to ask ye to run away with me for an evening ride," he continued, "but I'll admit, I found myself tongue-tied when I realized I'd be asking ye to put yer clothes back on for it. Part of me rebels completely at that idea."

He was chuckling again, his features transforming into a visage that was really quite handsome.

"No' sure yer reputation will survive such a thing?" she teased.

"No' if Marcus hears of it," he confirmed gravely.

"Or Angus?"

Bhaic nodded agreement. "Among others."

They were both smiling, clearly still unsure about being easy in each other's company.

There was a rap on the door, and Helen pushed it in a moment later. "Left those fools at the base of the stairs, and if they do nae want their skulls caved in, they'll stay there."

She stopped abruptly as she found herself facing Bhaic, but she didn't simper in front of him, only gave him a nod before scooping up Ailis's arisaid and beginning to fold it on the table.

With Helen's help, Ailis was soon finished. Bhaic offered her his hand. She didn't ponder the decision long. If there was an alternative to sitting through another supper in the hall, she'd take it.

Even if it included the rather unsettling persona of her husband.

He clasped her hand, his eyes flickering with enjoyment.

"Helen, ye have no idea where we've gone."

"I feel me memory clouding. However…" Helen crossed to them and unbuckled Ailis's belt. "Ye'll be wanting to leave these Robertson colors here, else everyone will take notice of yer passing."

Helen pulled her own arisaid loose and handed it to Ailis. Bhaic took the length of wool and slung it over his shoulder.

Bhaic pulled her toward the door, but looked back

at Helen. "And warn the laundress that I'll be having words with anyone who forgets Ailis is me bride."

Helen scoffed at him. "Ye may do that yerself." She scooped up the chemise and walked to the tub to dunk it. "I'd rather look after the lass meself than tangle with the lot of women ye have in this castle. Arrogant lot. It's no wonder most of the babes have red hair. No one is willing to wed an outsider. Mark me words, that sort of thing makes the blood thin."

❧

"I truly like Helen."

They'd crossed into the stairway. Bhaic looked back at her. "Because she told me nay?"

Ailis nodded.

He rolled his eyes, but the grin stayed on his lips. "Suppose she's entitled. I forgot she was here."

He pulled her up the stairs and across a landing before going down another set on the other side of the tower.

"How could ye forget something like that? And how long has she been here?"

"Since last spring." He shrugged and kept going, pulling her along behind him. "I was nae the one who took her. Marcus did." They made it to the bottom of the stairs. He pulled her close as he looked into the passageway. He tapped his lips with his finger, warning her to be silent. Finley and Lyel were leaning against the stone wall on the other side of the landing, both of them looking up.

"We're going to starve if she does nae get down here," Lyel groused. "Let's go and get her."

"Well ye can just go first. That way, that she devil of a Grant will use up her spite on yer skull."

Lyel hesitated, but he finally set his mind to it and started up the stairs, Finley on his heels.

"Now's our chance, lass."

She bit back a giggle as Bhaic tugged her through the passageway, hugging the walls to stay in the shadows. There was a swirl of excitement in her belly, a hint of anticipation stroking her insides. Other girls could sneak into the shadows for a kiss, but not her. No, not the laird's daughter.

But she'd thought about it more than a time or two.

It was strange to have Bhaic MacPherson helping her experience such a forbidden thing, but then again, maybe he was the only man who could take her away into the night.

For kisses...

She blushed, grateful he wasn't looking at her.

Well, maybe there would be kisses... What was wrong with that?

He was her husband, wasn't he?

He clicked his tongue when they neared the outer doorway. There was a snort in response. Fires were being lit on the walls so the sentries could keep watch, but the castle was still shrouded in darkness.

"Here now, lass, give me yer foot." He'd cupped his hands to offer her a step up. His stallion was eying her as she pulled her skirt out of the way and let Bhaic help her gain the back of the beast. The stallion was intimidating, in height and sheer bulk. Bhaic swung up behind her, sending a shiver through her as she ended up pressed against him. A light rain had started to fall.

"Do ye mind the rain, lass?"

He'd pressed the horse into motion, riding away from the castle and heading for the outer wall.

"Less than the scrutiny of the hall."

"Aye."

He covered her head with Helen's arisaid and locked his arm around her waist to secure her against him. They moved in unison with the motion of the horse, his body chasing the night chill away. The sentry eyed them but didn't cry an alarm as Bhaic rode through the gate.

⌀

"Ye'll get yer hand off me…"

Finley snarled something in Gaelic as he tugged Helen down the last few steps. Lyel was behind the woman, doing little good, because he was loath to actually put his hands on her.

Marcus stood there, offering her a glare that unsettled most men.

Helen tossed her head and boldly stepped up to face him. "Ye did nae need to have yer hounds collect me. I am no' afraid of ye."

"So ye have mentioned before, mistress."

Helen glared at him. "Well? What do ye want from me?"

Marcus's lips slowly curved. Helen's eyes narrowed. She started to flounce past him, but he put his arm out, cupping her shoulder and turning her around so her back was against the wall.

"Leave us," he said.

The position gave her an excellent view of Finley

and Lyel making haste toward the hall. Her insides twisted as she realized she was quite alone with Marcus.

"Where did yer mistress go?" he asked.

Marcus was accustomed to getting what he wanted, either by sheer force of will or cunning. Fortunately, she was immune to him.

"Me memory is clouded." She tried to slip along the wall.

Marcus pressed a hand on the wall next to her, caging her. "We can stay here as long as it takes for ye to recall."

His gaze dropped to her cleavage. "But if me behavior unsettles ye, best ye recall quickly."

"Unsettles?" she scoffed. "I hardly recall ye draw breath. Is that no' the same way ye feel about me?"

"Longing for me attention, are ye?" He continued looking at her cleavage, in defiance of every rule of decent conduct.

"I long to be free to return home," she shot back. "Ye dropped me in yonder courtyard without a backward glance, and a warning that ye'd burn me father's house if I went back there."

He raised his attention to her face, abandoning his attempts at intimidation. "Ye seem to have fared well enough."

She didn't care for the compliment. No, not at all, because there was nothing she wanted to like about the burly War Chief.

Nothing.

She lifted her foot and he curled in, expecting an attack on his groin, which left his shin wide open. He jerked and jumped back as she landed the blow. Helen made full use of the opportunity and escaped into the hall, where supper was being served. Marcus was on her heels. He cupped her elbow.

"We're nae finished, mistress. Ye can be sure of that." Yet he seemed loath to drag her back in the face of so many watching them.

"And ye may be certain that I will never help ye with a single thing so long as I draw breath."

She jerked her elbow from his grip, but not before she heard a husky chuckle.

Her heart was pounding as she made her way away from him. Damned brute. It always unsettled her to see the man who'd so easily ordered her abduction.

That was the only reason she'd allow into her mind for her accelerated heart rate.

The only one.

୶

"Here, lass…"

Bhaic had guided them across the land bridge and through the village until he could once again climb onto the high ground. A body of water stood between them and MacPherson Castle. The moon shone off its smooth surface as the stars came out.

"There used to be an astrologer here," Bhaic said. "He died a few seasons past."

There was a small building that might have been called a home as easily as it could have been labeled a workshop. It was an odd, two-story structure, perched on the highest point of land. There was even a single-stall stable built onto it.

"When he grew older, his knees were nae so good,

so me father had a horse here for him to use when he needed to get about." Bhaic slid off the back of the stallion and reached up to help her down. "Me father enjoyed the man's predictions and rarely made a business move without first consulting with old Maeburn."

He led the stallion around and into the stall. There was a trough Bhaic filled with oats.

"Ye keep the place stocked?" Ailis asked.

"Aye." He removed the bridle from the stallion and rubbed the beast's nose before the horse went looking for the feed. "Ye are nae the only one who feels the weight of those watching in the hall." He looked up at the building. "Sometimes I come here to look up at things that are far removed from anything MacPherson."

He offered her his hand, and she laid hers into it, earning a grin. Excitement glittered in his eyes. "The second floor is quite interesting."

He pulled her inside and shut the door, releasing her in order to lower the bar. He took a good look around the room before moving farther into it. As far as rooms went, it was a good size. There was a hearth, with an iron bar for roasting meat, and a hook to suspend a pot from. Wood was stacked up beside it.

"Lighting a candle will ruin the view," he said. "Do ye mind the darkness?"

"It is nae so dark."

In fact, the second floor of the structure seemed to be glowing. There was a loft with a steep stairway. Bhaic gestured her up behind him. "Hold on."

"Easy for ye to say," she said with a laugh. "Ye are nae wearing a skirt."

She struggled to keep her skirt out of the way of her feet. "I wish Helen had left me my belt."

Bhaic was watching her from the second floor. "Aye, I can see how that would have made things simpler. But I'm grateful she took yer colors from ye."

She'd almost reached the top when he grasped her waist and pulled her the rest of the way up. He held her against him, the scent of his skin filling her senses.

"Because now I have ye all to meself."

His tone had turned husky. She ended up resting her hands on his chest, her fingertips suddenly becoming far more sensitive than she'd realized they might be. His breath teased her temple, tempting her to raise her face for his kiss.

Instead, she turned to look at what was glowing. She felt him hesitate to release her.

"Aye...this is what I wanted to show ye."

He hooked his arm around her back, resting his hand on her hip as he guided her forward. There was a huge glass window that went from waist high to the roof. It was made of squares of glass, all set with thin lengths of iron between them.

"It's breathtaking."

It surely was. The moon was full and looked like a glowing ball across the lake. All of the stars were in view, but without the harshness of biting wind.

"Aye, a truly stunning sight."

Bhaic wasn't looking at the view. He was watching her. She turned her face toward his, drawn to the husky promise in his voice. It wasn't something she thought about. No, she was responding to something she felt deep inside her belly.

He cupped the side of her face, holding her steady for his kiss. She saw it coming, felt time freeze as he came closer and closer, finally making contact. He tried to start softly, but she lifted up onto her toes to meet him, craving the connection.

He shifted, pushing his hand along her cheek and cupping her nape to hold her steady. The kiss turned demanding, his mouth moving across hers in a firm motion that made her thoughts spin. She let it all go, kissing him back, searching for the motion, trying to mimic the way he was using his mouth against hers. Sweet sensation tore through her, racing down her spine and curling her toes. It stole her breath, leaving her feeling as if she'd been spun around and around until she was ready to fall down.

She pulled away, turning toward the windows. "I should…thank ye for offering me an alternative to supper in the hall. 'Tis truly a majestic sight here."

She was struggling to catch her breath, but so was he. That surprised her. She could hear him breathing heavily, heard the slight scuff of his boots against the floorboards as he came toward her.

"I had planned on stealing kisses after I fed ye, but well, what can I say? Ye're a Robertson. I feel the need to do me stealing first thing."

There was a playful note in his tone, and it touched something inside her. She'd never thought she'd feel this way with a MacPherson. She laughed and shoved him in the shoulder. "I should cuff ye for it. Did nae yer mother teach ye any manners at all?"

In that moment, he might have been anyone. Heat teased her cheeks as the moonlight highlighted his features.

He shrugged. "Nay. She died when I was still waist high."

He turned and picked something up. It was a large wicker basket with a cloth covering the top.

"I'm sorry," she said.

He shook out the cloth and let it settle on the floor. "Yers did too, did she nae?" He offered her a hand and eased her down to the floor.

"Aye. Just after me second brother was born. Childbed fever took her. I do nae remember her."

He set the basket between them and settled on the floor on the other side of it. He started rummaging through it. "I had to grab what I could before Duana noticed what I was about."

He started tossing things to her. A plate, a goblet, a napkin.

"Ah...port," he exclaimed victoriously as he held up a bottle.

"Better confess later," she said, "else some poor kitchen lad is likely to be blamed for thieving that." Ailis held out her goblet as Bhaic poured her some. "Duana is nae one to let something like port go unaccounted for."

"Aye, she likes to run the kitchens her way." Bhaic didn't find another goblet in the basket. He shrugged and took a swig directly from the bottle. "But she'll be doing some bending."

She was caught in an odd moment of both embarrassment and contentment. Both stemmed from the fact that he was willing to champion her.

"I can fight me own battles," she said with a touch of determination.

He took another swig from the bottle and put it down so he could rummage through the basket again. "Marcus would enjoy having you trying to kill him a little too much. He's a rogue, never doubt it."

"I didn't mean I'd actually try to…well, brawl."

He pulled another plate from the basket; this one had a roasted chicken on it. The scent teased her nose and made her belly rumble. A chunk of cheese was shoved onto the side of the plate, the heat from the meat melting part of it. Bhaic placed it between them and offered her an eating knife.

He tore into the chicken and sliced up the cheese. There was a round of bread and some sweet butter for it. The silence grew as the meat disappeared between them. The port was easy to turn to as a remedy for her nerves, but she stopped when she realized she was losing her wits.

"Aye," Bhaic said, setting the bottle away. "We'll both end up babbling like fools and wake up trying to remember if we consummated our union or not."

"Is that why ye brought me out here?"

His features tightened. "I did nae have to bring ye here for that, Ailis. Grant me a wee bit of credit for trying me hand at courting ye."

She looked up at the moon, feeling foolish and a bit unkind. "It *is* an impressive view."

"Aye." He lifted the basket away and took its place. "But we're no' enjoying it quite…right."

He scooted right up beside her. She shivered, feeling small beside him. He laid an arm across her back, slowly, almost hesitantly as he waited to see her reaction.

He didn't have to woo her.

Ailis drew in a deep breath and relaxed. It took all of her nerve.

He was overwhelming her again.

The smallest contact between them felt extreme. Her skin prickled, her heart pounded, and her breathing sped up when she caught the scent of his skin. Never once had she decided she liked the way anyone smelled, besides a baby.

She liked the way Bhaic smelled.

But in a completely different fashion.

Oh yes. What she liked about his scent was the way it made her feel small. He was stronger, and that fact didn't alarm her—it set her blood to racing as he teased the side of her neck with his fingertips.

"I brought ye here…so we might learn to be easy in each other's company."

His voice was a whisper, a soft suggestion that might just as well have been coming from inside her. She'd never been one for believing in spells, but at that moment, she was certain she was enchanted by him.

He didn't have to make the effort. She'd have done her duty if he demanded it. That made her cheeks heat even more, churning up a desire to be more than just his duty. She turned and reached up, laying her fingers against his jaw.

It was a powerful connection, making her glad she was sitting, because she was fairly sure her knees had gone weak.

"Since ye've done yer best to impress me, I owe ye a token of me gratitude."

His face was in shadow now, but she swore she saw his eyes glittering. He eased her forward with his hand, gently encouraging her when she hesitated.

It seemed to take forever to commence with the kiss. Time became a slow-moving thing that allowed her to be aware of every breath she took. Her lips tingled with awareness, anticipation twisting down her spine and pulling her insides tight. It was exhilarating.

Bhaic waited for her.

His jaw tightened, and the hand on his knee was clenching his plaid.

Waiting…for her to kiss him.

She pressed her mouth against his, feeling him adjust the angle of his head so that they fit seamlessly. Their breath mingled, hers catching as she pressed her lips to his, a soft motion that made her shudder with the intensity. It opened up a yearning for more, and she parted her lips, working them against his in a slow action of discovery.

His hand slid to her nape, cupping it and holding her in place. But he didn't take the lead from her. He followed her, letting her tease and taste his lips. Her thoughts scattered, leaving her a willing voyager on the waves of delight. She wanted to be closer, wanted to open his mouth wider. A moment later, the kiss was harder. Hungrier. It shocked her, and for one insane moment, she happily flung herself into it.

But it was madness, and everything was crumbling around her, leaving her with nothing to hold on to. She pulled back, gasping when she realized how brazen she was being.

"That was worth every damned blow Marcus landed."

His tone was hard. She eased away from him, suddenly shy. "It couldn't have been. I do nae know very much about…kissing."

He stroked her jawline. "Ye'll no' make light of it, lass. 'Twas a kiss freely given and I'll no' allow ye to take it back. Marcus is no' the only rogue in the family."

She shoved him playfully away. "I did nae doubt it."

But what now?

He had every right.

Every right…

He wanted more. She could feel the hunger between them. His grip on her nape was still solid, his jaw tight as he leaned close.

"*Ah, Christ…*" he swore softly. "I just recalled what I hate about courting."

He stood up in a swift motion and reached back down to pull her off the floor. For a moment, she was only an inch away from him, her hands resting on his arms as her skirt pressed against his body. His breath teased her lips, the darkness surrounding them a perfect cloak for the hunger flickering inside her.

"It's frustrating," he muttered. "Damned frustrating."

He found the basket and scooped up everything in a few swift motions. "I am no' having ye for the first time on the floor." He was down the steep steps in a swish of his kilt. "Let's go home."

He offered her his hand. She made it to the bottom floor before she let the word "home" hit her. It sat uneasily on her stomach as they left the astrologer's house and mounted. Bhaic pulled his plaid around them both as they rode back across the land bridge and through the gate.

Someone rang the bell, recognizing Bhaic.

"That will raise hell," he said before pulling up on the reins. Boys were running out of the stable, reaching up to tug on the corners of their bonnets. One of them reached up for her, helping her down as Marcus appeared on the steps of the keep.

"Tempting fate, Brother?" Marcus asked.

"What I was tempting is between me and me wife."

Bhaic pulled her behind him through the keep. There was an assortment of musicians playing now, the retainers enjoying mugs of ale as the household staff pinched out most of the candles to save them. The hallways were lit with torches. Bhaic took her up the steps and stopped in front of her chamber door.

"Do ye remember what is above this, lass?"

"Aye." She was breathless and unable to blame it on the rapid climb. No, it was Bhaic and the ideas he stirred in her that were making her heart race.

"I want ye in me bed, Ailis."

Her breath froze in her throat. His tone was dark and full of a promise that lured her closer to him.

He enclosed her in his embrace, sealing her completely against him. Letting her feel his body. Making sure she felt his strength.

"Yet I want ye there because ye choose to be, for more than the words ye were forced to speak with me inside that church." He stroked her jawline, his touch delicate and stirring. "Me brother will call me a fool, but I'll be waiting for ye to come to me."

She gasped, stunned.

He nodded once before leaning in and pressing a kiss against her mouth. It was hard and demanding, but he didn't linger over her lips. He pulled away, and she felt the night air rushing in between them, chilling her.

"Come to me, and I'll prove a patient lover. I promise ye that."

He was gone a moment later, the shadows swallowing him as he climbed to the next floor.

Ye want to go...

Aye and yet nae. She discovered herself smiling and smothering a giggle beneath her hand.

Hadn't she gone to May Day seeking courtship? It was surely a pleasant surprise to discover her husband willing to wait on her whim. There were footsteps on the stairs, Finlay's banter coming up ahead of him. Ailis turned and entered her chamber.

The tub was gone, and the room smelled fresher than it had before. Her chemise was fluttering on a drying rack near the fire, proving that Helen had returned to see the chamber righted. Beyond the arched doorway, a candle was burning on the bedside table, warmly welcoming her.

Bhaic had provided a warm welcome too.

She settled into her bed and pinched out the candle with a smile on her lips. She was suddenly exhausted. Far too tired to entertain the doubt that tried to wiggle past her contentment and remind her that Bhaic might turn mean whenever it suited him.

She wouldn't think of that.

No, instead, she recalled the ride to the astrologer's house and the fact that Bhaic hadn't needed to take her there. Never once had she realized how a man's pride might be something she'd be happy to contend with.

Tonight, she found herself very pleased to know

Bhaic MacPherson was stubborn enough to want only a willing woman in his bed.

Even a Robertson wife.

⁂

Helen had the paddle she'd chased Finley down the stairs with hanging from her belt the next morning.

Ailis was still rubbing her eyes. She was pretty sure she'd spent more time thinking about Bhaic than sleeping during the night. She stopped and looked at the paddle.

Helen noticed the attention and sent her a smug smile as she reached down to pat it gently. "The cook sent me out of the kitchens. Seems there's no place there anymore for someone who does nae loathe Robertsons."

Ailis made a small clicking sound under her breath. "How devastating for ye."

Helen snorted in response. "Deliverance, at last. Me father does nae have a castle, but he's a fine country home. One I was raised to run. Turning bread day in and day out was about to make me daft. I've never suffered boredom well."

"I know the feeling."

Ailis started to crawl out of bed. The bedding was so thick and the bed itself far larger than anything she'd ever slept in before.

"Tonight will be interesting," Helen said.

Ailis looked to Helen to explain.

"It's the laird's monthly court."

Ailis shrugged and picked up her comb. Helen took it from her and began to work the tangles from her hair.

"As the Tanis's wife, tradition dictates—" Helen continued.

"Holy Christ!" Ailis exploded.

Helen chuckled. "I see things are nae so different on Robertson land."

"No, but I did nae sit on the high ground during manorial court, because I was the laird's daughter."

Helen finished with the comb and pointed to a chair. Ailis sat down. Helen came up behind her and started to weave her hair into an elaborate braid.

"Well, ye're the wife of the Tanis now. It's yer place to rule on any issues between women that are of a delicate nature."

And only a handful of people knew the truth of her unconsummated vows. She was in a precarious position, one that might end in disaster, whichever way she went. Well, there was only one way her life was going to go.

"It seems I will no' be the only one doing adjusting," Ailis said, more to remind herself that she was staying than to answer Helen.

Helen began pinning up her braid. "Well now, it will certainly be a test of yer position."

"Aye," Ailis agreed. "It seems ye may have blighted yerself by being kind to me."

Helen finished and offered her a smug look. "Duana can kiss me Grant arse."

"Me Robertson one too."

The moment brought her the first hint of friendship. It wasn't MacPherson, but it was a beginning. Every new bride had to suffer through being a stranger. She'd heard such lectures since she was small, but they had lacked all reality until now.

Now things were very different. Suddenly, she understood how easily it might be to cling to her husband. Take the intimacy required of marriage as a sign of affection.

She smiled ruefully. It wasn't as if she had many other offers of companionship.

Well, she'd make a place for herself, by God.

And Duana could just become accustomed to it.

◦◦

"Is it bride or wife?"

Bhaic wiped the sweat off his brow and looked past the young stallion he was working with to see his brother leaning up against the corral fencing.

"I do nae care to get kicked because I'm talking to ye instead of minding what I'm about."

The stallion's ears perked up, a shrill sound coming from him. Bhaic turned, allowing the animal enough rope to feel comfortable.

Marcus pressed the issue. "Bride or wife?"

"Bride, if ye must know." Bhaic turned on his brother. "Because I will no' be a rutting bastard, jumping on her while going on about me rights."

"Yet it is yer right."

"Devil take that," Bhaic snapped. "And ye. I enjoy enticing a lass into me bed as much as ye do, and I will nae be having Ailis any other way."

His kilt flared out, his motion too swift. The stallion let out a snort and reared up. Bhaic cursed and dove through the rails, tucking his head and rolling over his shoulder and back onto his feet.

He ended up looking at his brother's feet. Marcus

stood there his expression grim. "She's skittish. If she bolts for her father's land, this feud yer marriage is meant to end might have new life breathed into it. Better to settle the business."

Bhaic got to his feet and glared at his brother. "Beware how little sympathy ye have for us, Marcus. Morton could easily decide ye would make a fine alliance with the bloody English."

"English ladies do nae transplant well into our highlands."

"I agree full well, but the good earl did nae ask neither me or me bride how welcome she'd be on MacPherson land. In truth, I doubt he cares."

Marcus grunted. "Aye, ye have that thinking right. The earl is set on securing his future. We're meant to fall into line."

"Let it be," Bhaic said. "If ye must know the details, she did nae refuse me. No' even the first night."

His brother slowly smiled. "I would nae be talking to ye if I did nae already know where the difficulty lie."

"Figured it out, did ye?"

Marcus shrugged. "Aye. The only one in this family more stubborn than ye, is meself."

"Agreement between us at last," Bhaic declared. Bhaic suddenly looked past his brother. "What in the name of Christ?"

Finley was coming up the road, dragging Ailis with him. Lyel had hold of Helen and even had his dagger pressed against her neck. Other retainers had joined in, some of them pushing Ailis when she resisted.

"I'd like to know the answer to that meself," Marcus said softly.

"Get yer hands off me wife," Bhaic roared.

Ailis hadn't been looking up the road. She jerked her attention toward the sound of his voice, and he was sure she snarled. Finley happily pushed her forward.

The retainer shook his head and stomped over to where Bhaic and Marcus were. He pointed an incriminating finger at Ailis. "She's been brawling with Duana. Turned over one of the tables in the kitchen. There's a hell of a mess down there. Ye should have heard the ruckus. Ye'd have thought the devil himself had set his arse down in front of the hearth."

Helen was shoved forward too, righting herself and turning to look at Lyel. He crossed himself and moved away from her. There was a swelling around his eye, enough to turn black in a few hours.

"Christ in heaven, Ailis. What are ye doing to me home?" Bhaic demanded.

She was beating flour off her skirt, but looked up when he spoke. The look in her eyes was pure hellfire.

"My duties," she snapped, stomping over to stand in front of him.

"Suddenly devoted, are ye, lass?" Marcus asked softly.

She clenched her hands into fists as she growled at his brother.

Bhaic stepped between them. "What sort of duties could possibly entail fighting with Duana?"

"The kitchen books. I was looking at them, and she took exception."

"Ye mean she walked right up and slapped ye," Helen interrupted. "As well as calling ye a spy. Yer damned men kept the mistress from giving that crone the slap she deserved."

"Well now…she'd already turned the table over," Finley said, defending himself. "There's a mess down there for sure. Cider and ale all over the floor, along with half the bread for supper. The hounds made good use of the time. Tore into the kitchens and ate everything they could. It will be a poor supper to be sure." Finley was shaking his head, Lyel joining his fellow retainer.

"The table turned over because I stood up so fast. God's breath! I certainly didn't think she'd actually hit me for looking at the books," Ailis said.

"Those are MacPherson books." Marcus spoke softly. She recognized the tone now as one of suspicion.

But what bothered her the most was the unreadable expression on Bhaic's face. Any hint of the man who'd teased her in the moonlight was gone. In its place was the man she'd feared her husband would turn out to be.

Suspicious and unyielding, because she was his enemy's daughter. She wondered if anyone would ever trust her enough to let her make MacPherson land her true home. More than one bride had faced such a fate, retreating to her chambers and weaving tapestries because there was nothing else for her.

She nearly gagged on the horror of how real a possibility such a fate was.

"So what is me place to be then?" she demanded. "Am I naught but yer mare for breeding?"

She reached out and shoved him. "Perhaps I shall just go make meself comfortable in the stable then, and wait for ye to decide it's time for me to foal."

Staying still was impossible. It felt as if a rock was

pressing down on her. She picked up her skirts and left, hearing Marcus mutter "spitfire" behind her.

She cringed. There seemed no hope of making a place for herself, as no one was willing to let her squeeze even a marginal spot open.

She made it to the stable and was inside before Bhaic hooked her arm and turned her about.

"Ye're putting words in me mouth, Ailis. Taking things too much to heart."

She balled her fingers into a fist and took a swing at him. "Too much too heart? More the fool I for trying to be anything other than yer enemy."

He avoided her easily, stepping aside and wrapping his arms around her when she stumbled past him. He pulled her against him and locked her in place in front of him.

"Let me go!"

"Nae a chance," he said next to her ear.

She strained against his arms, but he held her easily, carrying her back into a stall that smelled of fresh hay. He released her, and she spun away from him, but the stall had solid sides as high as her chest, so all she did was end up facing him.

"The books…is that what women do during the day?"

His question caught her off guard. "Of course. If they do nae balance, 'tis me failing. If any of the kitchen staff, right down to the smallest lad, go barefoot, it is me shame for no' keeping track of when they are due their measure." She spoke as though he were an ignorant child but stopped when she noticed he was truly listening to her. Shame nipped at her when she realized he truly had no idea what she was so angry about.

"Aye…I suppose I recall seeing Duana tending to some of that." He crossed his arms over his chest, gripping the fabric of his shirt as though he was fighting the urge to reach for her.

Her belly twisted, the privacy of the setting hitting her like a blast of heat. But giving into the impulse would make her little better than a mare. Duana would still be refusing to let her take her place when passion cooled.

She took a deep breath and locked gazes with him.

"Ye should know, for it will be yer name that is dragged through the muck if I fail. There will be plenty saying ye have a poor wife, and that ye are a miser who doesn't appreciate devoted service. I'd just as soon no' give any of them more reason to curse me name."

He grunted and uncrossed his arms. "Do ye know what I do during the day, lass?"

Her anger was deserting her, melting away as she was forced to shake her head.

"We both have things to learn about being married," he said. "I'll have words with Duana."

"Ye will nae," Ailis shot back.

He grunted and stepped toward her. "Ye're me wife. If she slapped ye, she'll be answering to me."

"If I am yer wife, then 'tis me place to see to the staff, and I'll be doing that without ye. I am no' a weakling. If yer cursed retainers had no' dragged me away, I would have given her what she had coming." She drew in a deep breath and searched her mind for a polite way to get her point across. "Would ye have me dealing with yer captains when they are unruly?"

His stern expression cracked, his lips twitching into

a grin that transformed his face into something far too roguish for her to be truly furious with.

"Marcus is correct. Ye're a spitfire sure enough."

"I am nae," she argued, but part of her enjoyed knowing he thought she had spirit.

His eyes glittered with anticipation as he started to close the distance between them.

She was cornered, but she tossed her head, refusing to surrender. Her cursed female body was warming, tempting her to recall just how much she enjoyed his touch.

"Stand aside. I am going back down to the kitchens and getting me house in order."

He only took another step toward her, opening his arms to make it harder for her to edge around him.

"If 'tis yer house, lass, that means ye're me wife…"

She nodded, understanding him perfectly. "Aye. I told ye, I keep me promises."

He shrugged out of his sword belt and hung it on the post that made the doorway to the stall, crocking his finger at her. "Then come here. Wife."

"Why?" She lost the battle to stand in her place, backing into the stall and trying to slip along its wall toward the opening.

His lips curved into a huge grin. "Because I want to roll in the hay with ye."

Her eyes widened, her attention shifting to the newly laid bed of hay beneath her feet. She was actually sinking into it, all the way to her ankles.

"Why so much hay?"

"I've got a mare ready to foal."

She jerked her attention up, but he was right in front of her. Just a half step from her. She might have recoiled if he'd touched her. But he stood there, waiting for her to do something. The only thing she could manage was a soft gasp.

She felt as though she was melting, everything inside of her warming to his presence. She'd never been so aware of a man before. Never felt her nipples tingle because one was near.

Bhaic was only a breath away. His scent mixed with the aroma of the hay, his blue eyes full of promise.

He reached out and stroked her cheek with the back of his hand. Her heart skipped a beat, her knees suddenly feeling weak.

"Is this another attempt to impress me?" She wasn't really sure what she was saying. Thoughts felt difficult to form, impossible to make sense of.

He slipped his hand into her hair and plucked a hairpin from it, and then another, and a third before he answered.

"I did nae crush ye to me and kiss ye quiet," he offered.

"Maybe that's what I wanted." It was a terrible thing to voice, but true nonetheless.

He chuckled at her. "Aye. I know it's what ye crave, lass. Give me credit for giving ye the time to be easy with it."

Easy? She couldn't grasp how being with him might ever be easy.

She shifted back, the hay rustling as she moved. He'd found more of her hairpins, and her braid started to sag onto her nape.

She turned around, completely unsure of why she was letting him take her hair down, only sure that she was enjoying the way it felt to be free with him.

"That's it, lass…" He stroked her neck, setting off ripples of delight that raised gooseflesh across her skin. "Let me woo ye gently. We'll get to the passion, once ye trust me."

His voice was deep and sensual, luring her past her reservations. He tugged the last pin free, and her braid dropped down her back. She felt the ribbon tie slipping loose before the strands of her hair started to free themselves.

"Ye've a fine mane…" He was combing her hair loose, her eyes slipping closed at the intimacy. She'd never realized how lonely she was. How much she craved being touched. It was as if a wall had been broken down inside her, in a place that she thought was as big as it might ever be. Now, there were more chambers, secret ones that she was eager to explore.

He buried his face in the strands of her unbound hair, inhaling and making a soft, male sound of enjoyment. She opened her eyes, turning around to see his expression.

"Ye doubt how attractive ye are?" he asked.

She lifted one shoulder in a soft shrug. "It's no' as if any of me father's men were allowed to tell me I was ugly as sin. I was nae vain enough to take such as confirmation of how pretty I might be."

"More likely, he spent a fair amount of time making sure they minded how they looked at ye."

He cupped her cheek, taking that last half step toward her. "For ye are a fine-looking woman." He slipped his hand into her hair, cupping her head, and tilted his head to the side so that he might press his mouth to hers.

It was a firmer kiss than she'd been expecting. His mouth claiming her with the passion he'd obviously been holding back. It stunned her, but it also stroked something inside her that seemed to be waiting for her to let it loose. A boldness that once recognized, refused to be ignored.

She reached for him, wanting to know what he felt like. He groaned, his chest rumbling with the sound as she flattened her hands on him and fought to undo the buttons on his shirt.

What she craved was his skin.

The kiss changed again. Bhaic pressed her lips open and teased her mouth with the tip of his tongue. She froze, trying to decide how to move her lips. He eased her into it, teaching her the motions.

He let her go, keeping his mouth on hers as he ripped open his doublet and shirt. He tossed the doublet down and scooped her up, cradling her against his chest as he lowered her to the ground.

Everything around them seemed so insignificant. The only details she seemed to have a mind to focus on were ones associated with Bhaic.

She reached for him, sliding her hands up his chest and threading her fingers through the crisp hair there. He came to rest beside her.

But he wanted to be on top of her...

She saw the strain in his jaw as he reined in his desire. His eyes glittered with it. But he leaned down and kissed her cheek, and then her neck, and then she really lost track of everything she'd been trying to think about. There was only the touch of his mouth against her skin and the yearning to have him kiss more of her.

He popped the lace on her bodice, freeing her breasts with a few sure motions of his fingers. Her insides twisted, but she decided she enjoyed it now.

God in heaven did she enjoy the way he touched her…

It was a wicked confession. One that made her open her eyes wide and stare at him. All she saw was his dark hair as he kissed his way across her chest. He gently cupped one of her breasts, sending a jolt of pleasure through her. He lifted his head and locked gazes with her.

"Do ye like that?"

He was smoothing his fingers around the globes of her breasts, watching her as he brushed his thumb over the tips of her beaded nipples.

"Ailis?"

She rolled her lips in, unbearably shy. He made a soft sound under his breath and kissed her until she relaxed her mouth.

"I want to know that ye like me touch"—he moved his hand to her other breast—"that ye lay with me out of more than duty."

Bhaic MacPherson had never struck her as someone who doubted anything. Yet she could see a flicker of need in his eyes.

"I like yer touch," she whispered. "And yer kiss…"

She reached up and cupped the back of his head, pulling him down as she lifted her head off the ground to meet him. The kiss was hard, full of passion, and she eagerly met him. He pushed her back down, giving her a taste of his strength, and she gave it right back to him.

She was twisting toward him, aching for something.

Her skirts felt impossibly heavy and hot, the air against her bare breasts absolutely perfect. He caught her hip and pulled her against him. She gasped, arching back as she raised her thigh to hook her leg over his hip.

It was so natural, so instinctual. So very necessary.

She was burning and completely uncaring of anything besides him. All that mattered was feeding the craving flickering through her insides. She wanted more, needed something deeper.

Bhaic pulled her skirt up, freeing her from its suffocating folds. He cupped her knees and stroked her thigh.

She arched toward him, humming with pleasure.

"Aye, lass, ye like being petted."

"By ye." She stole a peek at him, her breath catching when she saw his expression.

He wanted to possess her.

The desire was glittering in his eyes. His jaw was tight with need, shocking her. Exciting her.

He reached around and boldly cupped one side of her bottom, pulling her toward him as he settled between her open thighs. She closed her eyes, letting the heat consume her. Her hands had formed into claws on his shirt. She was straining toward him, certain satisfaction was within reach. If she only knew how to achieve it.

He slipped his hand over the curve of her hip and across her belly.

"Aye, by me," he whispered next to her ear, his tone dark and husky. "I'll show ye why coming to me bed is what ye need…"

His hand glided over her bare belly, beneath her chemise, down to where her curls guarded her sex.

"Bhaic…ye can nae touch me…*there*…"

But he was. His fingers teasing those curls, parting them, stroking that forbidden place until he boldly thrust one of his fingers right into the folds of her sex.

"A husband can… I'm going to show ye what pleasure awaits ye in me bed."

There was a confidence in his tone.

A dark, wicked, tempting confidence that sent her thoughts scattering. He'd touched some spot that sent a bolt of pleasure through her. In fact, the sensation redefined pleasure. She'd never experienced such a spike of pure delight. Her thighs opened for him, shamelessly eager for more. For certain, there must be something wrong with what they were doing, but she couldn't think of it. His touch was reducing her to a pile of quivering yearning.

She lifted her hips, feeling empty inside. He teased her folds, stroking over the pulsing spot hidden between them. Somehow, her flesh was wet, making it easy for his fingers to glide across that little pearl. He pressed against it, wringing a cry from her. Her body was pulling tighter, urgency filling her before it became true desperation.

He seemed to be in tune with the tempo of her blood, stroking her in time to her heartbeat. He caught her nape, holding her in place as he pressed a kiss against her mouth. It was hard and demanding, just like his fingers. Pressing her forward into something, something wild.

It wrung her out, twisting and pulling at her with a burst of pleasure that exploded inside her. He caught her cry, smoothing it as she twisted and bucked against him.

"There now…" he growled softly against her lips.

His words didn't really make sense. She was only half aware of the world, still floating on a cloud of sensation. He rolled onto his back, settling her head on his bare chest as she sighed. He toyed with her hair, stroking her arms as the sound of his heartbeat filled her ear. She recovered by degrees, becoming aware of her bare breasts pressing against his side, only the thin fabric of his shirt between them. She had her hand thrust through the opening of that same shirt, her fingers resting on his chest.

Her knee was bent over his thigh, her skirts raised and pushed up to bare her legs. Nothing between her sex but her chemise and his plaid.

Disheveled.

Oh, Christ, she was definitely that.

But, well…he was her husband. She took a deep breath, forbidding herself to fret.

"Well… I can nae see…"

She stiffened, recognizing Finley's voice, even in a whisper. There was a scuffle, and she jumped when he peeked around the opening of the stall.

"Get ye gone!" Bhaic snarled.

He tried to pull her close again, but she'd already rolled away, putting her back to the door as she tried to close up her bodice.

"Where's Helen when we need her?" Bhaic snorted. He was on his feet, braced in the doorway of the stall as he glared down the stable. "I'm going to let her beat ye senseless!" There was a scuff and a snarl as Finley ran for the outer door of the stable. Bhaic cursed before turning back to consider her. "Damned nuisance."

"Oh, they're that, but it's yer brother that set them on me." She'd managed to right her clothing, her cheeks on fire.

Bhaic grunted, but the sound was far too smug for her smarting sensibilities. He lowered himself to a knee beside her.

"Be easy, Ailis. We were nae misbehaving." His face split with a grin as surprise flashed across his eyes. "And that is a first for me. I think marriage is going to agree with me."

She swallowed the lump that had managed to lodge itself in her throat. "No' going to miss the lectures on hellfire and brimstone?"

He shrugged. "Know those, do ye?"

She couldn't help but smile. "Oh, aye. Women are the descendants of Eve, ye see, and therefore, by me very gender, I am predisposed to mortal sins." She shook her head. "Bunch of drivel. Men dally their lives through, but it is me blood that must be shown on me wedding sheets if I am to escape disgrace."

"Well now…" Bhaic was starting to chuckle and fighting to hold his amusement in. "A young lad's first time is marked only by the rather stupid look of bewilderment that is stuck on his face for hours on end afterward."

She rolled her eyes. "Have some decency. For all that I only met ye, I do nae need to be hearing about yer conquests."

"Well then…"

He reached out and scooped her up. She'd had no idea he might lift her so easily when he was still sitting as well. She landed in his lap, hay falling off her.

"I can certainly find something else to do…" He nuzzled against her neck, pressing several kisses along the column of her throat.

For all that he'd satisfied her, it seemed her appetite was yet to be truly sated. She let out a little sound of enjoyment, twisting her hands around his neck and arching back as he made his way to her cleavage.

"Such perfection…" He growled as he kissed the swells of her breasts. He cupped her bottom and lifted her up. She shifted herself, opening her thighs so that her knees ended up on either side of his lean hips when he lowered her.

Her breath caught on a gasp. The hard presence of his erection pressed against her sex. She opened her eyes and discovered Bhaic watching her.

Waiting for her.

It was a tender concern, one that stroked something inside her. He still cupped her hips, rubbing them with slow motions as she started breathing again.

"Ye're a kind man."

His lips twitched. "Do nae be sharing that little secret. It will ruin me fine barbaric reputation."

"We would nae be wanting that," she teased him softly.

"They're back at it…"

She stiffened. The sound of Finley's voice was like a bucket of icy water. Bhaic grunted with frustration.

"We are going to have to take this to a place with a solid door," he said before he lifted her off him. "Or risk having the details fodder for winter evenings."

Her face exploded in heat at the mere idea. Ailis kicked at her skirts, trying to gain her footing. Bhaic hooked her under her arms and lifted her.

"I can nae believe yer brother set them on us both."

"Meaning ye would understand them trailing yer heels, but no' mine?"

Bhaic scooped up his doublet and shook it to dislodge the straw. He shrugged into it. "Marcus takes his duties as seriously as ye do. Besides, ye can choose yer friends but no' yer family."

He reached out and plucked some straw from her hair.

"Where are me pins?"

He contemplated her for a moment as he worked the buttons halfway up his doublet. "I've half a mind to not give them back to ye."

"Then everyone will know—"

"Aye," he confirmed smugly. But he reached over and collected her hairpins from the top of the stall wall. "No' that we could expect Finley to keep his jaw shut."

He offered her pins to her. Reaching out to take them felt horribly exposing.

"I suppose 'tis a good thing we're wed, Ailis. For yer reputation is sure to be tarnished."

She looked up and locked gazes with him. "I've enough troubles without worrying I'll end up in the pillory for loose morals."

His grin faded. "Aye. Duana. She slapped ye?"

There was a look in his eyes that caught her by surprise. The man was feeling protective.

Of her.

It was a hard idea to grasp.

Yet welcome.

"Stay out of it." She was likely bound for the

pillory for being disrespectful to her husband now, but she didn't regret the words or her tone. "I'd have settled it meself if Finley and his lot had nae brought me up here. I will get me house in order."

"I suddenly see a bright side to me brother's orders." He nodded gravely. "At least I will nae have to worry about finding ye dead on the kitchen floor."

"Oh...enough. I am no' about to go sit in me chamber and cry because yer father's Head of House is as stubborn as yer brother." She went to pass him, but he captured her, binding her against his body as he buried his face in her flowing hair once more.

"Sweet Ailis, that was nae nearly enough. Come to me bed, and I'll show ye how much more there is."

He kissed her again, letting his passion free. It was a hard, blunt merging of their mouths. He mastered her, moving her to suit his needs. Holding her head in place while his lips ravished hers.

And left her sagging against the stall wall.

More?

She was certain she couldn't take anything else.

Yet very sure she was wicked enough to desire to attempt it.

❧

Clansmen started filling the yard early in the afternoon. They were men who had farms farther out from the castle. They set up cooking fires, suspending large black iron pots from tripods. More than one unlucky rabbit was hanging from a belt as they arrived. There were a few women, but Highlanders knew their way around a cooking fire. Many of them had bread cooked by their wives and chunks of cheese that always traveled well.

Ailis headed up to her chamber, needing to right her hair. Helen was nowhere to be found at the stable, forcing Ailis to walk back to the castle with her hair flowing down her back. A few men turned to look at her, their faces splitting with grins until they recognized the Robertson colors of her arisaid. Their expressions turned harsh, but they held their insults, likely due to Finley and Lyel following her with their hands on the pommels of their swords.

It was a welcome reprieve. One she would be best not to look at the details of.

"There she is."

Ailis stopped with her foot on the bottom stair of the staircase that led to her chamber. She turned to see Skene and Kam standing down the hall. Skene reached over and opened a door to one of the cells lining the passageway.

"Ye can come out now. Yer mistress is here."

Helen appeared, the two retainers backing well out of her reach. Skene tried to placate her. "Now, we were only following orders."

Helen gave him a look that told him' how little she thought of him before she turned to look at Ailis.

"Let's get ye put together, mistress. I'd certainly no' have made ye walk all the way up from the stables looking like a strumpet if I had nae been locked away. Little wonder no one respects ye."

"There will be respect as well as courtesy," Bhaic interrupted as he came down the aisle. He stepped aside, revealing Duana and two of the head cooks. They had the kitchen books in their hands.

Ailis felt her cheeks catch fire.

"It seems I did nae notice I was thrusting a duty on Duana that was no' hers to shoulder," Bhaic said. "I've asked her to forgive me ignorance in no' knowing it was the lady of the castle's duty to make certain the books were kept in good order."

"I enjoy serving ye," Duana said clearly.

"Aye but 'tis a poor laird I'd be if I did nae learn no' to overburden those who serve this castle. Forgive me," Bhaic informed her smoothly. It was clear to one and all what they were truly discussing. Duana didn't want to bend. Her lips were pressed into a hard line, but Bhaic didn't budge. The Head of House finally nodded and lowered herself.

"Naught to forgive. I knew 'twas only a matter of time until ye or yer brother took a wife."

Neither of them meant what they were saying, but the words granted everyone a measure of pride. Duana and the cooks brought the books to Helen and piled them in her arms.

Duana managed a nod before she turned and left.

Bhaic watched her leave, casting a look toward Ailis once the Head of House was gone. His lips curved just a marginal amount, and he winked before disappearing.

"Well, it seems we have something to set our attention to," Ailis said.

Her mind was already full, but the books offered a diversion from the matter truly weighing on her.

Come to his bed?

Bhaic MacPherson had best watch himself, because she just might take his offer. After all, a wife had rights too.

⁓

The household books were spread out on the long table in Ailis's chambers. The rows of numbers looked impossible to make sense of. There were half-finished computations and an entire basketful of slips of paper with amounts written on them that had yet to be entered into the books. All of it was smeared with flour and drops of dried sauces.

In short, it was a disaster.

Either there were some six hundred chickens penned up somewhere, or the slips of paper accounted for them. She had no idea how Duana had managed to keep a decent meal on the tables when there was no clear record of what was in the storerooms.

Ailis was fighting to make sense of it all when someone rapped on her door.

Finley pushed the door in. "The laird will be starting manorial court soon."

Clearly the retainer wanted to enjoy the spectacle. He was jerking his head toward the stairs, trying to encourage her to leave her chamber.

"We'll be along in a bit." Helen had appeared outside the chamber door, holding a large platter with a cloth covering it. "The mistress needs to eat."

"She's no' the only one," Finley groused.

"Off with ye then." Helen paused in the doorway.

Finley shrugged but aimed a pleading look at them. Considering the way he so often glared at her, it was nearly friendly. "I can nae. Lyel is nae here, likely down in the kitchen making wagers on tonight's cases, and Marcus said she's no' to be left unattended."

"I'm attending her," Helen responded.

Finley rolled his eyes. "As if ye are any different! Both of ye were brought here to keep yer kin under control. Naught but hostages."

Helen had brought her burden into the chamber. The scent of fresh bread came from beneath the cloth. She sat the tray down with a clunk as she turned on Finley.

"Why thank ye, Finley, for such a charming description of me new home," Ailis said.

He bristled. "I did nae bring either of ye here. Besides, Duana weighs double what ye do. If I had nae been there this morning, she might have crushed the breath from ye by just sitting on ye."

Ailis shook her head to dispel the image his words evoked.

"Nae, ye did nae bring me here," Ailis conceded, keeping her comments confined to the more important matters, such as doing her best not to make an enemy of a man who was going to dodge her footsteps whether she liked it or not. "Is it the kitchens ye wish to go to?"

His face brightened. "Aye."

"Well then." She walked through the door. "I suppose I can eat there as well as here."

Finley fingered his beard for a moment. "Ask ye?"

He was watching her, seeing what she'd make of his question. Ailis nodded on her way past him.

"This is to be me home, Finley. I do nae intend to be difficult about settling into me proper place."

She stressed the word "proper" just a bit. It wasn't

lost on her escort. His expression tightened, but she continued on down the stairs, not insisting on a formal agreement from him. He'd likely see that as treason, since she was a Robertson. It was certainly going to be a delicate thing, settling in.

But at the base of the stairs, she paused. Shamus was already at the high table. He caught sight of her and raised his hand in her direction.

"Come here, lass."

She couldn't very well ignore him. Finley groaned but followed her.

"Off with ye, lad," Shamus said with a gesture of his hand. "I'm still young enough at heart to want to have such a fetching lass to meself. Besides, there are plenty here to look after her if she wanders."

Finley considered the retainers watching his laird. He nodded and pulled on the corner of his bonnet before making haste toward the passageway. The retainer's hesitation sent a little chill through her, one that was familiar.

Shamus was clearly getting old. He might still be laird, but the MacPherson retainers answered to Bhaic and Marcus now.

Her father was in a similar condition.

"Sit with me."

For all his age, there was still a keen mind inside of Shamus MacPherson. Ailis caught hint of a calculating flicker in his eyes as a retainer pulled one of the huge chairs out for her.

"Eat something. I understand ye have put in a full day." Once more, Shamus was proving he wasn't as withered by time as his wrinkled face suggested.

No one waited for her to decide if she wanted to eat. Serving girls and younger lads who attended the head table began to fill her plate and goblet. It was done in a flurry of motion before they retreated to the back of the high ground. They watched those who were dining, waiting for any indication their services were needed.

"Do ye plan to call out me Head of House tonight?"

Ailis had taken a bite of bread. Shamus had spoken while looking straight ahead, and kept his voice low to keep the conversation private. Ailis shook her head.

"Why no'?" Shamus tilted his head to the side and looked at her.

Ailis swallowed. "Because I'd surely be a fool if I thought this union was going to be simple."

He considered her for a long moment. "'Tis yer right."

Three little words had never had such impact. They were certainly better than any words of welcome might have been. Those salutations she might have doubted. Her father's most hated enemy agreeing that she had cause to cry for judgment against one of his own? Well, that was a victory. One she'd best handle with care.

"I expect it to take time. Me being accepted here."

Shamus grunted. "Ye might just make a fine lady of this hall. I can see the making of such in ye." He reached under the table and boldly slapped the top of her thigh.

She jumped and witnessed a wicked flicker of enjoyment appear in his eyes. The same blue eyes that Bhaic had.

"Eat something, lass. I can nae have yer father saying I starve ye."

Because of the evening court, supper was being served more informally. The center of the hall was already cleared and ready for those clansmen who wanted to bring issues before their laird for judgment. Retainers were eating on tables along the side of the great hall, but most of them had gone outside into the yard. There was a buzz of conversation coming through the open doors.

But men started coming into the open doorway to peer at her sitting there with their laird. They stroked their beards and leaned in to discuss it with their companions.

Shamus grunted after a while. "I needs prepare, lass."

"Thank you."

She stood when he did, lowering herself before she turned and headed back up the stairs.

"Well now…" Helen joined her. "There will be talk a plenty about that."

❦

There were pipers at the manorial court.

Ailis enjoyed the sound of the music as she came down the stairs. The candles were all lit tonight, flickering above the hall in huge chandeliers held with ropes through pulleys, so they might be lowered and the candles replaced. There were also several standing candelabra to add more light. The scent of beeswax and smoke floated through the hall.

The hall was full. Men talked in hushed tones as they waited for the laird to take his place. The table was pushed back on the high ground, and three of the large chairs moved forward. No one was jesting tonight. There was clearly business to attend to.

Marcus was there, obviously recently groomed for the occasion. His plaid was secured with a costly brooch tonight, and there was a matching one on his bonnet. He was standing on the high ground, watching the passageway she appeared in.

"Mistress Duana."

The Head of House jumped when Marcus addressed her.

"Me brother is wed," Marcus continued as those waiting for the court watched. "Ye seem to have forgotten to direct yer staff to set a chair for yer new mistress."

The hall suddenly went silent.

Ailis was certain the color was draining from her face. Marcus kept his stare on the Head of House.

"Forgive me," Duana said at last. She snapped her fingers at two serving boys, but the chair was far too heavy for them.

Finley scoffed at them and climbed to the high ground. "In a few more years, lads."

He picked up the chair and set it off to the side, one pace back from the other three, in the position for the mistress of the castle.

The pipers began to play, signaling the beginning of the evening. Shamus started walking down the main aisle with Bhaic behind him.

How many times had she watched her father do the same?

She was suddenly homesick, but at the same time, enjoying the familiar sight that helped her confirm she wasn't so very far from home. Shamus settled in his chair before Bhaic turned and offered her his hand.

He was a handsome brute tonight. His chin freshly

shaved and his dark hair shiny from a recent washing. It was combed back, the tips of it just brushing his shoulders. His bonnet sported ceremonial feathers for the occasion. They were larger and fixed to his bonnet with a gold brooch. She felt disheveled, her gown grubby after so many days in it. She was also dressed like a girl, not the lady of the house. Clothing that had seemed stuffy just a few months ago now appealed to her. But there was nothing for it. She moved forward, trying to recall all the advice her nurse had instilled in her.

Chin always level.

Expression pleasing, yet serene.

Hips controlled so the skirts didn't sway.

Hands folded neatly into one another and held at the waist.

It was exhausting.

She laid her hand in Bhaic's, and he led her to her spot.

The pipers played again, signaling a beginning to the court.

But Ailis was pretty sure everyone was looking straight at her.

Well, let them. She wasn't going anywhere.

❦

He'd promised to wait for her.

Bhaic looked out over the land bridge that connected the castle to the main land. Everyone had settled down for the remainder of the night, the camp that had formed in the yard quiet now. The sentries were on the walls, slowly walking back and forth to keep themselves warm and alert. The view from his chamber often eased his mind, allowing him to see that the castle was secure, so that he might relax and sleep. Tonight, it wasn't affecting him that way. The reason was clear, and one floor below him.

He didn't want to wait.

But for all he knew, she'd come up to him, and he hadn't been there. He couldn't leave the hall until his father did, and his father didn't have anything enticing waiting in his bed.

Bhaic grinned, the fire in the hearth behind him making his reflection show in the windowpanes. He turned around and looked at his chambers. They'd always been his sanctuary. The one place he didn't have to share.

Tonight, they felt empty.

Well, he'd asked her to come to him. That wasn't the same as promising her he wouldn't seek her out.

Ye'll wait.

He scoffed at his own reprimand, but turned and pulled off his shirt.

Aye, he would wait, because if he didn't, he'd never know if she truly wanted him. He'd never realized what a burden it would be to have a dutiful wife. It was surprising to find himself reluctant to take advantage of the rights the law afforded him.

He didn't want her that way.

The memory of her sitting on the edge of the bed in their bridal chamber roused only his temper.

He'd never had a woman who didn't want him, and the few who had sought him out with schemes brewing behind their smiles were the ones he felt only contempt for.

The memory of the stable made him grin.

It also stirred his member.

He turned away from the door.

Aye, ye'll wait…

Ailis would be worth it.

❧

The bells along the walls started ringing at noon. It was a frantic call to arms. Ailis came out of the kitchen storeroom, along with the rest of the women. Retainers flooded the walls of the castle, some of them loading black-powder muskets.

Marcus was mounting his horse, the animal dancing in a circle in response to the flurry of activity in the yard. He spun around and then turned back to look at her.

"Get yer charge inside the keep and make sure she stays there," he ordered Finley.

Bhaic was already riding out of the gate, MacPherson retainers close on his heels. The sound of hooves was deafening. Fear pierced her heart.

Was it Lye Rob Gordon?

Perhaps another clan that had a feud with the MacPhersons?

There was no way to know. Her only option was to wait.

"Come along, mistress," Finley admonished her. "Do nae make me pick ye up."

She'd forgotten about her ever-diligent escort. Today it was Finley and Skene. They were frowning, and started walking toward her. She must move or be run over.

They forced her up into the keep with their arms spread wide. She turned around when she made it there, picking up her skirts and hurrying up the stairs to her chambers.

"Where are ye going, woman?"

She didn't pay Finley any mind, but went to the windows to see if she could see anything. Her chambers faced out over the lake, frustrating her.

Well, Bhaic's chamber overlooked the land bridge so he might keep an eye on anyone approaching the castle. She brushed past Finley as he gained the landing outside her chambers and headed up to the fourth floor.

"What's got into ye, woman?"

She only hesitated for a moment before opening the door and pushing it in. A tiny shiver crossed her skin as she strode into Bhaic's domain. She went across the receiving room and stood at the window. In the distance, she could see the MacPherson retainers. Marcus and Bhaic marked by pennant bearers behind them.

What made her gasp was the sight of her father's pennant flying. Her brother Duncan was riding with him too. Her blood ran cold, horror nearly choking her.

Stop! Ye do nae know why they are here.

That was true enough. She watched them as time crawled past. At last, the MacPhersons turned and stared heading back into the castle. Ailis felt her jaw drop as her father and brother followed.

Robertsons riding into the MacPherson castle.

She had to see it with her own eyes.

Still, she had to blink and force herself to believe what was right before her.

She dashed past Finley and Skene, holding up her skirts as she charged down the stairs.

"Now just wait for us!" She was already on the first floor by the time Finley's voice came down the tower to her. She ended up in the huge double doorway of the keep, panting from running, before Lyel stepped into her path and stopped her like a wall. She ran right into him and bounced back.

"Ye'll be staying here, mistress," he told her sternly.

Finley and Skene came barreling up behind her. They reached out and grabbed her arms.

"Are ye mad?" she hissed at them.

"Marcus's orders..."

She drew in a deep breath and made sure her tone was civil. She looked at Finley, trying to draw on the trust she'd been building with him.

"Me father is riding through the gate," she informed him smoothly. "Do ye really care to have him seeing ye yanking me about like a goat? Or for me to be nowhere in sight, so he can imagine the worst about me circumstances? Three generations of feud will likely take his thoughts to a very dark place."

"Yer father?"

Ailis jerked her head toward the gate.

Finley looked up, his eyebrows rising at the sight of Robertsons filling the yard.

"Fuck me," he muttered.

He wasn't the only one cussing. Or crossing themselves. MacPherson retainers hissed at the women to get back, but some of them were too frozen with shock to move. Her brother cleared the gate and found her. Duncan had the family blond hair, but his eyes were a light green color. His expression was stern as he swept her from head to toe. He was off his horse and moving up the stairs to stand in front of her before she really accepted that her kin were there.

"Sister."

He pulled her close, but it wasn't really a welcome hug. "Are ye well? Tell me the truth," he whispered against her ear.

Bhaic was suddenly there, close enough to hear what Duncan was whispering.

"I do nae mistreat women," Bhaic insisted.

Duncan released her and pushed her behind him. "I'll be hearing what me sister has to say on the matter, MacPherson. Make no mistake about that. If me father had nae sent me out to deal with some bastard Gordons, I would have been there to deal with the Earl of Morton and prevent this marriage."

Bhaic chuckled darkly. "There was a time I would have risen to that bait, Robertson."

Duncan pushed closer to Bhaic, clearly spoiling for a fight. She started to step between them, but Bhaic captured her wrist and held her back, turning slightly and pulling her behind him. Duncan didn't miss it. Her brother's eye narrowed with rage.

"And there ye see the reason why this marriage happened," Bhaic explained in a low tone. "Yer sister is more levelheaded than either of us. I offered me chest to the earl's marksmen, but she wasn't willing to see her father hanged when there was something she could do to prevent it. Even wed me. She shamed me well with the way she put the good of both our clansmen above her own preferences."

"Ye can bet ye were no' her choice for husband."

"Stop bickering," she said.

Her brother's gaze settled on the dark spot on her jaw, marking where Duana had slapped her.

"He was rough with ye," Duncan growled menacingly.

"He was no'."

But Bhaic turned around and looked at her jawline, his lips pressing into a hard line.

"Duncan," her father called from where he was standing in the yard. "Bring yer sister down here where I can see her."

"Better ye come into the hall," Marcus said.

Her father shook his head. "I've come farther than ever I thought to in this life, but I will no' be going into yer keep. I told ye, I'm here to see me daughter with me own eyes and make sure ye MacPhersons do nae have any reason to be saying she did nae arrive suitably outfitted as a bride should be."

Her father aimed the last part of his answer toward the yard where every doorway was filled with curious onlookers.

Ailis looked behind her father and realized there was a wagon. Marcus had his men helping to unload several trunks. She was grateful and yet at the same time, her breath got caught in her throat, because she realized her father had accepted her marriage.

Inside those trunks would be all of her possessions. While it would be wonderful to have her clothing, she was fairly certain she was going to cry when she looked at the pearl necklace her mother had left her, and her father had safeguarded for the day she wed.

Duncan reached out and took hold of her arm.

Bhaic glowered, clearly didn't care for the way her brother was taking charge of her.

"Ye have something to say, MacPherson?" Duncan asked.

"Ye'd like that, would ye nae?" Bhaic shot back. "Seems ye're in the mood to stir up something, alright."

"Oh, for Christ's sake," Ailis hissed beneath her breath so her words didn't carry. "Have done, ye two. Ye will nae undo what good has been done. Duncan, I am fine. Me husband"—she used the word on purpose—"has nae laid a hand on me that I did nae enjoy."

She shook off her brother's hold and shot Bhaic a hard look. "I am going to see me father. Ye should come as well and greet yer father-by-marriage."

Bhaic didn't care for the tone of her voice, but he stepped out of her path. Duncan made a noise under his breath that she snorted at. Bhaic stiffened but remained by her side as she went down the steps and into the yard.

"Marcus is correct. Ye are a spitfire," Bhaic said under his breath.

"Thank ye."

He choked back his amusement.

It was harder than she'd thought to see her father. Tears tried to sting her eyes, but she blinked them away.

"There's me lass…" Her father peered at her and frowned. "And ye have the nerve to tell me I did nae need to bring along her things? Me daughter is wearing the dress she left home in…a week later!"

Shamus MacPherson turned to look at her. "Well now, me daughter is nae home, and what would men know of such things? The lass might have spoken up."

"Ye've got a Head of House, do ye no'?" Duncan demanded. "If she were worthy of her position, she'd no' need to be told how to look after her mistress."

A ripple of conversation went through those watching. Many of the women looked at the ground out of shame.

"Maybe the lass has nae needed much clothing." Shamus puffed his chest out. "Any lass wedded to a MacPherson does nae."

"That's me daughter," her father insisted crossly, "so mind how ye talk about her."

"Oh, stop it," Ailis said, trying to end their argument. "As if ye have nae said something as...colorful about weddings before, Father."

Her father suddenly grinned and reached out to slap Bhaic on the shoulder. "Ye'll have yer work cut out for ye with me daughter. She's got spirit."

"That's the truth," Marcus said.

Duncan snarled softly at Marcus.

Bhaic stuck his hand out. Her father looked at it for a long moment. His gaze shifted back to her, sweeping her from head to toe before he clasped Bhaic's hand. A ripple went through those watching. Heads nodded; expressions eased. Surprise brightened Duncan's eyes before his complexion darkened slightly with guilt.

Duncan offered Bhaic his hand. The two stared at each other for only a moment before they clasped wrists.

Her father turned to her. "Now come and kiss yer father. I've got to get going. The sun is nae going to wait for me, and I will sleep better closer to me own land."

She went to his embrace, feeling as if a live coal had somehow gotten caught in her chest. Her father folded her in his arms, squeezing her before he sniffed and pulled away.

"Alright, me lads! Let's take ourselves home and prove we can go through MacPherson land without spilling blood. More than one wager is going to be lost over it, for certain. I think I'm going to enjoy knowing I am nae so old I can nae learn a new trick."

Duncan helped her father up onto the back of his horse before he took a moment to stare at her.

She was sure it was the hardest thing she'd ever done to look him straight back in the eye and smile. He nodded and mounted.

"But mind ye"—her father turned his horse around and looked at Shamus—"I'll be expecting me son-in-law there to be bringing me daughter home for a visit in a few weeks. Seeing as how I've come out here first to prove me commitment to this...peace."

It was a challenge. Cast down right there in the yard. Ailis couldn't help but be proud of her father for his brazen tenacity. It made her smile as they turned and left.

Her emotions started to boil though as she watched the last of her clansmen disappear. The MacPhersons were clustered around one another, talking intently about what had just happened. Shamus had both his sons near him.

Which left her standing alone.

Although on display might be a better description.

People looked at her, pointing, nodding—obviously discussing her. For certain, no one stuck in the pillory had ever endured more scrutiny.

She backed away from it. Retreating into the

keep. But that allowed her only to walk into a wall of women, all waiting to see what had happened. The suspicion in their gazes broke the hold she had on her feelings. Despair clawed its way up from where she'd locked it away on May Day.

Now, there was no way to shield herself from it. The tears she'd blinked away began spilling down her cheeks as she fled toward the stairs to hide her lack of composure.

Somehow, she ended up back in Bhaic's rooms, pressing against the window to gain the last glimpse of her kin. She didn't hear Bhaic arrive, but he was suddenly there, embracing her.

She shifted, shamed by her wet cheeks.

"Easy, lass…" he cooed against her head, tucking it beneath his chin.

She wanted to be stronger.

But fate hadn't been in the mood lately to grant her what she wanted.

Her tears fell, her breathing rough. "I'm sorry… I do nae know why I came here…"

She pushed away from his hold, wiping her eyes hastily on her sleeve before she turned to find her way to the door.

"I've been waiting for ye to come here, Ailis. Ye know that." There was a trace of promise in his tone.

She recalled it all too clearly from the night in the stairwell.

Behind him, his bed was lit with the rays of the afternoon sun.

"Somehow, I do nae think this is the circumstance ye were hoping for."

He chuckled, smoothing his hand down her arm. "Maybe because I'm new to being a husband. I've never had much dealing with women beyond…well…"

She slapped him on the shoulder, but since she was in his embrace, the blow lacked any real power. "I know what ye mean."

He tipped her chin up, but his gaze moved to the dark spot on her jaw. "I'm going to have words with Duana."

"Ye will no'. It's me house and me place to see to the running of it."

"And ye are me wife, Ailis," he countered. "I should be making it clear I agree with this union. Ye were right to wed me. Shamed me properly for no' thinking beyond what me father taught me of yer clan. Yer brother saw it just now."

"Aye. For the first time, I believe." She clung to the victory of that truth.

Bhaic stroked her cheek with the back of his hand. "Ye're a woman to be reckoned with, but Duana is taking advantage of yer tender heart. I aim to put a stop to that."

"I will do it in me own way and time," she insisted.

He wasn't going to allow her to sway him, but she dug her fingers into his kilt when he started to move away. His outer belt popped. Startled, Ailis released the fabric, and the wide belt slithered to the floor.

The sound of it hitting the floor made her eyes go wide.

Had she really just…undressed him?

"Well now, that's one way to win the argument," he said with a husky chuckle. "Taking me clothes off. Maybe ye're the spitfire Marcus claims ye are."

"I am not biddable," she admitted, "especially when I am dealing with pigheadedness."

His eyes narrowed as he contemplated her. "In that case, I need to make sure ye do nae find me too weak willed to handle ye."

He reached out and caught the lace holding her bodice closed. With a sharp tug, he opened the knot and pulled the lace free with his fingers from the first two eyelets.

"There," he said smugly. "Now ye see that I am no' too weak willed to face the challenge ye present."

"Oh?" She tugged on the front of his doublet, freeing several of his buttons. She almost stopped, but undid two more for good measure. "I like me challenges far more intense."

It was a ridiculous battle, but she was enjoying it too much to stop.

"Well now, I would nae care to see ye disappointed."

He reached out with both hands and pulled the lace through her eyelets with quick motions. She ended up reaching around and finishing off his buttons. Her bodice sagged open at the same time his doublet did. Bhaic shrugged out of it, letting it drop to the floor, and faced off with her in his shirt.

She hesitated, feeling the air against her breasts through her thin chemise.

Dare she continue?

"Come, lassie..." He tapped the button on his shirt. "Finish what ye started."

It was tempting.

Far better than waiting for him to decide when to claim her.

She reached out and opened the button, and then

another. Bhaic was slowly working the lace holding her skirt free. But he held her gaze. The passion shimmering in his eyes captivated her.

"Kiss me." Her voice was raspy and unsteady, her body starting to quiver. "Quiet me thoughts."

"It almost killed me to wait for ye to ask." There was a harsh edge to his voice that made her shiver, and in his eyes a hint of the desire he'd been holding in check.

He leaned down and kissed her with enough passion to send her thoughts scattering. She rose on her toes to get closer as he pushed her skirts down and over her hips. They puddled around her ankles as she went searching for the buckle on his second belt.

The metal was cold, but the plaid was warm from his skin. She pulled the leather tail free and then loosened the buckle. There was a soft sound as the wool hit the floor. A swift sense of satisfaction filled her as she let him press her lips apart and tease her tongue with his.

She shuddered, shaken to her core.

He scooped her up, carrying her away from their clothing. Kissing her with a hunger that ignited a storm of need inside her.

There was no reason to think. Sweet sensation reigned supreme, offering her a feast of delights. She had some dim awareness of him carrying her through to the darker room where his massive bed was and lowering her onto it. He cupped her head, holding her in place as he sent his tongue into her mouth.

It was so bluntly sexual.

And she loved it.

He gathered her close, holding her against his body as he moved her farther up onto the bed. It was soft, taking her weight as he let her down and lowered himself on top of her. He was hard against her thighs. He lifted her knees, parting them so he might settle between her legs. She was pulsing, throbbing with need, caught in a moment of anticipation as she waited for that first intimate touch against her sex.

He stroked her breasts first, soft, delicious strokes, before he leaned down and suckled one of her nipples. She gasped, arching up as it felt as though his mouth was burning her.

But it was a wonderful sort of torment, one she craved more of. She threaded her fingers through his hair, holding him to her. He kissed his way to her other breast, the sensitive skin of her nipple puckering tight in anticipation. Every little second felt impossibly long while she waited for him to claim that peak with his mouth.

"Oh…yes…"

She didn't know what she was saying, only that she was too full of churning delight to hold it all in. She needed to arch and twist and lift her hips toward him.

She needed…needed him.

"More," she demanded, opening her eyes.

His eyes brightened with hunger, his features drawing tight with need. It was frank and edgy, and her insides twisted at the sight. He smoothed his hand down her body, rubbing her belly before venturing lower to where her sex was spread open for him.

"Laird… Laird… Come quickly! That mare needs help…"

The lad was halfway into the chamber before he realized exactly what they were about. His face turned red before he spun around, his kilt slapping his knees because he moved so fast.

"Ye must come...*quickly*," the boy stressed in a squeak.

"Are they doing it?" Finley's voice came through the doorway.

"Almost..." Skene replied.

Bhaic roared, pushing off the bed and turning on their unwanted guests. Her chemise was still guarding her sex.

"No, they did nae get to it," Skene said as he turned away.

Ailis grabbed the bedding and rolled across the wide expanse of the bed until she was covered.

"But the mare... Hamas says she's going to die if ye do nae come now." The lad was trying to hide his sniffling.

"I'm coming," Bhaic bit out. He cast her a glance before grabbing his plaid and tossing it on the table to pleat it. "And then, I'm going to church to repent so the Lord can have done with tormenting me."

The boy turned around and looked at her, his eyes wide. "Has she bedeviled ye then? Like they say she has?"

Bhaic buckled his kilt and took a deep breath before reaching out to ruffle the boy's hair. "Only so far as a fair lass should, lad. Ye'll understand when ye're a man. For now, do nae be looking upon me wife when she's in me bed. That's a pleasure only a married man gets."

The boy turned his back on her, leaving her facing Bhaic. He pointed at her. "Stay right there."

She slowly shook her head, earning a grunt from him.

"Spitfire," he mouthed before he let the boy take him away.

Five

"WELL, COME ON NOW."

Helen had arrived.

"Ye aren't planning on waiting in that bed until that mare foals?"

Ailis raised her head and sent Helen a withering look. Helen laughed but turned away before Ailis got a good look at her face.

"What is it?" she asked as she crawled from the bed.

Helen waved her closer and cautioned her to be quiet as they got near the outer door of the chamber.

"They were just getting ready to do it!"

"I'm going to tan that lad's arse!"

"Damned mare!"

"Now we'll be stuck with her for at least another day…"

Helen was turning purple as she tried not to laugh out loud. Ailis rolled her eyes before going over to where her dress was puddled on the floor. She picked it up and wrinkled her nose.

"Here." Helen came forward with a surcoat. Ailis recognized it and slid into it.

"I've got a bath waiting down in yer chamber. Thought ye'd like to bathe before putting on some clean clothing."

"It's beneath ye to act as maid to me, but I appreciate it."

Helen offered her a satisfied smirk. "The truth is, I am enjoying telling every one of those arrogant cows who think they are something special what I want, and that I am going to get it for ye."

"Have ye been unhappy here?"

Helen shrugged. "I prefer to think of it as lonely, for it keeps me sane. But the lot in the kitchens is overly proud, and that's a fact. Ye've got yer work set out for ye, and no mistake. Tending to ye puts me in a fine position to watch. And that pleases me very much."

Finley and Skene shut their mouths when Helen opened the door. Ailis bit her lip when she saw how disappointed they both looked. Like a pair of boys who had arrived too late to get any jam with their bread.

Ye're the one disappointed...

She felt her cheeks growing hot with the thought.

But she *was* disappointed.

Bhaic had been too.

She was definitely growing warm by the time she made it down to her chamber. The memory of how hard he'd been behind the tail of his shirt was unshakable.

Ha! 'Tis the memory of how he made ye shiver in the stable that is making ye hot...

She couldn't deny it. Actually, she slowly smiled. It did seem that fate wasn't finished toying with her just yet.

She laughed softly because she realized she wasn't quite done toying with him either.

Perhaps she owed the Earl of Morton a kind thought or two.

Fate certainly did have a strange sense of humor.

Very strange indeed.

❧

Bhaic climbed the tower stairs well after midnight. He was fairly certain his boots weighed triple what they had when he put them on that morning. Kam and Lyel were sitting outside Ailis's door, playing cards. They looked up at him expectantly, hopefully—like a pair of puppies who wanted meat off his plate.

He shook his head. He stank of horse and sweat. Not exactly the way he'd planned to enjoy his bride.

Certainly not the way a maiden deserved to be deflowered.

He paused inside his chamber, staring at the slipper tub sitting in front of the fire. He walked across the floor to it and dipped his fingers into it. The water was warm from the heat hitting the metal. A length of toweling and a lump of soap were sitting nearby. A fresh shirt was neatly folded and waiting as well. Next to the soap was a small bottle of wine. The glow from the hearth turned it ruby red. A cloth covered a plate, and his belly rumbled, reminding him that he'd missed supper.

Ailis had remembered.

He suddenly grinned like a besotted fool.

Having a wife had benefits he'd never taken the time to think about. For certain, Duana had never thought to make sure he had a bath waiting for him. It was a personal thing. Something he realized he valued greatly. A quiet intimacy, one that stoked feelings he'd never associated with his female conquests.

He stripped and sank down into the water, still enjoying the glow of tenderness. It was truly tenderness, for a man was expected to shoulder what life demanded of him. A dutiful wife might be obedient, but he couldn't be cross if Ailis did only as he commanded.

She'd chosen to do more, chosen to think of his comfort and not just the requirements of her position.

He used the soap to wash the scent of horse off himself, rinsing his hair twice before crawling out lest he end up asleep in the water. Lifting the cloth from the plate revealed a round of bread and a chunk of cheese, along with some fresh berries. It tasted better than many a feast he'd sat through, because he was so hungry.

He crawled into his bed and stretched. There was a slight scent clinging to the bedding, and it stirred his cock even as he slipped into slumber.

Ailis.

Tomorrow, he was going to hunt.

And bring in his prey.

&co;

Ailis beat him down the stairs by an entire hour. Bhaic went searching for her and found her in the kitchens with every last lad who worked there lined up in front of her. He leaned in the door frame, watching her as she took stock of what each one was wearing.

She made them lift their feet to show her the soles of their shoes.

"Spending yer days idle, I see."

Bhaic turned to find Marcus behind him. "I thought ye were overly concerned about the status of me union."

His brother's lips curved into a smirk. "I'll admit, it's becoming amusing the way the two of ye can nae seem to…connect."

Bhaic sent his brother a profane gesture. Marcus slapped him on the shoulder. "Ye might as well come along with me to the crossroads. Yer bride is nae going to have any time for ye until tonight."

"Trouble?"

Marcus shrugged. "Maybe…maybe no. Heard Lye Rob Gordon was seen raiding."

Fifty men were already waiting in the yard. Bhaic mounted and rode out with them.

❦

The day was overly long.

Ailis discovered the afternoon sun moved at a snail's pace. She tried to focus but looked up from her lists more than she should have.

The cook finally rang the supper bells, but Bhaic wasn't at the head table. The hall was more pensive than normal—everyone was waiting to see if the laird's sons returned in good health. It was something she'd grown up accepting as a harsh fact of living in the Highlands. One reason men were so loyal to their clans was it was the only way to ensure safety. The farmers scattered across MacPherson land depended on the reputation of the MacPherson retainers. A lone man working his field might have his sons, but had little else to keep the neighboring clans from destroying his home.

Of course, that was why she was there. To end a feud that had placed a strain on those working the land near the border of her father's land and Bhaic's.

Just as Helen had been taken to ensure her father didn't retaliate. So imperfect a solution, and yet, there appeared to be no other way.

The bells on the walls began to toll. Ailis listened for a moment, catching the rhythm. She smiled, because it was a happy one, not a frantic call to arms.

"I suppose that would be yer husband returning," Helen said.

Ailis nodded and rose from her seat. They both walked down the aisle and out onto the steps. Bhaic, Marcus, and the MacPherson retainers had flooded into the yard.

But there was someone else with them too. Symon Grant was happily clasping hands with Shamus.

"And there is yer bride," Symon declared. The men in the yard parted to clear a path between them. The Grant Laird studied her for a long moment. He looked over at Bhaic and punched him in the shoulder.

"She looks as though she's had far too much sleep. Ye must no' be looking close enough at the lass to see what a prize she is."

"I'll thank ye to stop looking so closely at me wife." Bhaic made it to her and pulled her into his embrace.

He kissed her thoroughly, to the delight of those watching. "And just maybe, the rest of the world will let us have enough time to enjoy being wed."

She laughed softly, slipping her hand across his chest. He caught her gaze, and for a moment, nothing else mattered but the man holding her.

She was ready.

His expression tightened as his arms did. Then Symon was wrestling him away. The MacPherson retainers enjoyed the company of the Grant retainers. Flasks were pulled out of saddlebags and inner doublet pockets.

Ailis appreciated it, sitting at the head table for a time to enjoy a cup of spiced cider before the male conversation made her cheeks sting. She climbed the stairs to her chamber.

But Helen wasn't there.

In fact, she hadn't seen Helen since she'd gone out to see Bhaic return.

The state of her chamber further alarmed her. The bedding wasn't pulled back. The water pitcher wasn't refilled, and dirty dishes remained from the lunch she'd partaken of at the table.

Ailis turned and went down the stairs.

※

"Ye should be above stairs."

Ailis stopped. Marcus was leaning in the passageway's arched door frame. He was half-shrouded in shadow and looked as if he was very much at home that way.

"We told her that," Finley said from behind her.

"Helen is missing," Ailis said.

"Ye do nae know that."

"I do." Ailis looked to Marcus. "She always rights

the chamber, and it hasn't been done. I am worried something has happened to her."

Marcus listened with an unreadable expression. Beyond the shadowed doorway, Bhaic sat with Symon and Shamus at the high table. They were in deep conversation, their expressions tight.

"Go back to yer chamber, mistress. Ye'll see yer hand woman tomorrow," Marcus told her.

"Ye know where she is?"

Marcus looked back toward her and gave her a single nod. There was something in his expression that chilled her blood. She looked past him at Symon Grant.

"Did ye have her locked away because her laird is here?"

Her voice had risen. Marcus abandoned his lazy stance instantly, facing off with her and backing her deeper into the shadows. Had she not backed up, he would have barreled straight into her.

"Take yer mistress above stairs and see that she stays there. Bound and gagged if necessary."

The settled-in feeling she'd had shattered, cold, hard circumstances rushing in to torment her.

"Ye bloody brute." Insulting him wasn't going to gain her much. She made to dive around him but was caught from behind.

Finley and Lyel proved just how devoted to Marcus they were. She got out half a sound before something was wrapped around her head and tied across her mouth. They pulled her right off her feet and started carrying her up the stairs. She strained and twisted, but they tossed her into her chamber with ridiculous ease.

She ripped off the gag as they retreated, Finley eying her. "Ye heard him, mistress. Make a fuss, and I'll have to truss ye up like a pig on the way to market."

He closed the door in her face as her temper flared. She'd wrapped her hand around the handle before she accepted the harsh facts.

The gag was lying over her shoulder.

She'd end up bundled for market. There was no way to avoid it. A wave of helplessness went through her, washing out the foundation of trust she'd been building her new life on.

She and Helen were both hostages. Commodities to be traded and used to ensure peace.

Tears stung her eyes, and there was no way to hold them back. The sight of her personal things only made it worse, because it felt as though she was settling into her prison.

Marriage, prison. It seemed that for a Robertson, there was little difference.

❧

Bhaic crawled up the stairs, certain he'd never been so tired. Kam and Skene tugged on the corners of their bonnets when he passed Ailis's chamber.

It stung that she was there and not in his own, but honestly, he had to admit he was too tired to be patient.

So maybe she was wiser than he.

It was a humorous thought, one that had a smile curving his lips as he fell asleep.

❧

Ailis wasn't at the table in the morning. Bhaic had to wait for Symon to depart before he headed back up the stairs to discover her escort sitting outside her door, looking bored. Finley perked up the moment he saw him.

"I'm near starved," the retainer said.

"Go."

He didn't knock but pushed the door in. "Why are ye up here, madam? Ye need to think of the men assigned to ye. They do nae have a waiting woman to bring them their meals."

She flipped around. "I am here because yer brother had me imprisoned in this chamber last night, and Helen is suffering the same fate somewhere else."

Bhaic stopped halfway across the chamber. "Be careful what ye accuse me brother of. He thinks first and often only of the clan. I'll no' have ye disrespecting him."

Her face darkened with temper, but she made an effort to swallow it. "He had Helen locked away so she could nae seek out her laird while he was here. When I went looking for her, Marcus was waiting for me and told Finley to bring me up here. To bind and gag me if I didn't go quietly. I have been a prisoner in this chamber."

"But no' any longer." Marcus had come up the stairs behind him. His brother gave the door a shove closed before continuing. "Symon has cleared the gate."

"It is no' yer place to deal with me wife." Bhaic's tone was deadly.

Marcus didn't back down from him. "But she is no'

yer wife yet. Which makes it me concern when there is a possible way for her to escape the castle."

The two brothers shared a long look before Bhaic nodded. "Leave us."

Marcus gave her a quick glance, one that drove home how ruthless he might be in defense of the MacPhersons.

"Are ye really going to allow him to treat Helen like that?"

Bhaic clearly wasn't expecting her question to be about Helen. His brows lowered for a moment in contemplation. "As I said, Ailis, me brother will do whatever necessary to protect this clan. Ye can nae tell me yer brothers would do any different."

"So Helen must suffer being naught but a captured woman?"

"She looked well enough."

"How would ye feel if ye were prevented from seeing yer family?"

His expression softened. "Ye have a point there. I'll talk to Marcus about making sure the lass is wed, and then—"

"What if she does nae want to wed?" she demanded.

His eyes narrowed. "Ye ask too much. Me brother would no' have brought her here without good cause. I do nae need trouble with Symon. Helen will become a MacPherson. It's the only solution."

"The only one that favors the MacPhersons."

He didn't answer her, but his silence was confirmation enough.

It hurt.

He was everything she'd been raised to believe he was. She shook her head, nauseated by the stern stance he was taking. His expression softened.

"It has naught to do with us, Ailis. Our arrangement is proceeding well."

She bit back what she wanted to say, because everything was churning inside her. His words stirred up the passion that had been burning slowly inside her since they'd been interrupted. The memory of the pleasure he'd introduced her to in the stable tormented her too, but there was the ruthless look Marcus had given her that Bhaic clearly approved of.

She turned her back on him, needing to sort out her feelings. Needing to shield her emotions before he sliced them to the bone. She heard him grunt behind her.

"Yer kin would do no different, and Lye Rob would have raped ye."

Both solid truths. Duncan would have his own retainers posted about Robertson Castle. The knowledge made her feel less set upon, and at the same time, more overwhelmed than ever before.

He cupped her shoulder and turned her to face him. His eyes flickered with hard intent. "No Highlander can be weak, but I have chosen to be kind to ye."

Why was she drawn to him? She felt the pull, her flesh yearning for his in spite of her mental dilemma.

"Do I live in fear of the moment when ye decide ye have gained what ye wish with kindness?" It was an honest question, but one that vexed him.

He stiffened, his jaw tightening. "Clearly ye need some time to think matters through."

Overwhelmed was too meek a phrase to describe how she felt. Defeated was more fitting, and she couldn't seem to shake it even as she felt it rip at the last of her resolve to remain hopeful.

"Clearly," she muttered.

He nodded, obviously not pleased. But he turned and left. Something had torn between them, simply rent in two. The damage so great, there would never be a hope of mending it.

No hope at all.

❧

"I am Elise."

Ailis looked up at the girl who entered her chamber an hour later.

"Duana says I'm to see to ye now." Elise set a tray down on the table. "Since ye missed the meal below. I'll be back to help ye dress for supper. Ye're expected at the high table by the laird and yer husband."

Elise started to lower herself but stopped, uncertain how to proceed. She was facing a dreaded Robertson, after all.

"Thank ye, Elise."

Relief spread across her face a moment before she was gone through the chamber door in a flutter of blue wool skirts.

Ailis would not cry.

No, she forbade herself.

She wasn't a child.

But that left her noticing how silent the chamber was. She missed Helen's companionship. Well, better to know what would become of friendships she forged.

Aye, better, for all that much sooner to learn to embrace a solitary life.

❧

"Bhaic," Shamus called out. Dinner was not even halfway finished.

Not that Ailis was eating very much. She felt the weight of Marcus, Bhaic, and Shamus too keenly for any true appetite.

The high table quieted down. Shamus looked down its length at his son. "Good night to ye."

There was more silence. The retainers behind Shamus started to pull on his chair. "I am no' going to bed. Me son and daughter-in-law are."

Ailis's chair started moving backward. She was fairly sure her face went up in flames. A moment later, Angus was beating the tabletop as he laughed, and his amusement caught like fire, running through the hall as the retainers actually tipped her out of her chair. Her choice was to stand or be dumped onto the floor.

Bhaic ended up no better. They both stood there for a moment, surprise holding them frozen.

Shamus looked at his son. "Enough uncertainty. Take yer bride to bed."

The hall erupted again. Bhaic's complexion actually darkened.

All Ailis felt was the noose tightening around her neck.

Well, there was no help for it. She lowered herself out of habit before moving past Shamus. She ordered herself to pick up her feet.

Ye're a Robertson. No' a coward.

Somehow, she made it to the fourth floor without really realizing it. She paused for only a moment before pushing the doors of Bhaic's chambers open. The sound of Finley and the rest of her escort filled the stairway, making it easier to step far into the chamber.

She ended up almost to the entryway to the bedchamber, facing the huge bed.

"Must it be this way between us, Ailis?" He'd closed the door, but not before she got a glimpse of Finley settling in on the landing. "It's for sure we'll disagree sometimes."

"Apparently, we've been put to bed. I'm sure the Earl of Morton would approve." She pinched out one of the candles, the light making her feel unbearably exposed. At least in darkness, she might embrace the yearning her flesh had for his and be content in the fact that his touch didn't leave her cold.

It was more than some had.

She turned to look at him, searching for the man she'd so brazenly disrobed the day before. Maybe he was in there. "Did ye take Helen away from me?"

His jaw tightened. "I agreed with the decision."

Well, it seemed sure that he wasn't going to be that playful man tonight.

"I need help with my laces." She turned her back on him. Elise had returned and helped her dress for supper, but this dress was one that laced in the back. She reached out and extinguished another candle as she waited. She'd thought turning her back on him would be easier. Instead, it heightened her awareness of him, of the time passing and the way she was waiting for him to touch her.

Darkness was a balm for her wounded feelings, allowing her to hide how lonely she felt. She took a step farther into the shadows of the bedchamber.

"Aye, I suppose darkness suits us both tonight."

His voice was a raspy whisper. Part of her heard

companionship in it, a hint of another soul that was just as caught in the tangle of circumstances as she was.

Was he?

She clung to that idea, tilting her head to the side when he stroked her nape, sighing as a ripple of sensation went across her skin.

She felt his fingers brush across her back, stopping when he found the lace holding her dress closed. It tightened just a bit as he loosened the knot. The soft sound of it being pulled free of the eyelets seemed to ring in her ears.

She worked at the cuffs of her sleeves. By the time he'd finished, her bodice and sleeves slipped easily to the floor. He tugged on the tie that held her skirts closed, and a moment later, they had fallen into a heap around her ankles. Her heart was racing, her lungs trying to keep up. She hesitated, uncertain of the next move.

Bhaic settled the issue by kissing her neck. A soft pressing of his lips against her flesh that sent her thoughts spinning. She bid them farewell happily, backing up and digging her fingers into the pleats of his plaid. She wanted to find him. Just him. She wanted everything else gone.

So she pulled the lace of her corset free. It was a relief to be free of the stiff garment, her breasts feeling heavy and swollen.

"Christ, it seems like forever since I've seen these." He was looking over her shoulder, stroking his hands up her belly until he cupped her breasts.

His touch set off a pulsing between her legs. It was far from startling tonight. Instead, she felt some part of her welcoming the rising hunger.

She turned around, seeking out satisfaction. His first belt pulled free as simply as it had before. She went looking for the second one, but he cupped her chin and raised her face. For one moment, their eyes met. She could see him contemplating her, trying to think of something to say.

"Kiss me." She didn't want to talk. She reached for his shoulder and rose up to take what she desired.

He drew in a stiff breath, and she captured it when she pressed her lips against his. Her toes hurt from stretching to meet him.

"I can nae think when ye do that, Ailis."

She had to sink back down, but she drew her hands along his chest, finding the buttons on his shirt and opening them so she might touch his skin. "I do nae want to think. I might just go mad if I do."

He made a soft sound under his breath. "Aye. I suppose ye have a good idea at that."

He backed away, working the second belt that secured his kilt. It dropped with a soft sound as she took another step into the dark bedchamber. He followed slowly, opening the cuffs of his shirt before he pulled it over his head.

Her breath caught, shyness overcoming her. But that didn't stop her from looking at him and letting her attention slip down from his chest to the taunt muscles of his belly, and farther still until she was looking at his groin. Her cheeks heated, but she reached out, wanting to be bold instead of submissive.

She couldn't bear being submissive tonight.

He stiffened where she touched his length. It was hot, but the skin incredibly soft. She stroked him, hearing his breath rasp between his teeth. She looked up, catching sight of his jaw being clenched.

"Aye, yer touch drives me near insane."

He reached out and tugged her chemise up and off. It fluttered toward the floor like a ghost in the darkened room.

"I want to do the same to ye." He cupped her breast, and she gasped.

He chuckled softly. She closed her hand around his member, enjoying the way he ended up sucking in a harsh breath.

Her body was hot, their lack of clothing bothering her not at all. In fact, she was enjoying being bare. There was a wicked sense of pleasure weaving its way through her, one that overrode every lecture she'd ever heard on propriety and modesty.

His neck was corded, his eyes narrowing. She would have sworn she felt his control growing thin, just as her own was.

She wasn't sure who moved first. All that mattered was that he gathered her up against him, and he gave her his kiss at last.

She craved it. Felt as if she was starving for it.

Bhaic seemed to be as well.

He captured the back of her head and held her still as his mouth ravished hers. It was a hungry merging, his lips claiming hers and pushing her mouth open so he could boldly thrust his tongue inside. She moaned and tried to stroke his tongue with her own in return. Her body twisted against his, seeking a deeper connection.

He suddenly broke off; she made a half sound of distress before he was lifting her off her feet and carrying her around the footboard of the bed. The ropes groaned as he bore her up onto the bed. They were both straining, crawling into the center of the huge mattress. And at last, he covered her, sending a jolt of delight through her from the contact.

He pressed her thighs wide, settling between them. A dim thought surfaced, one she'd contemplated when she first learned what a man and woman did in bed together. But there was nothing awkward about the position.

It felt right.

Almost perfect, in fact.

Still, something was missing.

She lifted her hips, seeking out that last thing she craved. At last, there was trust between them.

Bhaic didn't disappoint her. He reached between them, teasing her slit and drawing the fluid pooling at the entrance of her passage through her folds. He stroked over that throbbing nub at the top of her sex, sending her arching and gasping with delight. He toyed with it, rubbing it as her insides clenched and twisted.

But she felt empty.

She opened her eyes and found him watching her. "That is nae enough."

His lips curved. "Nay, lass, it is nae."

He left off teasing her and guided his member to her open sex. The first touch made her tremble. He pressed forward, sinking inside as her body stretched.

He pulled free, waiting for her to draw in a breath. He smoothed the hair back from her face.

"Again," she said, her voice more sultry than she'd ever imagined it might be.

"There's the lass who stood up to Morton and me on our wedding night." His expression tightened as he thrust forward. "Ye are fearless, Ailis."

His words pleased her, but not as much as the hard flesh pushing deeper inside her. She let her eyes close because she was only interested in feeling. His hardness pleased her in ways she'd never suspected possible. There was pain, but what she really wanted to know was how good would it feel when he was sheathed completely?

She lifted her hips, eager for that connection.

"Let me—"

He didn't get to finish his warning. Her body gave under the pressure he'd been using and her own motions, something tearing inside her before he penetrated to the hilt. She gasped, caught between a moment of white-hot pain and intense enjoyment.

"Christ, Ailis...I did nae mean to hurt ye..."

He was petting her, smoothing her hair back from her face. She opened her eyes. "I do nae think there was a way to avoid it."

His expression changed. For a moment, she witnessed the respect he'd mentioned on that night that seemed so long ago. But his eyes began to narrow, his lips thinning as he started moving. Need shimmered in his eyes, making her breath catch.

He was holding himself back, moving in and out of her with slow thrusts. The effort cost him, the muscles along his neck drawing tight. She lifted for him, gasping when his length slid along that pulsing pleasure point at the top of her sex.

"Aye..." he ground out as he withdrew and pushed

back in at the same angle. "We have to find the right...position..."

She had no inclination to think about what he was saying. Only to feel. She lifted her hips, straining toward him because it felt so incredible. She was poised on the edge of something, something that was twisting tighter with every downward plunge of his body into hers. All that mattered was meeting him, moving in unison with him until she felt the world shatter. It was far more intense than it had been in the stable. This time she cried out, unable to contain it all inside herself. The moment seemed to hold her, keeping her inside it as pleasure burned through her.

Bhaic held her down, the only solid thing in her universe. He rode her through it, his pace becoming wild in the last few thrusts before he arched back and strained to bury himself inside her. She opened her eyes as his seed began to flow, spurting deep against the mouth of her womb while he rocked her a few final times before collapsing beside her on his back.

His breathing was harsh, his arm shaking as he reached up to stroke her face. She suddenly noticed the silence in the room. Their breathing was slowing down, the blood no longer roaring in her ears. Her body felt more relaxed, more sated than she'd ever felt.

So unexpected.

While she hadn't worried that marriage duties would be so painful she'd dread them, she certainly hadn't expected to feel so elated when it was all over and done with. The darkness was the perfect place to experience it, allowing her the privacy to simply be honest.

Of course, the sun would rise.

That hard certainty soured her mood.

Bhaic was still beside her. His breathing had slowed. She waited for a bit, listening to the deepening sounds of his breath. At last, when she was sure he was asleep, she pushed away from him, easing from the bed and slipping onto her feet.

She ached.

The pain surprised her, stopping her for a moment. Her chemise was lying on the floor. She reached for it and put it on. She pinched out more candles on the way to where her dress was. There was no point in getting into it, so she wrapped her arisaid around herself and gathered up her things.

Finley jumped when she opened the door, staring at her in surprise. She passed him and made it to her chamber before the first tears escaped her eyes. She let them flow, the strength to hold them in beyond her.

It would be better tomorrow.

Of course it would.

But that was a lie, because she'd still be a Robertson.

❧

She awoke at first light again.

Although, it was barely first light.

Still, she hadn't slept much, so what was the point of remaining in bed? She got up and found a chunk of bread left from the day before. The edges were hard, but she tore them away and ate the rest. The pitcher still had some water in it too.

Helen would have taken it away.

Ailis scoffed at the tray. Most any chamber would

have been righted. But of course, she was a Robertson. It felt as though the walls were closing in on her. She went through her clothing and found another dress that laced in the front. Made for days when she needed to work as hard as everyone else, it was sturdy green wool that went with her blond hair.

She tied up the front and put her arisaid on. Gaining a sense of satisfaction from seeing to herself. At least no one would be labeling her helpless.

Don't be peevish… Ye knew full well where ye were heading when ye wed.

She drew in a deep breath to steady herself. Aye. She'd known and struck her bargain, so she'd have to be keeping it. Besides, she couldn't very well expect to win over many hearts in a single week.

What she needed was a ride. Some fresh air would see her feeling right again.

She pushed her doubts aside and headed down the stairs. The hall was still full of sleeping retainers. They had their plaids pulled up and over their heads to stay warm. More than one of them had a serving lass sharing those plaids.

She caught herself staring at them, trying to decide if she longed for the same. If she were to be practical, she'd expect nothing more than contentment from her marriage and be grateful for the pleasure Bhaic had made sure she found in his bed.

Was there more? The couples in the hall looked more intimate somehow. The sight stirred up some longing she hadn't realized she had. The couple she was spying on started to move, stroking each other beneath their layers of wool plaid. The man cupped his consort's breasts as she reached down and boldly grasped his member. Their legs entwined as they kissed, and finally the man rolled the woman beneath him. He shrouded her with his plaid, but not before Ailis spied her clasping him between her thighs.

She'd done that too…

Her cheeks heated as she ducked out of the castle and headed up to the stables. It was quiet still. But her mare gave her a warm welcome, tossing her head and pawing at the ground.

"I've missed ye too."

❦

Marcus was in the hall when Bhaic made it down the stairs.

"I did nae expect ye to send the lass from yer bed," Marcus said softly. "A bit harsh."

"She left after I fell asleep," Bhaic bit back under his breath. "Likely due to the fine sense of welcome she's been shown."

There was a delicate scoff. Bhaic looked beyond his brother to see Helen sitting in a chair. She had her arms folded over her chest and was perched on the edge of the seat. Marcus was watching her, daring her to move.

"As if either of ye know a single thing about a woman's feelings."

Marcus's lips curled. "Me brother knows something about moving a woman to ecstasy. I have that on good report."

Helen pushed her lips into a pout as Bhaic punched him in the shoulder. "Have done with us, Marcus. Ye've had yer way enough."

Marcus continued to look at Helen. "I always get me way."

Helen looked right back at him and arched one of her eyebrows. "Every spoilt child has an encounter with disappointment. Ye're no' different."

Marcus looked past Bhaic. "What are ye doing down here without yer charge, Finley?"

Finley had a fresh mug of ale, his beard frothy with it. "The lass came out last night looking well ridden. Ye said to watch her until the union was consummated."

He drew off a long sip and belched, clearly thinking the job well done. Marcus started toward him but turned back around when Helen moved.

"Sit back down, Helen." Marcus spoke softly. It was a warning, one Bhaic knew well.

"I am no' agreeing with this."

Bhaic looked up to see several of their retainers lined up.

Marcus shrugged. "Ye can choose, or I'll let them compete for ye."

"Ye're a bastard," she snarled.

"I am."

"Ye're thieving from me father. That's the truth about what ye're set to do. Forcing him to give me dowry to one of yer own."

"Ye've been here too long," Marcus countered. "Yer reputation is ruined if ye are no' wed."

"That's yer shame, no' mine."

"Which way is going to be, lass? I've got other things to see to today."

She lifted one hand and gestured at the men who had stepped up. "What? Do I no' even get the chance to check their teeth? Should I select one simply by the way he leers at me?"

Marcus slowly grinned. "Well now, lads. It seems the lass desires a bit of courting. Make sure ye are attentive to her and do nae lose sight of her."

His last words were delivered in a solid tone his men recognized well. They grinned, several of them chuckling. Helen slowly stood. She turned to look at the men eyeing her like a treat. Marcus had turned to look at Bhaic. Helen struck in that small moment of inattention, claiming a pitcher from the tabletop and swinging it in a wide arch. She caught Marcus on the side of the head, knocking him flat.

Bhaic stared incredulously as his brother landed in a heap. There was silence in the hall for a split second before laughter erupted. People turned around in time to see Marcus jumping to his feet. Helen had the pitcher in both hands, facing off with him.

But it was the sound of their father's amusement that made them both turn. Shamus was halfway up the steps. He'd stopped because he was laughing so hard, his age-worn body was shaking. He struggled to make it up the last two steps.

"Just like yer mother," he said at last. "She was never afraid of anything. No' even the church. She was a member of the new kirk. That's why she never wed me."

"He's trying to force me to wed." Helen appealed to Shamus. "Allow me to go home."

Shamus made his way to a chair. He settled back into it and gestured her forward. "Why are ye on me land, lass?"

"Yer son stole me to force me father to no' make a fuss. He had me locked away when me own laird was here so I could nae seek his protection. I am a Grant."

"Me son Marcus, ye mean?"

Helen nodded. Shamus considered her for a long moment. "Well now, I stole his mother too. A Highlander does that from time to time when he sees a lass worth keeping for himself."

Helen's face paled, but she wasn't ready to give in just yet. She took a deep breath and considered her argument.

"Yet he is trying to force me on his men." Helen gestured behind her. "I'll have none of it."

People were moving closer, frowning at the tone Helen was using with their laird. Shamus was pensive, clearly thinking the matter through.

"If ye stole her, Marcus, ye'll keep her or return her to her father," Shamus said firmly.

"Her family was making trouble," Marcus informed his sire. "Better one woman change her thinking than blood spilt."

Shamus took to stroking his beard.

"I was giving the men leave to court her," Marcus added when his father didn't speak.

"After listing me dowry," Helen argued. "Ye've given them a fine reason for rough wooing sure enough."

There was a rise of sound from the back of the hall—women were shaking their heads in disapproval.

"Me son's choice to take ye was valid. Unless ye would like to tell me that ye would prefer spilled blood over a peaceful settlement?" Shamus suddenly sounded exactly like the laird he'd been ten years earlier, before age had stolen his strength.

Helen opened her mouth but shut it without utter-
ing a word. She nodded a single time, clearly frustrated
by her circumstances but wise enough to see the
matter for what it was.

Shamus grunted with approval and turned his attention to Marcus.

"Ye stole her. If ye can no' convince her to wed
ye, it falls to ye to return her to her father and account
for yer actions. Her father will account for his actions
if he persists in causing trouble. It's true a Highlander
may steal a woman, but no' to make a mockery of her
and her father's good name. However, if she does nae
favor ye, she may choose another."

Marcus opened his mouth to argue at the same time
that Helen did. Shamus slapped the table, making it
clear the matter was closed. Which left them staring at
one another. "Now. On to yer brother."

Shamus took a drink from his mug before he
looked around. "Where is that sheet?"

"Father..." Bhaic said quietly.

His father paid him no mind. Duana finally came
into sight, her breathing labored and sweat trickling
down the sides of her face. But she came up onto the
high ground and held up a sheet. The dark stain on it
was clear in the morning light.

"Well now." Shamus nodded approvingly. "That's
settled." He slapped the tabletop again but looked
around. "Where is the lass? Still sleeping? Well
now...that's me son after all! Let her rest. She'll be
needing it."

The hall filled with laughter.

Duana started to direct the serving of the high table.

The retainers moved the tables and benches into position so they might enjoy breaking their fast.

The day was beginning, but his wife never appeared.

Well, tonight he'd see about making sure she had reason to seek him out.

∽∾

Her mare was eager for a ride, setting off the moment Ailis gave her leave to. The hills were covered in green, and the heather was blooming. Ailis leaned low and let her mare run. The castle fell out of sight before she pulled up on the reins.

Her chest felt lighter. Her circumstances no longer seemed so overwhelming.

Well, she wouldn't say she felt hopeful, but at least she wasn't hopeless any longer.

It was something.

She smiled ruefully.

Well, her marriage was something too. Something she'd best avoid putting a label on. It was done now, and there was part of her satisfied by the knowledge. Part of her hoping for another night of passion. Was that to be the way she found meaning in her new life? In those dark moments when she surrendered to the bliss Bhaic's touch unleashed?

Well, it had certainly been better than what the marriage bed held for some daughters of lairds who needed to marry with alliances in mind. He wasn't old enough to be her father—more than one bride had suffered such a fate.

She wasn't wed to Marcus.

That idea made her snicker. Bhaic's brother was

well suited to his position as War Chief. Ruthless to his core. She couldn't see him taking her to the astrologer's house, and the idea of Marcus courting her was laughable. He would hunt his wife, not court her.

At least her mood was lightening. She eased her mare up an incline, coming to a crest. Below her, a river was roaring with spring melt off. The power of the moving water was incredible. It was churning so much, it created its own mist. The sun was coming up now, chasing away the night shadows. The moment was magical, that time between night and day when fae roamed and the specters of night were no longer able to move about.

There was a crack behind her. She started to turn but was suddenly falling off the horse as pain ripped across her shoulders and a shower of splinters rained down on her. She hit the ground, more agony tearing through her. Her mare reared up, and Ailis willingly let herself start tumbling down the incline. The newly risen sun flashed off the horse's hooves as the animal pawed at the air before coming down.

Ailis lost sight of her as she tumbled head over heels, her skirts blinding her and trapping her arms. She couldn't stop, couldn't get her bearings, and a moment later, she plunged into the river, the chill biting into her.

She let out a shriek, but her mouth was full of water and fabric. The current tore at her clothing, dragging her into its heart and downstream as she fought to break the surface and draw breath. She was straining, fighting with all her strength, but the water was too powerful. The pain in her back was stolen by

the chill of the water, but still she fought to escape
its power.

&

Helen was a bold woman.

She appeared in the training yard later in the day in
defiance of the tradition of it being a place for men.
Some of the younger retainers blinked as they tried to
decide if she was truly there. She gave them no attention, continuing on to the man she sought.

"Save yer breath, Helen." Marcus cast her only a
short glance before returning his attention to the men
training in the yard. "I will nae be taking ye back to
yer father, and ye do nae belong in the training yard."

Marcus and Bhaic were standing on a stone platform at the front of the training yard. It was set off
from the main yard in front of the keep. Helen picked
up her skirt and climbed the stairs without hesitation,
a stern look on her face that promised Marcus hell.

"No' that I am surprised to hear ye saying such, but
I did no' come here to talk to ye."

Helen stepped right up to him but looked at Bhaic.
"I can nae find Ailis."

"Who gave ye permission to go near her?" Marcus
demanded.

Helen bristled. "At least I went looking for her. No'
a single one of yer household cares to notice that their
mistress is gone, and it past noon."

Bhaic turned to face her. "Where did ye look?"

"She is no' in her chamber, or yers, or the kitchens.
And no one has seen her. That lot ye had trailing her
has no idea where she is."

"Elise should know," Bhaic said slowly, trying to think the matter through. But his emotions were rising.

"That useless creature dropped a tray in Ailis's chamber this morning and left, considering that service enough for a Robertson. She never checked to see if her mistress was in the bedding," Helen informed them both. "I checked. The tray is untouched, and a dress missing from those her father brought her. I hung them and took an inventory."

Bhaic locked gazes with Marcus.

"The mare," they said at the same time.

Bhaic was down the steps and on the back of his horse in a flash of thigh and plaid. Marcus was right behind him. Men scrambled to pull horses around from where they were kept ready during the day. They dug their heels in to catch up with their leaders.

Helen was left standing on the stage from which training was conducted. The youths had stopped and were staring at her, some of them with gaping jaws. She held her chin steady before making her way down the steps and away from the training yard.

❧

"Well now, that mare was gone before first light."

"And ye did nae think to tell me?" Bhaic demanded of his stable master.

The man shrugged. "Yer stallion was missing too. Thought the pair of ye went off to the astrologer's house again. Or someplace else ye might enjoy being newly wed."

Bhaic cursed, feeling his own choices nipping on his heels.

"Pull the hounds out," Marcus instructed. "Looks like it will be a good thing she went back to her own bed last night. Best get that sheet. We'll start with the mare, but might need something of Ailis's."

"Aye." Bhaic swung back up onto his stallion and headed back to the castle. By the time he made it back to the stables, thirty men were readying their horses. Marcus had chosen well. They were all hardened Highlanders, their saddles packed light but with what they needed to survive.

The hounds were large ones, their coats gray. They were eager for the hunt, pulling on their leashes. The hound master took the hounds into the mare's stall.

There was a low whine as one of them picked up a scent. Another hound joined in, and then the pack was jumping against their leashes, trying to break free. The hound master let them go, the pack taking off into the afternoon light.

Bhaic was right on their tail. He avoided thinking about what Ailis's absence meant.

But that didn't stop his temper from rising.

The hounds led them over the ridge and into the village. The most confounding thing was that they were heading away from Robertson land. Someone started ringing the church bell as they neared. People came out of their homes, goodwives standing in their doorways wearing aprons as children peered through open windows and men looked out from workshops. The streets cleared to allow for the retainers' passage.

Marcus whistled at Bhaic and pointed ahead of them. Ailis's mare was tied up outside the tavern. Bhaic slid from the saddle as several of his retainers struggled to release the hounds. They tossed slices of meat to the animals to praise them for a duty well done.

Bhaic went inside, pausing in the doorway to get a look at what was happening, his hand wrapped around the pommel of his sword.

The place was filled with laughter. It died away quickly as the occupants gained a look at who was arriving. They reached up to tug on the corners of their caps.

"The mare," Bhaic began. "Who tied her up?"

There was a hoot from several of the men sitting at the tables. One of them lifted his mug toward his companion. "See there? Even the Tanis has heard of yer talents!"

"Who?" Bhaic asked again.

The men were all drinking again. Bhaic ended up waiting until they lowered their mugs. One of them wiped his mouth on his sleeve before standing. "The mare is me prize. Shot a Robertson off her back this morning, I did. Damned bastard was sneaking around at first light. Up to no good for certain. Saw those Robertson colors clearly."

"Ye shot her?" Bhaic demanded. Marcus put out his arm, holding him back.

"No' the mare." The man sniffed indignantly. "Horse can't be held accountable for what stable it was born in."

"The rider," Marcus snapped.

The man shrugged and reached for something on the table. "It was a Robertson sure enough." He held up a tattered piece of wool, the Robertson colors clear in spite of the mud dried on it. "I know me enemy when I see them. Even in the dim light of early morning," the man declared. He patted one of the pistols stored in his belt. "Keep these loaded just in case I needs them."

"What is yer name?" Bhaic asked. Marcus recognized his low tone for the threat it was, standing half in front of him.

"Haddox."

Bhaic flattened a hand on his brother's chest and pushed him aside. "Did ye hear of me recent wedding?"

The men in the tavern all started nodding.

"Aye. Indeed I did," Haddox stated proudly, but his eyes widened as he realized exactly what Bhaic was getting at.

"Did ye shoot me wife?"

Haddox lost his color, his mouth working like a freshly caught fish. "It was only barely first light... I saw...saw the colors..." he looked down at the mangled piece of wool, dropping it as though it burned his hand.

Bhaic grabbed the man up by his clothing. *"Where?"*

"Up by the river... He went into the river..."

Bhaic tossed him toward the tavern door. "Take me there."

❧

It was his failing.

Bhaic looked at the ground, the place where Ailis had fallen, marked by gouges in the new spring growth. It was a steep incline, the earth worn away by the water. It was hard to keep his footing. If he'd fallen from a horse, there would have been no hope of stopping.

"I let ye down," Marcus said quietly, disgust edging his tone.

"No. I should have seen to her. She's me wife."
Bhaic moved down the slope, following the path she'd
taken on her way to the riverbank. He looked at the
current and peered down the ravine.

"If she's alive, she's on her way—"

"To Gordon land," Bhaic finished for his brother.

"God help the lass."

"No," Bhaic snarled. "God help Lye Rob if I find
him anywhere near me wife."

The Earl of Morton and his threats about feuding
could rot in hell if Lye Rob put one hand on her.
Bhaic yanked the sheet off his saddle and gave it to
the dogs. They sniffed at it and started to search along
the riverbank.

❧

Obviously, she wasn't dead.

No, she was clearly alive, because there wasn't sup-
posed to be pain in heaven.

Maybe ye're in hell…

Well, she was freezing. So she wasn't in hell.

She coughed out another mouthful of water and
wheezed. Pain shot through her. There was so much
of it, she was fairly certain it would be simpler to list
what part of her body didn't hurt as opposed to what
did. Her back was on fire, as though there was a red-
hot poker across her shoulder blades. She wiped at her
face, but there was so much mud, she had to roll over
and scoop up handfuls of water to wash her eyes out
before she could open them.

And when she did, she wished she were dead.

"No' happy to see me, Ailis Robertson?"

She blinked, but Lye Rob Gordon was still standing there, looking at her as though she were a freshly downed doe. "I'd have preferred Satan."

Two of his retainers hauled her off the riverbank. She cried out, her back in agony as they moved her.

Lye Rob cupped her chin, bringing their gazes together. "Ye're on me land now. Forget who is master here, and ye'll suffer for it." He slapped her. She staggered only because her legs were so unsteady.

"I am wed." She straightened up, pushing the pain aside.

"So was Bothwell," Lye Rob answered her. "A little gold in the right hand, and we'll have ye divorced quickly enough."

"Wedding me will nae gain ye me father's support."

Lye Rob moved toward her. "Ye'll be the one to tell him how savage yer MacPherson husband was. Beating ye…" He hit her again, this time using his fist against her shoulder. She went skidding into the dirt. Some of his retainers looked disapproving, but none of them were willing to cross the laird's son.

"I will nae."

Lye Rob grinned, coming down on one knee next to her, because she couldn't stop shaking enough to stand.

"We'll see about that."

There was a twisted flicker of enjoyment in his eyes. She stared at it, sickened by the sight. He grinned at her horror.

"Ye're right." He tapped her on the chin. "I will enjoy it."

She didn't doubt him. Her belly twisted with nausea, but it gave her the strength to struggle to her feet.

"We need to build a fire," one of his men said.

Lye Rob looked up. "Ye do nae tell me what to do. Me father may have stuck ye to me, but I'm too old for a nurse."

He was an older man, his head shaved but his whiskers well kept. "She's no good to ye dead. I've seen men pulled from that river who died a few hours later from the ordeal. The chill stops the heart. Hers is slowing now, that's why her fingers are blue. With the sun setting, ye'll need a fire, or she'll no' see the dawn. Mark me words."

Lye Rob looked down at her hands and cursed. "All right then."

He started up the incline, leaving her to his men. The older man took her in hand, laying an arm around her back as he half-carried her up the incline. Their horses were on the other side of the rise, leaving the sound of the river behind them and making sure they could hear anyone approaching them. There was a wagon, stuffed full of bags and other items.

But that didn't horrify her as much as the three women tied to the wheels of the wagon. Their clothing was dirty and their faces smudged with dirt. One was a Robertson, but the others were MacPhersons. All of them had pinched expressions as they tried to hide their fear.

"Add her to the plunder, Naughton," Lye Rob directed. "She's a fine prize to be taking home. Me father will have to take notice of me now."

Naughton took her close to the fire. He pushed her down gently. He knelt as Lye Rob tossed a length of rope over to him. It landed in the dirt because he was busy rubbing her feet.

"Got to get some warmth back into ye, lass."

He looked up at her, trying to tell her something. For a moment, she thought she was only seeing what she wanted to. That panic was pushing her to desperation. He was rubbing her feet, and she realized both her shoes were missing. One stocking was torn completely away, and the other was tattered. Her skin was scraped and cut, but he palmed something and pressed it against her calf. She blinked, trying to decide if she was really feeling that cold metal against her skin. Naughton gave her a hard look before he began to move it up her leg.

She bit her lip, sealing her protest inside her mouth as he reached all the way to her garter. No one except Bhaic had touched her thigh. She felt him slide whatever it was under her garter before pulling his hand down. He shot her a warning before he picked up the rope and looped it around her ankles. The knots he tied were snug but not too tight.

"Now give me yer hands. I've no care to handle ye, seeing as ye're another man's wife."

She forced herself to comply, focusing on the feeling of what was secure in her garter. It was a small eating knife. Like the one Marcus had insisted she not have. Her brother had shown her how to use one years ago.

It would be a last effort to keep herself from rape. Good only when her attacker was close enough to hit his vital organs and distracted enough for her to land her blow.

Yet, it was something.

She simply didn't know if it would be enough.

Six

"WE'RE ON GORDON LAND," MARCUS SAID, BUT Bhaic knew his brother well. He was saying what had to be said, even though he didn't care for it.

"He's got me wife," Bhaic cut back.

"Tied up, too." Marcus had a small spyglass in hand as he considered the men below them. "Not to mention a couple of other lasses. He'll still cry innocence when it's all said and done."

"Only if he's alive."

Waiting for true darkness took a long time. The moon was only a sliver in the sky. The perfect time for raiding. It was also the perfect time for an ambush. Bhaic eased closer, stopping often as he watched the horses tied up near the camp. If it wasn't for the captives, he'd have ridden into the camp and cut them down. But Lye Rob was no fool. Neither were his men. Some of them had rolled up in their plaids, right next to the women. The fighting was going to be hard if they wanted to avoid spilling innocent blood.

He looked back at the horses and eased closer.

❧

Lye Rob was getting drunk.

Ailis watched him tip a leather flagon up to his lips again and again. The other men with him had drink, but they took only a few sips to warm themselves. They knew better than to dull their wits.

Lye Rob? Well, he was obviously accustomed to having others look out for him.

She shivered and sent up a silent prayer of thanks for the circumstances that had prevented her from falling under the spell of the man. The courtship would have been grand, but the union a horror. More than one bride learned the true nature of her husband after the vows were spoken.

She shifted and realized the knots Naughton had tied were all loose. She had to hold onto the rope to keep it around her wrists. The fire had started to dry her, making her aware of all the dirt on her skin. She wanted to scratch and brush it off but had to remain still. She lowered her head to her bent knees and watched Lye Rob through her eyelashes.

He was looking at her, tipping the flagon again. His lips set into a smirk. He suddenly flipped his kilt up, exposing his swollen organ. She flinched, turning her head away.

"Knew ye were toying with me," Lye Rob said.

She heard his steps crunching the gravel on the ground as he came closer. His breath smelled of whisky when he hunched down beside her.

"Ye'll learn to enjoy me cock." He reached up and caught a handful of her hair. He yanked her head up so that their lips were only an inch apart. "Since I have to wait until ye bleed, I'm going to enjoy fucking yer mouth first."

She gasped with horror. He held her in place as his words sank in.

"Has yer husband no' gotten to that little delight?"

She tried to shake her head, but the hold on her hair was too painful. Lye Rob snickered.

"He would have. A pair of lips around the cock is just as sweet as shoving deep into a cunt."

He yanked his kilt up, exposing himself again. "It's a fine way to start our relationship, Ailis."

She turned away in spite of the pain shooting through her scalp, but he only tightened his grip, yanking her around. She reached for the dagger, pulling it free. One of the horses screamed in the distance. Lye Rob straightened and dragged her up in front of him, pressed a dagger against her throat as the camp was overrun.

She wanted to be relieved at the sight of the MacPhersons, but Lye Rob dug the tip of his dagger into her skin.

"I'll slit her throat!"

Bhaic pulled up out of the lunge he'd been in. She'd always known he had a savage side. Tonight, she faced it. He'd sheathed his sword in favor of his long dagger. Its blade was already bloodied, but the look in his eyes made it clear that what he truly craved was Lye Rob's blood.

It was the most beautiful sight she'd ever seen.

Lye Rob was twisting the knife, cutting into her neck. She could feel his heart hammering against her back as panic set in. Around them, men were dying, but it seemed insignificant, fading away as she became conscious of the details.

Like the feeling of the knife in her hand. She let the rope drop to the ground. Bhaic noticed it. He gave her only a fraction of a glance, but she knew he noticed.

He lifted his hand higher, drawing Lye Rob's attention. "Leave now, Lye Rob. Let me wife go, and I'll get off yer land."

"If I let her live, how long before the Robertsons and the MacPhersons unite and overrun Gordon land?"

He was dragging her backward, looking over his shoulder for an escape route. His voice was tense, telling one and all that his grip on reality was slipping.

Marcus appeared behind them. "Let her go," he warned softly.

Lye Rob turned to look at Marcus. Ailis tightened her grip on the dagger and drove it into his neck. She couldn't see her target, but she felt his blood covering her hand. Bhaic was a blur of motion, springing on them and grabbing the knife at her throat. She fell down, blood flowing over her shoulder before someone grasped her wrist and yanked her free of the fight.

She looked up into Finley's face, his expression harder than she'd ever seen it. No hint of the playful buffoon he'd so often appeared.

"Up with ye now, mistress."

He lifted her off her feet and set her behind him. She looked around him. Bhaic had Lye Rob on the ground, his hands wrapped around his throat. It was a violent struggle, both men powerful, but Lye Rob was losing. The smell of his blood was everywhere, and his body went taut a moment before he went limp.

Bhaic snarled something in Gaelic, squeezing Lye Rob's throat a few final times before Marcus was able to pull him off the body. He turned, searching for her. She stumbled around Finley, suddenly feeling every ache.

But being in his embrace soothed it all away. He trapped her against him, muttering against her hair. She buried her face against him, inhaling the scent of his skin. He cupped her face, raising her head so he could look at her. For a long moment, he just looked at her, the hands on the side of her face trembling just the tiniest bit.

"Ye can nae go riding alone."

She let out a snort. It was unladylike, but she was far past caring about appearances. "As if I could nae come to that conclusion meself."

"She might look rough about the edges, but she sounds right," Marcus said. "What do ye want to do with the survivors?"

Bhaic turned her loose, but kept her close with one solid grip on her wrist. The camp was in shambles. Bodies were slumped to the ground, the female captives freed. The surviving Gordons were herded together, the MacPhersons holding them under guard. Bloodlust was still running high.

She suddenly saw Naughton. His shoulder was bloodied, but the older man stood proudly, his chest puffed out as his fate was being decided.

Ailis curled in toward Bhaic. "Ye have to let that one with the silver beard go. He gave me the knife."

Bhaic looked down at her in confusion. She nodded. "No one chooses what clan they are born into."

"Aye."

He leaned over to discuss it with Marcus. Her brother-in-law cut her a curious look before he nodded.

She suddenly felt every scrape and bruise. Bhaic and Marcus moved off to deal with the Gordons as Finley stayed near, clearly resuming his post as her escort. She looked down and realized the rope was still knotted around one of her ankles. She sank down, intending to work the knot free, but her hands were covered in blood.

She stared at it, starting to shake.

Her belly twisted with nausea.

For some reason, her back felt on fire.

And she was unable to focus on anything.

"Here now, mistress."

She ended up staring at Finley's head in confusion as he gently brushed her hands away and finished untying the knot.

"Since when do ye call me mistress?" She probably shouldn't have asked the question, but she couldn't think. Couldn't seem to stop shaking either. She didn't wait for Finley to reply but became fixated on the blood on her hands.

"Did I kill him?"

"I did." Bhaic was suddenly there, scooping her off the ground. "Do nae think about it, lass. Ye did what ye had to."

He carried her over to the wagon, settling her in a spot that had been cleared. The other women were there, relief on their faces, but all Ailis could do was shake. She tried to unbuckle her belt and free her arisaid.

Bhaic ended up doing it for her. He lifted her again, and she sighed, the scent of his skin the only stable thing she could grasp. "Ye found me."

He held her for a moment, their gazes locked. "Ye're me wife."

"But—"

He settled her back down among the grain bundles. She rolled onto her side because her back was still on fire. He tucked her tattered arisaid around her.

"I'm no' letting ye sleep on Gordon land."

He smoothed the hair back from her face, considering her for a long moment. Something flickered in his eyes. Something that both warmed her and made her shiver. He removed the brooch holding his plaid onto his shoulder. He used a dagger from his belt and rent the fabric, tearing off the half that he might use to shield his shoulders from the night's chill. He laid it out on top of her, satisfaction showing on his face as the MacPherson colors covered her Robertson ones.

She started to say something, but he pressed a single fingertip against her lips to silence her.

"Let's go home," he said.

He was gone a moment later, his powerful stride holding her attention as she watched him mount and raise his hand to bring his men into line.

"He's a fair bit more attractive than the tales I've heard."

Ailis turned her head to look at the Robertson woman who had been one of the captives. She was young, not much more than a girl really. She smiled at Ailis as the wagon started moving, the MacPherson retainers surrounding it.

"Never thought I'd be happy to be traveling with MacPhersons," she said.

"I am," Ailis said as she started to slip away. She didn't fight against the darkness, letting it envelop her and snuff out the pain.

But she was glad.

Very glad indeed.

❧

She knew his scent.

Ailis sighed and rubbed her cheek against Bhaic. She felt as if she was floating or rolling around inside a cloud. There was daylight and darkness and voices that were far away. Time seemed impossible to grasp, and honestly, she just didn't want to.

And sometimes there was Bhaic.

Or maybe not.

She wasn't really sure.

❧

"It was only a little fever," Ailis said firmly.

"As if I'd be willing to risk yer health because ye were fortunate," Helen said, still standing in front of the chamber door.

"Ye were very fortunate," Senga said softly from where she was changing the bed sheets with Elise. The young Robertson had been there when Ailis woke up, settling in with Helen.

Now that her head was clear, Ailis looked toward Senga. "Are ye sure ye wish to stay?"

Senga stopped and let Elise finish. "I've no home to go back to. The Gordons burned it and killed me father. Even if I were to rebuild it, how would I protect meself? Besides, I've no intention of arguing with the good Lord's will. He sent me father's enemies to rescue me. So, I think yer marriage is what he's wanting." She smiled. "I'll prove meself to ye, mistress."

Elise bit her lip, obviously realizing she'd lost her opportunity to secure a higher position in the household. Now, she was a chambermaid, holding stacks of fresh linens for Senga.

"I need fresh air." Ailis was sick of looking out the window. "I am going for a walk."

Helen grunted but moved aside. Ailis's memory was cloudy, and she wasn't even sure what day it was.

All the more reason to take a walk and get her blood flowing.

Ha! Ye're running away because ye're in yer husband's chamber.

It was the truth. One she had no idea how to wrap her thoughts around.

But she'd woken up in Bhaic's chamber, and that was a hard fact.

Finley was leaning against the wall with Skene. They both reached up and tugged on the corners of their bonnets when she opened the door. She offered them a soft smile as she started down the stairs.

"Here now… Mistress…wait for just a wee moment…" Finley cupped her elbow.

"I am very well," she assured him.

He didn't release her. "Well now, I can nae be having yer husband thinking I let ye take a tumble."

They reached the bottom of the stairs, and Skene tugged on his cap as he hurried off somewhere. Finley fell into step behind her, but it felt as though he was hovering. People looked up as she passed. The day was half gone, and the scent of baking bread came down the passageway from the kitchens.

Had she really slept so late?

She moved through the great hall, drawn toward the door by the sunlight. Two more retainers fell in with Finley.

"I do nae need to be taking up yer time," she assured them.

They tugged on their caps but made no move to leave. She was torn between them and the sunlight.

Freedom won.

She made it out the door and sighed. The yard was full of activity, and it felt as if she'd been locked away from it all. Her brain seemed to be working slower than normal, but she could feel the stiffness leaving her joints.

A horse came through the gate, Bhaic leaning low over its neck. He pulled up at the base of the steps and swung his leg over the horse's head before sliding to the ground.

He was up the steps in a flash.

"Should ye be up, lass?" There was concern in his eyes that confused her.

"Why shouldn't I be?"

He studied her for a long moment. "Because ye've been fighting a fever for the better part of two weeks."

Her eyes widened. "I didn't realize it had been… well, I'm quite well."

He flashed her a smile and slid an arm around her waist. She felt his breath brush her ear as he tilted his head close to hers. "Ye're shaking."

She was.

But she couldn't bring herself to admit it. "I just wanted to stretch me legs."

Bhaic's expression softened, a hint of compassion flickering in his blue eyes. "I've something I wanted to show ye."

He guided her down the steps and lifted her up to the saddle. He mounted behind her and pulled her against his body. He looked back at her escort. "Taking her up to the stables."

Finley nodded before Bhaic turned his stallion and sent it toward the gate. She was suddenly surrounded by him, shivering as he enclosed her with his embrace.

The stallion carried them easily beyond the walls of the castle and up toward the stable. He slid from the saddle first, reaching back up to help her down.

"I'm not delicate."

He raised one dark eyebrow. "I do nae want to argue with ye, but ye look as though a stiff wind might blow ye over."

"It was only a little fever."

He looked at her as if she'd gone simple. "Do ye remember yer father coming to see ye?"

"Me father?"

Bhaic chuckled softly and reached up to tap his jaw, where she noticed a dark bruise.

"How could me father land a blow on ye?" she scoffed.

"I let him."

"Oh," she said softly, completely at a loss for words. "But why?"

She'd stopped next to a stall and realized her knees were weak. She leaned on the railing as a young lad took the stallion.

"It was me failing that allowed ye to end up fighting for yer life."

She tried to think. "I just went for a ride to clear me thoughts…oh…someone shot at me." The memory rose up from what seemed like a long passage of time she couldn't recall. But bits and pieces were starting to take shape. They were flashing through her memory, startling her as though she were experiencing them for the first time.

Bhaic nodded. "At yer colors, Ailis. The man thought ye were raiding."

She looked down at her arisaid. "Oh, I suppose… well…"

"Aye. It's something more than one man would think in the predawn light."

She looked back at his jaw. "Ye shouldn't have let me father hit ye." She reached out and touched the dark spot.

Touching him dusted off another memory, and another and another. "Did ye…were ye there with me? I recall ye."

"Of course I was. Every night."

She pulled her hand back, but he caught it, folding his fingers around hers. The touch was strangely intimate and surprisingly familiar. She stared at their fingers. "Ye were. But why?"

He kissed the back of her hand. "I did nae send ye from me bed, Ailis, and we're going to be discussing things when ye're a bit stronger. On that, ye can count. But no' just now."

He pointed out one of the wide doorways. She followed him outside and smiled at the young colt playing in the sunlight next to his mother.

"I would have brought ye up a bit sooner if fate were nae having such a fine time toying with us."

"So this is the fellow who interrupted us."

He was a black colt. His coat shimmered in the morning light, his eyes glittering with spirit. He would dance away from his mother's side, kicking at the air before returning when she snorted at him. Someday, he'd be a powerful stallion, worth a fortune if he could be trained to take a rider. She avoided using the word "broken," because there was something in the colt's eyes that told her he was far more valuable with his spirit intact.

Bhaic took her to the rail of the corral, and she sat down. "Aye. I plan to remind him in a few years when he spies himself a pretty mare and I tell him she's no' ready for him. But I'll likely end up commiserating with him, for I know the frustration of waiting out a lass."

She reached out and slapped him on the shoulder. "Ye had to wait an entire week to have me. What suffering ye have endured."

"Ye think that's all I'm waiting for?" He clicked his tongue. "There's more to a good marriage than passion, but I'm no' complaining about the fact that ye can nae keep yer hands off me."

He flashed her a grin, and she discovered her cheeks heating. They might have been anyone. In that moment, there was only the warm spring day, the scent of growing crops all around them, and the twisting in her belly as she looked at Bhaic. He was watching her, his gaze full of hunger. It shifted to her mouth, making her breath catch. He leaned toward her, his breath teasing her lips.

Finley's voice intruded. "There they are."

Bhaic grunted. "I always thought getting married would end the need to sneak off into the shadows with a lass."

"Can nae ye tell them to simply go away?" she asked as she blushed. "I thought it was only a matter of us…um…"

"Making things official?" he teased her.

She nodded, certain her cheeks had never been so red. Bhaic noticed, reaching out to tap one of her crimson cheekbones.

"Do nae enjoy yerself so much," she warned him.

His grin grew until his teeth were flashing. "I plan to enjoy meself quite a bit with ye and make sure ye like it too."

"Well no' at the moment, it would seem." She looked over to where Finley was leaning against the side of the barn. He was looking off to the side but keeping them in his sight.

"Aye. Ye may thank me father for them this time."

"I thought it was Marcus setting them on me heels," she said. "Is nae he now satisfied that I am no' planning to take secrets back to me father?"

"Aye," Bhaic answered. "But now yer father made me father swear ye would nae be at risk."

Her jaw dropped. "Me father…*made*…yer father?"

Bhaic nodded once, obviously suffering from injured pride. "No' that I was nae planning on taking ye in hand."

"What do ye mean 'in hand'?"

He grunted and stood up. "This is no' the time."

"It is indeed a fine time," she argued.

"Ailis," he warned her in a low tone.

"Do nae sound like yer brother." She stood up to face him, actually poking him in the chest with her finger. "Ye'll be telling me what ye want from me now. I've had quite enough of worrying over ye and me circumstances."

Something flashed through his eyes before he leaned over and tossed her right over his shoulder.

Her belly twisted, and she realized it was with excitement.

Well, what's the matter with that? He's yer husband, isn't he?

She was giggling when he let her down in another stall freshly made with a bed of sweet-smelling hay.

"A much better place to be telling ye what I want from ye, lass," Bhaic informed her. He was big and imposing, just like the first time she'd seen him. Sensation rippled across her skin, but this time, she knew anticipation when she felt it.

Aye, "anticipation" was the right word.

She was nervous, twisting her hands as she tried to decide what to do. She felt the buckle of her belt and unfastened it. She pulled her arisaid free and shook it out so that it lay on the straw.

He pulled off his sword belt and left it hanging on the stall post. He reached out and cupped the top of her breast. "Ye enjoy me taking ye in hand…"

"Sometimes…"

He leaned down and claimed her mouth in a kiss. She hadn't realized how starved she was for it. The memory of her tumbling in the river returned, bringing with it a need to live.

No, a desperation to survive.

She kissed him back. Opening her lips and thrusting her tongue up into his mouth. Her passage ached, too empty to endure. She needed him. Needed him to fill her. Fill her with life.

And she wanted him right now.

He was pulling on her laces, opening the front of her dress until he could get at her. He scooped her up and cradled her on the way to the ground. Coming down to nuzzle against her breasts.

"I'll make sure that ye like it every time, lass, I swear that to ye."

The husky promise made her twist with anticipation. He kissed his way across one plump mound until he captured the puckered tip between his lips. She gasped, feeling as though his mouth burned.

But it was a sweet agony. One she wanted more of. She plunged her hands into his hair and held him in place. He suddenly lifted away from her.

"Does it hurt? Yer back?"

She'd been sinking into a vortex of heat and had to blink before his words made sense. "Why should it?"

"Because the bullet tore across yer shoulders. The healer had to stitch it."

He lifted her and rolled over so she was sitting on top of him. He grinned, reaching up and cradling her breasts in his hands.

"It doesn't hurt, but I've half a mind to tell ye otherwise." Her knees were on either side of his hips. She should have felt awkward, but a sense of control was sweeping through her, filling her with a confidence she'd never suspected she might feel. He was hard, his member a solid presence beneath the thin layers of his kilt.

His expression became hungry. "Like being in the saddle, do ye?"

"Possibly." She lifted herself up and settled back down to see what it felt like. "But I'm fairly certain I haven't successfully mounted ye just yet."

She rose up again and made sure her skirts were out of the way. Bhaic grabbed handfuls of the fabric and tossed it up so her thighs were bared. He gripped the bare skin above her garters, his expression tightening with hunger.

The sight sent confidence roaring through her. She'd never felt so much in control, so much a match for anyone.

She lifted off him again, and this time, he yanked his kilt up. His member sprang up, and he held it steady as she lowered herself onto it.

"Now, let's see if ye can stay in the saddle."

She'd started to close her eyes, the feeling of him inside her overwhelming. But his words were edged in challenge, and she opened her eyes and considered him.

"I'm a Robertson."

"Ye are indeed." He reached around and cupped her bottom. "But ye are also mine."

He lifted her and thrust up into her. She gasped, reeling in a wave of sensation before she tried to regain control. It became a battle, Ailis trying to set the pace while he met every downward thrust and held her bottom in place so he might impale her. Frustration grew inside her at the same pace that the need to surrender to him did.

Sweat beaded on her skin, her heart pounding frantically as she tried to hold back the building explosion until she'd pushed him to the same extreme. But he wasn't going to let her. He suddenly released her bottom, letting gravity slam her onto his length as he slid his hand across her belly and found the little pearl at the top of her sex. He fingered it, pressing hard on it as she rose and fell on him again. She was fighting back her climax, riding him hard as she tried to push him into one as well.

But she was losing her grip, her body refusing to obey. Pleasure spiked through her, twisting her as it exploded beneath his fingers. Her passage contracted, gripping his flesh as she cried out. He sat up, taking control as he flipped her over onto her knees and started hammering into her.

She ended up braced on her elbows, Bhaic gripping her hips as he took her. It was the hard possession she'd craved, setting off another, deeper wave of satisfaction. It was too intense to contain, her cry echoing inside the stall.

Bhaic growled a moment before his seed began to flood her. He pumped himself against her a few final times before they ended up in a heap of quivering limbs. Somehow he rolled over and pulled her with him, pressing her head onto his chest as they lay there, trying to recover.

Ailis didn't really care if they ever did.

In those moments, she didn't have any doubts. She was floating on a wave of satisfaction and could feel Bhaic quivering with the same feeling. The circumstances of their forced union were finally irrelevant. What mattered was the way they took each other into ecstasy.

Somewhere in the distance, Finley laughed. Bhaic smoothed a hand over her shoulder before moving to right his clothing. She found the ends of the tie threaded through her chemise neckline and tugged it tight again.

But she froze when she realized Bhaic was watching her.

"Do nae begrudge me yer private moments, lass." He was sitting in the straw, one knee raised and his arm resting on it.

Her fingers were clumsy as she worked the lace through the eyelets on the front of her bodice. She tugged them tight, suffering from embarrassment when she had to adjust her breasts with him watching.

"Becoming yer maid suddenly has merit."

His gaze dropped to the Robertson plaid spread out beneath them. "Yer colors…"

He stood up and lifted her to her feet. She reached back down for the length of wool, but stopped when she realized there was a hole torn through the fabric. It was large, and the edges charred.

"Ye can nae wear them."

He pulled the fabric from the floor and held it over his arm.

"Haddox will no' be the only one who sees these colors and thinks we're being raided."

It seemed she wasn't finished settling in. His words were logical, the charred hole lending weight to his argument. She offered him a single nod and turned toward the stall doorway.

Bhaic pulled her back. "I'm sorry, Ailis. I know what I'm asking of ye."

He did.

She witnessed the proof of it in his eyes. The sight touched something inside her, some need she wasn't able to define. It felt as if he might be able to fill it, if she were willing to surrender completely to him.

Of course, it would be an unconditional surrender.

But then again, she doubted a MacPherson knew any other way.

Or that she could bend so very completely without snapping.

"I think I'd like to bathe." It was an excuse. A place to hide while she sorted out her thoughts. He knew it too. His expression tightened, but he let her remain silent as he took her back to the castle.

But he kept her colors.

She turned at the top of the stairs and looked back at him. She lifted her hand for her arisaid. Bhaic shook his head.

The distrust stung.

Oh, aye. "Unconditional" was the right word.

She honestly doubted she could manage it.

Which left her with a bitter taste in her mouth.

Trust. Such a small word for so large an idea.

❧

She was starving.

When the cook rang the supper bells, Ailis wasn't sure she wanted to stay awake long enough to eat. But the sight of her bed didn't look inviting, so she went down to the hall.

At the first whiff of food, her belly rumbled.

Her mouth actually started watering.

She was shaking as she climbed the stairs to the high ground and sat down. The staff was putting the supper out, the aromas driving her nearly insane. Her belly was so empty it hurt. Waiting for Shamus seemed like a torment. Time moved at a snail's pace as she grasped handfuls of her skirt to keep from grabbing at the food before he blessed the meal.

"Now there is a fine sight," Shamus remarked as he gained the high ground. He sent her a wink before settling down.

Bhaic followed with Marcus. Below them, the retainers were moving the benches around, filling the hall with laughter and jesting.

Her belly rumbled again. But the meal began, granting her relief from one of her torments. Her appetite might have been raging, but it was soon satisfied. She wanted to eat more, but her insides felt as though they were near bursting.

A moment later, her eyelids felt too heavy to hold up. The meal was only half over, but she feared she was going to end up snoring on the tabletop if she didn't get up. Bhaic raised an eyebrow when she started to move, but nodded and looked back at his father, who was in the middle of telling some tale from his youth.

Her own father would be doing something similar.

Finley noticed her from where he was eating at the bottom of the high ground. He reached for a round of bread. He tore it open and stuffed a thick slice of meat inside it before sliding his bench back.

"I'm going straight up. I promise," she said.

He'd stopped halfway off the bench. "A promise, is it?"

Ailis nodded. Finley considered her for a moment before he settled back down. "Straight up then, and I'll be looking in on ye when I come up. I'll knock, mind ye."

It was a small thing, but she was discovering that trust was something very necessary. Bhaic didn't trust her.

The knowledge hurt.

❧

She started to pull the pins from her hair, setting them carefully on the small table next to her mirror. The chamber was neat and ready, showing that everyone was as unsure of her place as she was.

"Why are ye here, Ailis?"

Her comb went clattering to the floor. She was off the stool, stumbling back because of how deeply she'd been in her thoughts. Bhaic reached out and caught a handful of her skirt to steady her.

"Ye do nae sleep here." His tone was solid, his expression tight. "Ye know where ye sleep."

"Why?"

His eyes narrowed. "Why do ye sleep in me chamber?"

She nodded. "Ye do nae trust me no' to wear me arisaid, so why would ye trust me beside ye at night."

He muttered something under his breath. "I took yer arisaid because I can nae stand the thought of ye in peril." He offered her his hand.

She stared at it for a long moment, earning a soft chuckle from him.

"I am no' the only one learning to trust, lass."

"Ye give up much less than I do." She probably

shouldn't have spoken. Shouldn't have let him see how exposed she felt.

"Aye. But I can nae be changing the way the world works. Ye are here." He reached a little closer, still offering his hand.

"Aye, and ye've had me today. I'm tired."

He dropped his hand and made a soft sound. "Ye think all I crave from ye is the release I gain from coupling with ye?" He closed the distance between them and scooped her off her feet.

"Put me down."

He'd already carried her out of the room by the time she finished protesting. The flight of stairs between their chambers passed in a flash, before he was angling her through his doorway and kicking the door shut with his foot.

"Now I will," he said. He set her on her feet but stood in front of the closed door.

"What do ye think ye're proving?" she asked.

"That ye are more than a duty."

His words caught her off guard. He moved closer and cupped her shoulder, turning her around. "This is the only place I can be meself, Ailis. Something I think ye know a little about from being yer father's only daughter."

"Aye, I do."

He was so solid behind her.

Her attention settled on something. She blinked and peered closer. Sitting on the table was her arisaid, folded neatly but not hidden away. Most unions, such as hers and Bhaic's, would have allowed her to continue to wear her colors, while their children wore his.

"Marcus advised me to burn it," he said.

She snorted.

Bhaic smoothed his hands over her shoulders. "It's his way of protecting ye. Harsh, aye, but ye would no' make the mistake of riding out in the predawn light with it again. Marcus will always take the method that allows no opportunities to catch him unawares."

"I suppose there is logic to that way of thinking," she conceded. "Why didn't ye take his advice?"

"Ye're right when ye point out I am nae expected to give up so much of meself in this union. Burning yer father's colors seemed more like stripping ye of yer identity. There may be times ye'll want to wear them. *Inside*."

He stressed the last word, gaining a soft sound of amusement from her.

"Since ye were willing to give Finley yer word, perhaps ye can ease me mind as well," he said.

"I'm no' foolish," she said. "Even if fate seems to be having a merry time at me expense."

"Aye, she has been making the pair of us dance to her tune sure enough. I'm no' sure any other couple has had more trouble consummating a wedding."

The chamber echoed with the soft sound of their amusement. It was balm for her wounds, soothing the hurt and offering the companionship she'd felt so deprived of.

But from her husband?

Was such a thing possible?

Men and women were simply so different.

Her hair was sagging, since half the pins were removed. She reached back to finish the job, but Bhaic brushed her hand aside and began searching out the remaining pins.

"Well, we did manage it…after all." The words were past her lips before she realized what she was discussing so openly.

"Aye."

Her hair fell down her back. He threaded his fingers through it, leaning down and inhaling its scent. His tone was husky and possessive, but she liked it. He kissed her nape, and a shiver went down her back.

"Is it so wrong of me to want ye to settle in at me side?" He turned her slowly but kept her close.

"I suppose I never thought ye'd care to have me so close."

He lifted her chin, their gazes locking. "I know I nearly went mad while ye were locked in the grip of that fever." He stroked her cheek, his eyes flashing with hard purpose. "Ye're mine, Ailis Robertson, and I plan to keep ye close at hand."

He didn't give her time to respond. He tilted his head and pressed his lips down on hers. She rose on her toes to kiss him back. In his embrace, there wasn't a boundary between them.

There was only the need to be joined completely.

He was more accomplished at disrobing her than she wanted to dwell on.

"The number is no' that high," he said.

She stepped back, feeling as if he'd read her mind.

Bhaic chuckled as he reached out to pull the lace on the front of her bodice free from the last two eyelets. "But I do admit to enjoying more than a quick toss of the skirts against the wall."

Her eyes widened. "How...never mind." An image burst into her head, dispelling all innocence.

Bhaic laughed. "Yer father deserves more credit than I'd ever have thought. How did he control his men so completely that ye never saw a couple in the passageway after sundown?"

"Well..." She was moving away from him, slowly retreating from the intimate nature of the conversation. Her bodice fell down her arms and ended up abandoned on the floor. "I suppose...me brother Duncan is more like Marcus than I realized. His men were forever with me."

Keeping her innocent, so she'd be useful.

Bhaic reached for the tie holding her skirt closed. She slapped his hand away. It was a light blow, but the sound echoed in the quiet chamber. His expression tightened.

"I think I've had enough of being groomed..." Her tone had turned husky, the confidence she'd felt during the afternoon at the stable returning in a rush. She let it flood her.

"In fact..." She forced herself to move toward him. Surprise flickered in his eyes as his lips curved. "I'm so very tired of everyone deciding what is best for me."

He nodded as she reached for his belt and very boldly worked the buckle until she was able to let it fall to the floor.

"I'm tired of being...settled in..." She pulled the edges of his plaid free of the brooch that held it over his shoulder. "Tired of being watched..."

She found the second belt holding his kilt around his lean waist and opened the buckle. The wool slipped easily down his body, leaving only the soft linen of his shirt. His member was standing up, pushing the fabric away from his groin.

"Really tired of being innocent."

She reached beneath the tail of the shirt and closed her fingers around his length. He sucked in a breath, hissing through his teeth. She was mesmerized by the way his jaw tightened. Against her palm, his member was hot, and covered in satin-smooth skin. She drew her hand up from the base to the tip and smiled at the groan that escaped his lips.

"It will be me pleasure to help ye become a woman who gives as much as she receives," he said.

He reached inside her open chemise, cupping one breast. It was her turn to gasp, sensation swirling through her. He brushed his thumb over her nipple, the sensitive tip drawing tight beneath his touch.

"And I'm going to enjoy having ye in me bed…"

He popped the lace on her skirt and pushed it down and over her hips. She jumped back, ending up in nothing but her chemise and stockings.

"Bare yerself for me, Ailis…"

He was working the buttons on his cuffs. She was still backing up, grasping for the control that had filled her with such boldness. But she realized it was a struggle between them, and it always would be. It was in both of their natures.

So…she'd just fight fire with fire.

She pulled her chemise over her head. Her heart pounded, warming her so the night air felt good against her skin. His eyes narrowed as he contemplated her, taking a long time to study her.

"Ye're beautiful." He reached behind his neck and pulled his shirt over his head.

She set her teeth into her lower lip as she let her gaze slip down his body. He had a light coating of dark hair across his chest that tapered to his belly. His member was thick and long. She really hadn't realized how large it was.

He was closing the distance between them, and the fine hairs on her skin were rising up as his body heat teased them. Moments became tiny eternities, time slowing down to allow her to be cognizant of every little detail.

He touched her forearms first. Just his fingertips, gliding up the outside of her arms, to her elbows and on up until he was sliding his hands across her shoulders.

She reached for him, completing the moment. She was trembling and fighting for breath as she threaded her fingers through his chest hair.

"I do nae deserve the fact that ye waited for me… while I did nae keep meself to the same standard…" His tone was hard, edged with possessiveness as he gathered up her hair in one hand and stepped up to bring their bodies into full contact. "But I'd be a liar if I did nae admit how much I enjoy knowing ye are mine and mine alone."

The kiss he pressed against her mouth swamped her thoughts. It was full of hunger, and she matched it with her own appetite. She was twisting in his embrace, needing more contact between them. He held her captive to his will, kissing her hard and long before he scooped her up and took her to his bed.

They rolled across its huge surface, and he flattened

her beneath his body. She let out a cry as she opened her thighs to cradle his hips. It seemed the most natural position, and another sound of enjoyment hit the canopy above their heads as he lowered himself onto her, the head of his member slipping between the wet folds of her cleft.

"Sweet Christ," he groaned as he pushed deep inside her. "I truly…meant to…let ye rest…"

"Later," she said, lifting to take his next thrust and listening with surprise at the sound that came out of her.

Breathless.

Carnal.

She didn't care. All that mattered was working in time with his rhythm. Rising to meet each downward plunge. Taking his member as deep as she could, all the while being pushed further and further into a churning storm of sensation.

She was twisting, straining toward the end. Craving it, and at the same time, wanting to enjoy the journey. But self-discipline was completely beyond her grasp. There was only the current and its grip. It pulled her along with it, into the center of the storm, pleasure exploding through her and pulling every muscle she had tight enough to break. She cried out.

Or maybe it was Bhaic.

In truth, it seemed as though they were a single being.

Both strained toward each other; both tried to grip the pulsing heart of life. It dropped them back into reality with a jolt, leaving them listening to their own harsh breathing.

❦

Someone was next to her.

Ailis opened her eyes and stiffened, sitting up. The room was dark, the hearth embers putting out only a tiny red glow.

"Naught is amiss, lass."

She jumped and heard Bhaic chuckle. He reached up and stroked her arm before rising from the bedding and closing his arms around her.

"Go back to sleep."

He didn't wait for her to comply, gathering her close, pulling the bedding around them as he settled her against his body.

She didn't know what to think of it, but his scent soothed something inside her. Awakening a memory of him being beside her, holding her. Honestly, she didn't need to think.

⁓

"Still in bed, little brother?"

Ailis squealed, jumping as Marcus's voice boomed in the early morning. Bhaic snarled and flipped over, coming out of the bedding to shield her. It wasn't necessary. Marcus was in the outer doorway, his back to them.

"Ye need a wife!" Bhaic shouted before the door shut.

"A demanding one," Ailis added. "To slow him down a bit."

Bhaic looked toward her, but his gaze settled on her bare shoulders.

"Ye make a fetching sight."

He made a soft sound before he grabbed a shirt and put it on. The morning sun was streaming through the windows, shaming them both with how long they'd slept. Ailis crawled out of the bedding, her body stiff.

She scooped up her chemise, but froze when she caught sight of herself in the long mirror. Across her shoulder was a dark, jagged line, impossible to miss. She started to turn, slowly, until she was looking over her shoulder at her reflection. The path the bullet had traveled across her back was marked with a half-healed line an inch wide in places. Her skin was sewn together, the edges uneven and red.

"It will look better in time, lass." Bhaic moved toward her and looked at the healing wound. "There was so much dirt in it from the river. Little wonder ye were taken with fever for so long."

She was fortunate.

She tried to focus on that as she put on her chemise, but all she could see was the jagged scar.

Bhaic cupped her chin, raising her face so their eyes met. "Ye're strong. That's what that scar says about ye. The healer had ye given last rites."

"I didn't realize…"

He slid an arm around her when she tried to step away. "Did nae realize how close ye came to leaving this world?" He locked her against him, keeping their gazes fused. "I recall every last moment of it. I've never spent so much time on me knees."

"Ye prayed…for me?"

There was a flash of something in his eyes that touched off a storm of emotions inside her.

"I treasure ye, Ailis."

No one, outside her family, had ever treasured her. He pressed a hard kiss against her lips.

"And I have no idea what it means, only that fate seems to think ye and I belong together. So perhaps we should try doing as we're being directed." He released her and walked back to where he'd been pleating his kilt.

"Ye mean kicked in the tail until we fall into line."

He looked up from his pleating and shot her a wicked grin. "Into bed, ye mean."

Considering she'd spent the night in his bed, she shouldn't have blushed. But she did, turning away to fumble with her skirt. He buckled his kilt and captured her while she was busy trying to avoid his gaze.

"I'm beginning to see why the French lock new bridal couples into a chamber for a month with all the honey mead they can drink." He kissed her soundly until she melted and kissed him back.

"Ye need to learn to be easy in me company," he said.

He released her, grabbed his second belt, and secured it around his waist before retrieving his bonnet from the table. With a wink, he headed for the door and disappeared, giving her a glimpse of Skene waiting outside.

Easy in his company?

She was fairly sure her hair would be gray before such a thing came to pass.

Seven

SUMMER CAME, AND THE CROPS RIPENED.

Ailis spent more time in the kitchens, overseeing the enormous task of preparing the castle for the lean months of winter. Wagonloads of fleece came in from where Bhaic and his men were supervising the shearing of the sheep. Days passed in which all she did was catalog load after load of wool.

They built fires near the banks of the river, setting huge caldrons on them to warm. They all tucked their skirts up to kept their hems from the flames as fleece was dunked into the hot water and washed.

Her hands were rough from the lye soap, but the bundles of drying fleece pleased her. It was the sight of prosperity, of life. The fleece would be sold south, bringing income. It was so valuable, Bhaic took over half the retainers with him every morning to safeguard the incoming wagons. Some nights, he didn't return.

Her brothers would be doing the same.

But for the first time, Bhaic and Duncan wouldn't be raiding each other.

Aye, "hopeful" was the word for her mood.

Even Angus wasn't shooting her suspicious looks anymore. The burly captain had settled into a silent contemplation she might have called a glare if she wasn't feeling hopeful.

At least until the night she caught a whiff of her supper and ran from the hall. Two serving maids had to jump out of her path, or she would have run them over. Finley stood up so fast, he turned over the bench he'd been sitting on. Men looked up, and Lyel took off after her, but all Ailis could manage to focus on was not throwing up in the hall.

She ended up in her chamber, draped over the chamber pot that was thankfully empty.

"Here now…" Helen said as she and Senga arrived.

"Give me a moment…"

They both ignored her, coming around the privacy screen. Helen wiped her face with a cool cloth as Senga helped her off her knees.

"Really, I do nae need help," Ailis protested. What she needed was a corner to hide in.

Lyel had the outer door of the chamber pushed open, looking in, trying to judge her condition for himself. There was shuffling on the steps as Finley brought up the healer.

"I'm fine," Ailis said.

She was completely ignored.

"Ye'll sit, mistress." Marcus took several long steps into the chamber, making it clear he wasn't leaving until the healer had seen her. "And we'll hear what the healer has to say."

"What are ye doing in me chamber?"

Marcus hooked her upper arms and lifted her right

off her feet. She gained a brief moment of shocking firsthand understanding of just how strong he was before he deposited her on a stool.

"Yer husband is nae here. So yer health is me concern."

The healer was a thin man who wore a leather skullcap. It came down over his forehead, hiding all of his forehead and almost all of his eyebrows. He squinted at her as he held a candle up to her face. He examined her hands and fingernails, turning them over several times with his lips set into a hard line.

"No poison."

Ailis gasped. "I never thought there was."

But Marcus clearly had. He looked toward the open door and nodded at Lyel. "Tell Duana she can finish serving supper."

"Really, it was just a queasy belly."

The healer grunted before standing. "I suggest ye send a midwife up."

Marcus had been watching with an unreadable expression, his arms crossed over his chest. The first genuine smile she'd ever seen appeared on his lips, lasting only a moment before he turned and disappeared through the doorway.

A midwife?

❧

Bhaic and his men escorted the last of the fleece. The village was full of cheering when they were sighted on the road, and someone even rang the church bell.

In response, the men on the walls of the castle began to ring the bells. Ailis left the drying bundles of wool and started down the road toward the castle with the rest of the women.

But she stopped, watching the stallion charging up the road toward them. Bhaic was leaning low over the beast's neck, letting him have his freedom. The stallion made good use of his strong legs, sprinting up the road until Bhaic pulled him up, slowing him with a firm hand. The stallion snorted, clearly unhappy. Bhaic leaned over and hooked her about the waist. He pulled her off the ground and onto the stallion.

She ended up gripping him for dear life as the women around her laughed.

All Ailis cared about was the way his scent filled her senses.

Bhaic.

She shivered, feeling as though the scent touched her. How long had they been separated? Was it really long enough to feel so needy?

She dug her fingers into his clothing, uncaring if she tore it off him. He growled next to her ear, the sound raising gooseflesh along her body.

They reached the stable, and he rode right inside it, slipping off the back of the stallion before he reached up to help her down.

She slid happily into his embrace.

"I can nae wait…" he said, his tone as strained as she felt. He pressed her back, kissing her as he plunged one hand into the neckline of her dress.

"Christ, how I've missed ye."

She bumped into the wall but didn't care. She was too busy trying to find his skin. She tore at the buttons on his doublet, and then the ones on his shirt, purring when she bared his skin at last.

"Want me, do ye?" he asked.

He'd grasped a handful of her hair and pulled it just tight enough to send a prickle of pain across her scalp. His eyes were full of need, and she would have sworn his nostrils were flared.

It was blunt.

And carnal.

She raked her fingernails down the bare skin of his chest. "I want ye to satisfy me."

He shuddered, his body flinching before he kissed her.

Hard, savagely, and completely satisfying. She rose on her toes, pressing her mouth to his, opening her lips and boldly thrusting her tongue.

He growled and bit her softly on the side of the neck.

She arched against him as desire slammed into her like a lightning strike.

He grasped her skirts, dragging them up until he could cup her bottom. It was pawing, but it twisted her insides with an intensity that forced a gasp past her lips.

He was lifting her up, using his body to push her against the wall. She clasped his shoulders and locked her legs around his waist.

"That's it, lass…cling to me. I swear to Christ, I'll die if ye do nae."

He pressed into her, plunging his length deep. She gasped, arching toward him as she used her legs to pull him to her. The wall was rough against her back, but it gave her a solid place to take the hard ride Bhaic gave her.

She didn't care. Honestly didn't have any room in her head for thoughts.

There was only the need and the delight churning inside her. Like two sides of a coin, it was impossible to separate them. She craved him, and he satisfied her with every hard thrust. But the moment he withdrew, she hungered again. Bhaic felt it too, riding her with more strength, greater speed, until it all burst. She clung to him because the alternative was to fly apart.

He ground himself into her, his seed hot against her insides.

"Christ…" He nuzzled against her neck, kissing the spot he'd bitten. "I should nae have done that."

"I am no' complaining." She sounded husky, and he chuckled softly.

"Well now…ye were doing a fair bit of yelling…"

She slapped his shoulder and unlocked her legs. "There's the thanks I get for giving ye a warm welcome home."

Her skirts settled, but she was still leaning against the wall. Bhaic stroked her cheek, his eyes flickering with a warmth that touched her deeply.

"It was a fine welcome, lass. One I'll no' forget."

For a moment, she was struck deeply by how tender his gaze was. The loneliness that seemed her constant companion evaporated as he stroked her cheek with the back of his hand. It was as though he was the other part of her. She hadn't realized she'd longed for him until he'd returned.

Men were starting to make their way into the stables

now, horses snorting, happy to be home. Bhaic's stallion had found an empty stall and was busy eating.

Bhaic backed away from her, turning to begin relieving his stallion of its saddle. She watched for a moment, soaking him up.

⁊

Shamus was in good cheer at supper, slapping the table and laughing as he retold stories. The hall was full of more life than it had been. Ailis sat at the high table longer than she had in weeks, nibbling on a piece of bread. The staff knew not to fill her plate, but Bhaic stared at the empty place with a question on his face.

She shook her head, not wanting to pull him away from his father. But Shamus caught her motion.

"Have eyes only for yer wife?" he demanded. "Well now, I recall being much the same way. Off to bed with ye. I'm looking forward to a grandson."

Bhaic pushed his chair back, and hers as well. He clasped her hand and pulled her above stairs at a speed that had her heart pounding.

For all that she'd slept in his chamber while he was gone, she felt shy with him there now. There was still so much about him she didn't know.

Like what he'll do now that his seed has taken root...

It was a fear, and she couldn't deny it. More than one man left his wife to the duty of growing his babe while he enjoyed dallying with others. It was possible Bhaic might think his duty complete, at least as far as sharing her bed.

The slipper tub was still in the chamber, the water emptied.

"I should have bathed before having ye welcome me home," he said softly, "but I could nae help meself."

He came up behind her, closing his arms around her. "But now…"

He nuzzled her neck, pressing a soft kiss against it and then kissing his way to her collarbone.

"Yes?" she asked. "Now…what?"

A soft chuckle was his response before he stepped away from her just enough to get at the laces on the back of her dress.

"Now, I am going to enjoy spending the night in bed, with me wife." His voice had a wicked promise in it.

Her bodice sagged, and he eased it over her shoulders and down her arms.

"I'm sure the Earl of Morton would be pleased."

He grunted behind her and found the lace that kept her skirts tied about her waist.

"Fate has a strange sense of humor," he said. "I'd have cheerfully run the man through a season ago."

Her skirts puddled around her ankles, and she turned around as she stepped free of them.

"Go to me bed." His tone was edged with demand, but a needy form of it she never would have thought she'd ever crave. "I want to see ye waiting there for me."

She tugged off her chemise, standing for a moment in nothing but her skin. His gaze swept her from head to toe, his features sharpening as he began to disrobe. Ailis took a step back when his kilt hit the floor.

And another step when he unbuttoned the cuffs of his shirt.

Two more when he reached behind his neck to

yank the garment over his head, leaving him standing in only his boots.

He still didn't look vulnerable.

No, not Bhaic MacPherson.

He propped his foot on a chair and started to pull the lace that held the antler-horn buttons closed on it. Her attention slipped to those buttons, a sudden memory surfacing of Lye Rob's silver ones. Bhaic wasn't one to cater to fashion or vanity.

It was that strength of character that drew her to him. He dropped the boot and worked the other one loose.

"Hmmm," he said softly as he came toward her, "what will it take to make ye properly submissive?"

She chuckled. "Ye do nae truly want such."

He was looming over her now, his greater height making her breath catch. "Telling me what I want now as well?"

She reached out and stroked his thighs. His lips thinned, the reaction fascinating her.

"Enjoying yer power over me?"

She lifted one shoulder. "It seems only...fair."

He stroked the sides of her bare body. She'd never realized her skin might be so sensitive.

Or a simple touch so erotic.

She shivered, allowing her eyes to close as she savored the moment.

There was another thing she'd never realized before. How a single moment might be so soul moving.

"Surprising...is nae it..."

Ailis opened her eyes to find Bhaic watching her face. He drew his fingers down her sides again, slowly, so very slowly as he gazed at her.

"Is it no' always this way?" she asked, her tone a breathless whisper. There had to be something wicked about discussing such a topic.

"No."

He drew his hands around and stroked her belly until he closed his fingers over her breasts, cupping them and holding them. She shuddered with delight, her heart pounding.

"Believe me, I have never been so captivated by a woman reaching for me as I am by ye," he said softly.

She rose up on her toes, seeking out his lips, needing his kiss. There was a haven in the intimacy, one she craved above all others. It was some mixture of physical pleasure and spiritual intimacy A place where she was no longer alone.

He lifted her up; she wasn't even sure just how. Only that they were soon among the bedding, his body hard and heavy against hers. She twisted against him, spreading her thighs in welcome as he kissed her long and deeply, taking his time with the cover of darkness to cloak them, just the embers from the hearth glowing.

The need built in her, rising to a slow boil this time. Her passage was sore, but he eased his length into her, withdrawing and thrusting in slow motions until her body relaxed. By then she was wet and welcoming, her bud pulsing with hunger. Bhaic didn't leave her unsatisfied. He moved against her, his jaw drawing tight as he held back his own release. She arched up to take him. He held her hands down to keep her in place as he pushed her toward release with a final few strokes.

They were hard.

Possessive.

Perhaps even arrogant, but she tumbled over the edge into bliss under the motion of his demanding thrusts. Her body was eager to be the vessel for his seed, every muscle she had straining upward, toward him in a bid to make him as mindless as she was.

He growled when he lost the battle, his body drawing tight as he buried himself to the hilt. His seed flooded her before he rolled over, the bed ropes groaning as he dropped heavily onto the bed.

"I meant to be…more caring…"

She turned to look at him. "Ye were. Ye always have been."

He reached out to smooth her hair away from her face. "I thought about it…about ye every night." His eyes flashed with something, some emotion that touched off a similar one inside her.

He rolled onto his side and propped his head on his hand. "I thought about how much I missed the sound of yer breathing next to me."

It was an unexpected compliment.

It warmed her. She rolled toward him, filling her senses with his scent, and sighed.

❧

"Ye seem to have neglected to tell me brother yer news."

Marcus was leaning in the passageway, concealed in the shadows as supper finished up. For how large a man he was, he was rather well accomplished in the art of hiding in the shadows.

"And ye continue to be very well-informed on the personal details of my marriage," Ailis said.

Marcus had his arms crossed over his chest. "Ye must admit, mistress, having a Robertson wed to me brother is something unexpected enough to draw attention."

"It's been months now."

"Aye," he conceded, "and ye've done well."

She had. Ailis didn't counsel herself against the rise of pride, because it was hard earned. "It is the first spring I have no' had to attend a funeral in a long time."

Marcus nodded, his expression grim with memory. "Of course now, we're feuding with the Gordons."

"Were ye truly at peace with them?" she challenged him. "Lye Rob seemed intent on wedding me in order to have the numbers to match yers. I know me father always forbade me to be in the hall when he was there. He often said, with the Gordons, he never knew just where he stood."

"Well, there is that."

Marcus wasn't going to concede any further. Ailis decided it was part of his nature. Helen moved past them, drawing his attention.

"When are ye going to take her home?" Ailis asked, feeling just a bit guilty about using Helen's plight to change the subject.

Marcus stiffened but clamped his mouth closed.

Ailis smiled. "Well now, ye are no' the only one who can be pushing their noses into the private affairs of others, saying it's on account of wanting to protect those ye care about. Helen is important to me."

Marcus chuckled softly. It was a menacing sound and reminded her of Bhaic.

"Is it a bargain ye want, lass?" he asked her. "An agreement to let ye deal with me brother in yer own time, and in return, ye will forget to mention to me father that I have nae heeded his command concerning Helen?"

"I wish to tell me husband meself," she admitted. "And I am no' sure why it concerns ye. There is no threat from waiting a few days more before saying anything."

"Providing ye do nae do anything foolish." His gaze dropped to her belly. "That is me blood growing there. MacPherson blood, which I'm sworn to protect."

She gasped, slapping her hand over her mouth to smother her horror. "I would...*never*..." She gagged.

She wasn't so sheltered she didn't know what he was talking about. There were ways to unseat a growing babe. Plants that would see the job done.

"Well then." He straightened up. "I suppose I can stop having yer maids watched. But I do confess to being curious as to why ye have nae told me brother. The pair of ye do seem to be getting along far better than anyone might have hoped for. I simply wish to be sure, before raising yer brother's hopes."

And that was the very root of why she hadn't told Bhaic about the baby growing inside her.

She knew it was true now, even if she hadn't yet felt it move. It had been over two cycles since she'd bled, and her queasy belly still hadn't settled. She couldn't stand the sight of raw meat. Even after it was cooked, her belly still rebelled most of the time.

The midwife claimed it would pass as her belly began to round. Bhaic would know when that happened. The question that weighed on her mind was what would he do? Would he put her from his bed? Consider his duty satisfied?

It shouldn't have bothered her so much. Men often did such things.

But it tore at her heart. Just the thought made her eyes sting with tears.

She climbed up the stairs, the sight of the chamber she'd first used making her sniffle.

Men had so many more rights than women when it came to marriage. No doubt if Bhaic put her from him, she would have to be content with her place.

Stop it! Ye are convicting the man without evidence…

She tried to concentrate on the fact that Bhaic had always been kind to her.

Well, he's always wanted ye in his chamber too…

Yet, it still seemed like his chamber as she entered it. Even though rooms didn't have genders, she looked at the large wooden chairs and tables and just felt like it suited a man. The bed was huge, the canopy a dark green.

Once she'd disrobed and crawled between the sheets, she noticed Bhaic's scent. It was soothing as she drifted off to sleep. But her mind was still full of turmoil, picking and poking at the unknown future coming her way.

But her dreams were kind. Full of sunshine and bliss. She warmed as though in the middle of an August day, feeling perspiration break out on her skin.

And it felt good.

So very delicious.

She was twisting in the grip of pleasure, craving it, straining toward it. All of it centered under her bud.

She gasped and opened her eyes, realizing she was more awake than asleep. The room was only faintly light, the predawn light falling over Bhaic's head of raven black hair where it was nestled between her spread thighs.

"Bhaic…"

Her voice was a raspy whisper.

"Hmmm?" He swept his tongue along her open folds, sending a jolt of intense need through her. She wanted to argue.

Needed to say…something…

But he was teasing her little pearl, worrying it with his tongue. She was arching up, lifting toward him, her hands twisting in the bedding as her eyes slid shut.

It had to be wrong.

But it felt so good. She was on the edge of climax, her own little sounds of enjoyment filling the chamber. Her body drew tight as he sucked on her, adding just enough pressure to send her spiraling out of control. The pleasure gripped her and wrung her like a wet cloth. She forgot to breathe because it was so intense, twisting and jerking as it spread through her.

When she came to her senses, Bhaic was watching her, his fingers still playing softly over her tender folds.

"Ye…should…nae have…done that."

He rose up, giving her a glimpse of his hard body. The sheer erotic nature of the moment made her breathless once more. Details fell aside, becoming meaningless. She lifted her arms in welcome, earning a growl from him.

He came to her, covering her and settling into her open thighs. He nuzzled her hair, the scent of her own body clinging to him as he seated himself deeply inside her.

His member was hard, but she was so wet from his attentions, he slid smoothly into her. He was breathing hard, the sounds harsh and so very male. She lifted toward him, feeling him draw tight, his member hardening further before his seed was flooding her.

"Sweet Christ..." He rolled over, pulling her along with him and settling her head against his chest. "Ye have become an addiction, Ailis."

She traced one of the ridges of muscles on his chest with her fingers, trying to absorb every detail about him. Tiny things she had never noticed about other men fascinated her when it came to Bhaic. She felt as if time was slipping through her grasp, just as the grains of sand flowed through an hourglass.

It might be their last moment together before he learned of the babe growing inside her.

"I am going to do that to ye again, lass..."

She tapped his chest with her fingertip. Shyness gripped her, but so did the unmistakable knowledge that she'd enjoyed it full well.

She'd be a hypocrite to argue.

His chest rumbled with amusement. "No agreement? Good. Me charms are working on ye." He stroked the hair back from her face.

"None that would nae make me a liar."

He made a low sound under his breath, one that said he was unmistakably pleased. "As I noticed when I met ye, ye are most definitely a woman."

She choked on her amusement. "And as ye informed me on our wedding night...ye enjoy companions who are women enough to enjoy being intimate with a man."

He rolled her over, coming up on his elbow while she was on her back. His blue eyes were pensive. "Would ye rather have cold duty?"

She fought the urge to look away. It was a private moment, and yet, one she realized she needed to share with him if she didn't want to feel the bite of loneliness. "No. Truly."

His lips curved, victory shimmering in his eyes.

"Do nae be so smug now," she warned him.

His grin became only more roguish. "I earned it. No' just any man can take the time to be a good lover." He leaned down, hovering over her lips as he cupped one of her breasts. "And ye enjoyed it full well,"

She ended up looking away, uncertain. He reached out and stroked her cheek, gently bringing her face around to him again.

"We truly need a honeymoon."

She laughed. "This is the Highlands, not some palace."

He looked up at the stonework that formed the tower they were in. "Still, it's a fine chamber, is it no'?"

She realized what he was asking. "Finer than the one I was raised in. But me brother has ideas about adding to Robertson Castle."

He nodded, toying with her hair as the room brightened with the dawn.

"I enjoy most of all that ye took the time," she said. It was a confession, one that came from her unsteady emotions. One born inside her desire to find herself at home in his world.

His expression became sensual, his eyes flickering with pleasure. In that moment, she felt settled and cherished. She lifted her shoulders off the bed, seeking his mouth with hers. Kissing him to keep any thoughts from spoiling it.

Reality would return soon enough.

❧

Ailis looked up in the late afternoon. There was something happening in the yard.

"What is that?" Ailis asked.

Duana surprised her by answering, "A party of Grants. Looking for shelter for the night, no doubt."

There was still a line of clanswomen waiting to see her. Most of them had children with them that they intended to discuss apprenticeships for. Serving in the castle started young because it instilled loyalty, and those who knew no other home were far less likely to agree to poison the laird. She couldn't leave them without hearing their cases, but failing to welcome guests would also be looked on as a slight. The women watching her knew it, their expressions becoming strained. Some of them had spent days on the road, traveling from the villages that dotted the MacPherson land.

"Duana, please welcome our guests and tell them I shall attend them as soon as my duties permit."

The Head of House hesitated for a moment, but her features remained serene. She slowly lowered herself. "Yes, mistress."

It wasn't so much what the Head of House had done or said as the reaction to it. The women turning bread nodded, the young lads who helped out in the kitchens watching it all with their impressionable eyes.

Three months. So short a time.

Well now, ye did get shot…

She smiled and focused on the little girl in front of her.

Ailis didn't make it back to the hall until the cook was setting out supper. Her belly was still queasy, but she had to make an appearance. Near the high ground, there were Grant retainers tonight. Only about a dozen, but their plaids stood out.

She'd almost made it to the stairs when she spotted the woman sitting at the high table. Whoever she was, she was stunning, her cheekbones high and her skin flawless. She had sparkling blue eyes and a head of auburn hair that looked as though the setting sun was trapped in it. Men were watching her, enchanted by her. She had a soft laugh and seemed to know exactly how to mesmerize the men.

But what chilled Ailis's blood was that she was aiming her eyelash flutters at Bhaic.

And her husband was enjoying every moment of it.

Someone cleared their throat, and then several others did the same. Bhaic looked up, catching sight of her.

"Ah…me wife, at last."

He got up and pulled a chair out for her. Ailis settled into it, happy to be between the woman and Bhaic.

❧

Supper seemed to last for a small eternity. Tonight it was Brenda Grant who made Ailis long to escape the high ground. She toyed with her meal until at last she could excuse herself without drawing too much attention.

She didn't escape Bhaic's notice, though. He followed her into the passageway, catching her wrist and pulling her to a stop when she'd been intent on going above stairs to hide.

"Ailis?" His keen stare was cutting into her. "What's wrong?"

She bit her lower lip, trying to find a way to state her concerns without sounding jealous.

Well, ye are jealous…

Still, she didn't want to sound like a harpy. But she certainly felt like one. Brenda was beyond lovely. Half the men in the hall had drooled over her fair features. What had bothered Ailis the most was the way the woman seemed to know exactly how to keep those men hanging on her every word.

So, there was no reason to be a harpy. She swallowed and smoothed her expression as Brenda had been doing. Bhaic's lips curved into a grin. A little spark of victory warmed her, burning away some of her concern.

At least until Brenda arrived.

"Oh…there ye are. There is going to be music," Brenda said. "A delightful way to spend the evening. Come, Bhaic."

Her voice was sweet temptation. She walked out into the hall, the candlelight making her hair shimmer. She gave Bhaic a come-hither look over her shoulder.

It was the first time Ailis truly understood what a come-hither look was.

And it was aimed at her husband.

"Ye do nae need to be jealous of Brenda," he said.

There was a touch of amusement in his voice, but his attention remained on Brenda. It tore something inside her. White-hot pain piercing her heart.

"And there was no reason for ye to be so concerned about me dancing on the green with Lye Rob," she said.

He snapped his attention back to her.

"Ye're missing the fun…" Brenda's voice was lyrical. She stepped into the passageway, taking a moment to glance over her shoulder. When she turned her attention back to Bhaic, her lips were set into a sensual smile, which froze when she spotted Ailis.

"Shouldn't ye be off to bed?" Brenda asked. "Ye've both done yer duty well enough. So long as ye are strong enough to carry that babe to term. Best take yerself off to sleep now. Do nae worry about yer husband's needs. I'll see to those."

Of course she would.

It was the thing Ailis had feared and had told herself not to worry about. Men had more rights in a marriage. It was simply fact.

Yet it did bother her. So greatly she turned around and headed up the stairs, tears filling her eyes. She stopped at the second floor, pushing in the doors before her breath caught on a sob.

Ye'll no' cry!

She wiped her eyes on her sleeve and drew in a deep breath to clear her head.

"What are ye doing here?"

She turned around, finding Bhaic in the center of

her chamber. He pushed the door shut behind him, blocking Helen outside.

"What are ye doing here?" she echoed his question.

"Wondering why ye are here and no' in our chamber."

He stepped closer, something flickering in his eyes. "Are ye with child?"

She couldn't help but smile a bit. "The midwife believes so."

"Christ, Ailis." He closed his eyes, his expression tightening. "Ye should have told me...before I handled ye so roughly."

The memory of him coming up the road teased her cheeks with heat. But it also filled her with lament, for it might have been the last time he paid her such attention. "Ye did nae give me much chance."

He stepped toward her. "I would have listened to ye. 'Tis never been my way to be harsh with ye."

There was a hard note in his voice, one that reprimanded her justly.

She shrugged. "I was as heated as ye were."

And worried that he'd no' want ye if he knew his duty was satisfied.

He muttered an oath in Gaelic and caught her close, wrapping his arms around her and holding her when she tried to wiggle away.

"Do nae be jealous of Brenda. I can nae change what I did before we wed."

She pushed him back. It was like trying to move a wall, but he snorted and released her.

"Are ye planning to take her as a mistress?"

Surprise flashed across his face before his expression hardened. "No. But I'm planning on carrying ye back to me chamber, since ye seem to be trying to escape it again."

He scooped her up and carried her past Finley and Helen. The flight of stairs between the two floors was gone in a flash. Bhaic didn't let her down until he'd moved far into the bedchamber.

"It bothers me to see ye doubting me, Ailis."

"Well, it bothers me to see ye flirting with yer mistress."

Bhaic crossed his arms over his chest. "Brenda is no' me mistress."

"She was yer lover," Ailis retorted. "And she clearly came here the moment she heard I was carrying. There is only one reason for her arrival."

Bhaic suddenly chuckled, his lips splitting into a grin. His amusement frayed her already sore feelings. She swatted him and slapped his arms when he tried to enclose her in his embrace. He wrapped his arms around her anyway, pressing soft kisses against her temples and cheeks until she quieted.

"It is not…amusing," she said at last, horrified by the rough sound of her voice.

He cupped her chin and raised her face so their gazes met. "No, lass, the fact that ye care for me is no' amusing. It is precious. Very precious to me. Never doubt it."

She pushed against him, hissing when he wouldn't release her, but the sound came out as more of a whimper.

"I did nae invite Brenda."

Ailis stilled and searched his eyes. Nothing but sincerity stared back at her. "Then why is she here?

And so certain ye will put me aside now that yer duty to me is finished?"

"Because everyone in the Highlands seems to think they need to be involved in our marriage," he exclaimed. "Why should this moment be any different?"

She couldn't help but smile at his words.

He grunted. "Me duty to ye will never be finished. Not in this lifetime or the next." He placed a soft kiss against her lips. "And I am going to have the bed taken out of the chamber below us so ye understand I will nae be having ye anywhere but by me side."

It was everything she'd been so sure she'd never hear from him. She rested her hand against his chest, feeling the beating of his heart and trying to make herself believe him.

"Ye are the keeper of me heart, lass. I must hold ye near and hope ye'll soften toward me."

The tears she'd tried so hard to fend off trickled down her cheeks. He caught them with his fingertips. "Ye've already stolen me heart, MacPherson."

His lips curved into a roguish grin. "In that case, be very, very sure that I have no intention of ever returning it."

She reached up and stroked his cheek, settling against him completely. "I'll just keep yers in its place."

"Ye do that."

She would.

Because there was nothing she craved from him more than his love.

Eight

"YE LIKELY HAVE HARSH THINGS TO SAY TO ME."

Brenda was waiting for her the next morning in the passageway, out of sight of the retainers breaking their fast in the great hall.

Ailis touched her foot down from the last step and considered the woman. She was beyond striking, a true beauty.

Brenda smiled knowingly. "I came here because I'd heard ye were breeding. It's true. I'm not going to run away and pretend I did nae. I suppose it's no' very important to tell ye how clear it is that Bhaic is content with ye, but I know he never looked at me the way he does at ye. So here I am. Say what ye will."

"Really? He never looked at ye the same way? Ye are…"

"Beautiful?" Brenda shook her head in disgust. "It's more trouble than it's worth. Believe me." A knowing gleam entered her eyes. "There's something I know about. The way men look at women. It's different when they merely want a ride. Bhaic…well now, he wants to possess ye. I was merely a plaything, maybe a challenge once or twice, but nothing beyond a diversion."

There was lament in her tone that touched something inside Ailis.

"Be grateful, Ailis," Brenda said softly. "I know ye most likely want none of me advice, but ye are a fortunate woman to have more than duty and respect in yer union."

"I know it well," Ailis agreed, deciding to count her blessings instead of quibbling over her husband's past.

"Even if ye doubt yer husband's feelings?"

Ailis shrugged. "I suppose, I'm surprised is all. Still trying to believe it."

Brenda smiled and laughed. "Aye. Every now and again, life is too good to believe. I met a man once who struck me in such a way."

A far-off look entered her eyes. It tugged at Ailis's heart—she knew the sting of loneliness.

"Where is he?"

Brenda looked startled, her cheeks turning pink. "I was promised. He was honorable. It doesn't matter where he is, for my life is still no' me own. I am Symon's cousin. Me mother was his father's sister. So I was used to settle alliances. As ye know well."

"I do."

"Me husband had no affection for me, but I can nae fault him, for he was ordered to wed me as well."

"I begin to understand why I should nae judge ye," Ailis said.

Brenda offered her a naughty, knowing look. "Good. For it would have been very unfair of life if I had ended me days without ever knowing what it was like to have a man in me bed who made sure I enjoyed it as much as he did."

Ailis ended up returning Brenda's smile. It was a strange conversation to say the least, but she didn't have it in her to think badly of Brenda. Her own fate might have been very much the same.

Aye, she'd be grateful.

Someone began ringing the bells on the walls. Finley appeared from outside the passageway, making it clear that he wouldn't be giving her any privacy when there might be danger.

But it was Brenda who drew her attention. The normally poised woman looked pale. She watched the entrance of the great hall with a nervous expression on her face. A few moments later, Symon Grant appeared, his men on his heels.

"What's the matter?" Ailis asked.

Brenda steadied herself as she clenched two handfuls of her skirt. "For all that yer marriage seems to be a happy one, I have no desire to be used as a pawn again." Her voice lowered to a mere whisper. "Forgive me. Bhaic is one of the few men I knew I might hide behind."

"But ye would have had to trade yer favors for it." Horror was nearly gagging her, but it wasn't jealousy this time. It was Brenda's plight.

Brenda cast her a forlorn look. "Bhaic is a rare man. He's kind when seeking his pleasure and returns it measure for measure. Be sure, most men are not the same. And I would nae have had to wed him."

"Brenda," Symon called out. He'd stopped in the hall, looking toward her. "Do nae make me come and get ye. I rode through the night, and it rained too."

Brenda stiffened, but she moved out of the passageway. "I force naught upon ye."

Marcus was with Symon, and Bhaic appeared in the passage doorway.

"Me father sent me to fetch ye, Brenda," Symon said gruffly. "And I do nae appreciate being taken from his side."

"Ye should have sense enough to realize a fool's errand and refuse it."

Symon drew in a deep breath. "Alliances are nae a fool's errand."

"When it involves forcing me to wed a Gordon because yer father is too far gone to realize naught will settle Colum Gordon's rage except time, I say it's a fool's errand. The man's son was just killed. He wants vengeance, and I'll no' be going as the lamb." Brenda shook her head. "Go home. Yer father is dying."

"He's yer uncle."

Brenda pressed her lips into a hard line. "That may be, but I will no' be going to Gordon land. So it looks as though I can nae be going to Grant land either."

"Brenda is me guest," Ailis said clearly, "for as long as she wishes to stay."

Several crashes came from the back of the hall as the women listening dropped things in shock.

"Are ye sure about that, lass?"

Ailis turned to find Bhaic behind her. Brenda sent her a disbelieving look, but the desperation in her eyes made Ailis nod firmly. "Of course I am. To do otherwise would be to doubt yer sincerity."

Bhaic slowly grinned. His eyes flickered with an emotion that was bright enough to blind her. He stepped toward her, capturing her hand. "Well now, we couldn't be having that."

"No, we couldn't," she agreed.

The hold he had on her hand sent her doubts crumbling. She was suddenly so sure she held his heart, it filled her with a sense of joy that made her want to spin around and around like a gleeful child.

"Brenda…I did nae ride through the night to go home empty-handed," Symon said.

Bhaic's expression tightened. Ailis could see the indecision in his eyes. Symon would soon be Laird of the Grants. Bhaic had to tread carefully.

But she didn't.

"Well now, ye do nae need to." Ailis turned around to face Symon. "One of yer kinswomen has need of escort back to yer land. Ye will be lifting a burden from Marcus's shoulder. Yer father will be happy to hear what a service ye performed."

Marcus sent her a cutting look before Symon turned to lock stares with him. "What woman is this?"

"There was some sort of misunderstanding… I'm no' sure of the exact details…" Ailis continued. "Yet Helen has asked to return to her father's house, but couldn't very well go unescorted."

Symon wasn't a fool. He crossed his arms over his wide chest, aiming his topaz eyes at her. The man was pure Highlander, but amused enough by her cunning to indulge her changing the topic.

"Where is this Helen?"

Marcus's knuckles were white. But he nodded toward Skene. "Fetch her up here."

"Ye're playing with fire," Bhaic warned her softly.

"As if he has nae played with us enough to be deserving of it."

Bhaic snorted in her ear. "Ye're going to be a very good mistress of this hall. Ye give as good as ye get."

She warmed under his compliment as Marcus glared at her.

Lyel appeared with Helen in tow.

"Helen," Ailis said, "I was just telling yer laird's son how ye wished to return to yer father's house."

Helen pulled her arm from Lyel's grip with a satisfied look on her face. Symon didn't miss it. He turned to look at Marcus.

"Did ye steal her from me father's land?"

Marcus lifted one shoulder, completely unrepentant. "I did, and I kept her from ye when ye were here before."

People were shifting closer, making sure they got a good view. Bhaic pulled Ailis back when she started to move forward again. "Nae, lass, there is going to be a fight," he whispered in her ear.

Symon slowly chuckled. "Ye always have been a rascal when it comes to the lasses."

He turned and gestured Helen forward. Lyel adjusted to his new duty of taking her to her laird's son. Symon considered her from head to toe for a long moment as the hall remained in silence.

"There isn't going to be a fight," Ailis argued.

Bhaic leaned down and nipped her ear. "I know me

brother, lass. He's no' going to let Helen go, and if he does, I will never let him forget it."

Ailis jabbed him with her elbow, but the beast only wrapped his arm around her to keep her from doing him any damage.

"What's this now?" Shamus made his way into the hall from another passageway. He peered at Symon, starting to grin until he realized that Helen stood there too.

"So ye did nae take the lass home?" Shamus said to Marcus as he shuffled into the hall and sat down on the high ground. "I suspected ye might not. She's a fetching sight and no' afraid of ye. I do nae think I've seen another lass stand up to ye the same way. Certainly never seen one knock ye to the ground! The lass wields a pitcher like a broadsword."

There was a rumble of amusement in the hall, but Marcus merely grinned, the curving of his lips far more promise than anything else, and he was looking straight at Helen.

She lifted her chin and looked back at Symon. "It's far past time for me to go home."

"Oh... I see..." Symon smirked at Marcus before turning his back on Ailis. "We have a difficulty here."

"So it seems," Marcus agreed.

"I am only a laird's son." Symon spoke slowly, menacingly.

"As am I," Marcus answered firmly.

"Which means...we're equals."

Marcus nodded, starting to walk in a half circle around Symon. The retainers fell back, taking Marcus's doublet when he shrugged out of it. Symon was doing the same, both men stripping down to their shirts and kilts.

"So this is a matter between men," Symon concluded.

"It is," Marcus confirmed.

"It is no'!" Helen interrupted. She stepped right up to Marcus, tilting her head back so she could make eye contact. She stood up to him with her jaw steady. "I will nae have the pair of ye fighting over me. I choose to go home."

Marcus's lips split and curved into the biggest grin Ailis had ever seen on his face. "Ye can choose me, Helen, or I'll fight for ye." He reached out and caught her arms, pulling her to him as he tilted his head to the side and pressed a hard kiss against her mouth.

She stiffened and shoved away from him. There was a loud smack as she laid her hand across his cheek. "Toad! Arrogant bastard! As if I'd fall down at yer feet simply because ye told me to."

He chuckled at her temper before jerking his head at Lyel and Skene. They hooked Helen by her arms and pulled her out of the way.

"Ye can nae let him do this…" Ailis implored her husband.

Bhaic only tightened his arm around her. "Ye will nae be getting yer way with both Brenda and Helen. Me brother has his fair share of pride. Just as ye do."

She couldn't argue with him.

Symon and Marcus circled, sizing each other up. They connected with a harsh grunt and the sound of flesh hitting flesh. It was brutal. They were like huge bears, well matched in both brawn and spirit. Blood brightened their noses, and eyes began to swell. The men around them threatened to raise the roof as they cheered and placed wagers.

Neither man went down easily, and both of them got back on their feet, even when they were staggering. Marcus finally caught Symon, pinning his arm and slamming him to the floor. Symon growled, trying to gain his footing.

"It is done!" Shamus shouted from the high ground.

Marcus held on for just a moment longer before he snorted and got off Symon.

"Shake hands, ye devils."

Symon cocked his head to the side before he put out his arm. Marcus was grinning, his teeth bloody. He clasped Symon's wrist. The men around them cheered.

"Well now, that's the business," Shamus said. "Join me at the table, Symon Grant. And where is Bhaic?"

Bhaic started off to join his father.

"Thank ye," Brenda said, her voice only a whisper. "I do nae deserve it from ye, Ailis, but I'm properly grateful."

"Everyone deserves to be happy," Ailis said. "Maybe ye can find the man ye remember."

Her expression became pensive. "He's likely long wed now."

There was a note of defeat in her voice, but the tension was easing from her expression.

"Well, at least ye will no' be wedding this month."

"Aye," Brenda said. "One day at a time. I think young Helen needs ye more than I."

"Actually…" Ailis leaned back so Finley wouldn't hear her. "I'm wondering how grateful ye might be. Ye have two waiting women riding with ye, do ye nae?"

Brenda regained her poise. "Indeed I do."

"And ye have some relations ye might wish to go visit?" Ailis suggested.

"I certainly do." She sent Ailis a long glance. "And indeed I *will*. Ye have me word on that."

"Good."

"Yes. Whenever….my ladies are ready, that is," Brenda confirmed.

Brenda moved down into the hall and took a seat at the high table. Ailis waited for Helen to find her. She was fuming.

"Worry not, my friend…" Ailis leaned in to whisper in her ear. Helen slowly stopped grinding her teeth, her expression becoming one of victory instead.

"It will nae take Marcus very long to reason out where I went and how it happened," Helen warned her.

"That's a warning for ye as well. Be sure ye want to leave, because if ye do, I believe he might come after ye," Ailis warned quietly. "But the choice should be yers."

"I thank ye for that," Helen answered. "Truly."

Her husband wasn't going to be pleased.

Of course he'd also be amused.

That thought put a smile on her lips as she made her way to the high table. Bhaic lost interest in the conversation as she came close, rising to pull her chair back.

He'd be both annoyed and impressed. Which was right in keeping with their union.

She discovered she liked it full well.

And loved him above all else.

How could she not? He was a MacPherson after all.

❧

"Ye do nae have to worry about Helen." Bhaic was stroking her hip, his hands gentle now that they were both satisfied. "Marcus will behave himself."

Ailis choked and raised her head from where she'd been resting against his chest. "If he does, I will be most impressed. Yer brother is a savage."

Bhaic pushed her head back down but not before she got a glimpse of his arrogant grin. "That's part of his charm. He's a Highlander through and through."

"Ye likely think it only fitting, since ye have managed to steal me heart," she said softly.

"Ye're a Robertson. I am duty bound to steal everything of value from ye. But ye have it right about Marcus, he has a savage streak in his nature. Helen is no' afraid of him. That's what fascinates him, ye know. The way she stands up to his growling."

"I am still no' going to approve of keeping her here and insisting she wed."

"Has it turned out so badly for ye, then?" He rolled her onto her back and settled beside her, one of his thighs covering hers as he cupped one of her breasts.

"I am completely yer captive."

"Good, because I could no' allow the keeper of me heart to leave." He smoothed his hand down to her belly that was just beginning to round.

"No more than I could stand to leave," she said. "But…"

He raised his attention to her face. "There is the little matter of yer father informing ye that ye would have to pay him a visit."

Bhaic gave her a pinch. She poked him between the

ribs in retribution. "Are ye saying ye are nae as bold as me father, who has come here…twice?"

"Nae, I'm saying I'm no' as great a fool as yer father—"

He rolled back as she slapped his chest, following the blow with several more playful ones. He clasped her to him and rolled her over onto her back once more. There was little point in struggling. She was already opening her thighs to allow him to settle between them.

"Yes…" He pressed a kiss against her mouth. "I will take ye to see yer father." He pressed a longer kiss against her mouth, teasing her lips before lifting his head. "But I am no' going to let him hit me again."

Ailis raised an eyebrow.

He flashed her a grin, and she laughed.

Complete…perfection.

With a MacPherson.

Fate had a very fine sense of humor.

About the Author

Mary Wine is a multi-published author in romantic suspense, fantasy, and Western romance. Her interest in historical reenactment and costuming also inspired her to turn her pen to historical romance with her popular Highlander series. She lives with her husband and sons in Southern California, where the whole family enjoys participating in historical reenactment.